The EPHEMERAL SCENES of
SETSUNA'S JOURNEY

The Former 68th Hero and the Beastfolk Apprentice

1

Alto | A beastfolk boy.
Setsuna takes him
in as an apprentice.

Setsuna

Former 68th hero. Inherited power and knowledge from the 5th and 23rd heroes.

contents

The Ephemeral Scenes of Setsuna's Journey

The Former 68th Hero and the Beastfolk Apprentice

1

Rokusyou • Usuasagi

Illustration by sime

YEN ON

NEW YORK

The EPHEMERAL SCENES of
SETSUNA'S JOURNEY

Vol. 1

©Rokusyou and Usuasagi

Translation by Andria McKnight

Cover art by sime

SETSUNA NO FUKEI Vol. 1 ROKUJUHACHI BANME NO MOTOYUSHA TO JUJIN NO DESHI
©Rokusyou • Usuasagi 2020
First published in Japan in 2020 by KADOKAWA CORPORATION, Tokyo.
English translation rights arranged with KADOKAWA CORPORATION, Tokyo through TUTTLE-MORI AGENCY, INC., Tokyo.

Yen On
150 West 30th Street, 19th Floor
New York, NY 10001

Visit us at yenpress.com • facebook.com/yenpress • twitter.com/yenpress
yenpress.tumblr.com • instagram.com/yenpress

First Yen On Edition: June 2023
Edited by Yen On Editorial: Shella Wu, Maya Deutsch
Designed by Yen Press Design: Madelaine Norman

Yen On is an imprint of Yen Press, LLC.
The Yen On name and logo are trademarks of Yen Press, LLC.

Library of Congress Cataloging-in-Publication Data
Names: Rokusyou and Usuasagi, author. | sime (Illustrator), illustrator. | McKnight, Andria, translator.
Title: The ephemeral scenes of Setsuna's journey / Rokusyou and Usuasagi ; illustration by sime ; translation by Andria McKnight.
Other titles: Setsuna no fukei. English
Description: First Yen On edition. | New York, NY : Yen On, 2023. | Contents: v. 1. The former 68th hero and the beastfolk apprentice —
Identifiers: LCCN 2023002882 | ISBN 9781975363871 (v. 1 ; trade paperback) | ISBN 9781975363895 (v. 2 ; trade paperback) | ISBN 9781975363918 (v. 3 ; trade paperback)
Subjects: CYAC: Fantasy. | Adventure and adventurers—Fiction. |
LCGFT: Fantasy fiction. | Action and adventure fiction. | Light novels.
Classification: LCC PZ7.1.R6646 Ep 2023 | DDC [Fic]—dc23
LC record available at https://lccn.loc.gov/2023002882

ISBNs: 978-1-9753-6387-1 (paperback)
978-1-9753-6388-8 (ebook)

10 9 8 7 6 5 4 3 2 1

LSC-C

Printed in the United States of America

Preface

✿

I want to see *the world*.
That was *my* wish.
All *I* wanted was to learn more about *the world*.
And
At the end, *I* wanted
to *flutter down* and *fall* like the *camellias*.
I wanted to die like the *camellias*.
I wanted to live like the *camellias*.
I wanted to live *gracefully* and die *gracefully*
as *Setsuna Sugimoto*.

But…
Neither of *my wishes* came *true*.
No one in *this world* knows the real *me*.
No one in this world knows *my* real *name*.
The only thing *I* got in *this world*
was a *white world* just like in the *previous one*.
A *place* called a *hospital room*, cut off from the *outside*.
I was about to *lose myself* once again in this *white world*.
I had *given up* on *everything*.
…Until he came along.

"What do you want to do?"
he asked.
And *I* wished to see *the world*, too.
Even if it wasn't *mine*, but *another*.
To find *my* ____, I tucked the single remaining *camellia*
into my heart.
And the *present me* became ____.

✿

Prologue

That day will be etched into my memory forever.

I was bathed in the light of the blue moon that hung outside my window.

It was the day the real me vanished and a new me was born.

And what I received from it was freedom.

He had left me all of himself.

It was the day when everything was erased, save for the camellias that bloomed inside my heart.

I lost you.

I lost the first friend I'd ever made.

I etched a new promise in the camellias that survived.

I vowed to abandon everything, including my name, right here on the spot, and live here in this world.

Chapter One
Camellia ~ A Gentle Kindness ~

◇Part One: Me

Would twenty-four years generally be considered a long time or a short time? Surely anything that lasted for twenty-four years would be considered long. So in that case, wouldn't a life that lasted twenty-four years be long? After all, you'd carried on living during that whole time.

I remembered the term *average life span*, a nagging thought in the back of my mind arguing that it was not, in fact, a long time at all.

I continued searching for a reason I could accept, even though the answer was already inside me. Because I had no choice *but* to accept it. I had been sick ever since I was a child, and my life that had lasted for twenty-four years would end today.

I never made any friends. I never fell in love. I never got married or had any children. I'd just lived, slowly drifting toward death. It was fairly difficult to say my life had been blessed in many ways. But I was blessed with the environment and family in which I'd grown up. My parents were both doctors who ran a prestigious hospital. I'd lived my entire life in one of those patient rooms. They had prepared it especially for me.

Since it was a hospital, the walls were painted white, but it had been decorated appropriately for my age. I thought it probably wasn't much different from the rooms of other boys my age. Of course, I'd never seen anyone else's room, so I couldn't be sure, but I just had a feeling it was similar. If I had to name one difference, though, it was that I was not allowed to leave my room, for my own safety.

There were times when I'd wondered why I'd ever been born to begin with, or why my life had to be like this. But once I discovered my parents had been deeply hurt by the fact that they hadn't been able to cure my illness, I resolved to just accept the reality of my situation.

I had so many places I wanted to go and things I wanted to see. I never gave up hope for a possible cure, so I read many books and even studied to become a doctor one day. I wanted to follow in my parents' footsteps. I held on to that hope deep in my heart, right up until the end. My parents never gave up on curing my illness, so I truly believed I would be rid of it one day. The only thing I could do was trust them and work hard.

I'd lived my life to the fullest, the best that I could, for twenty-four whole years.

So that's why... That's why...
Mom. Dad. Kyoka. I was happy.
So I don't want you to cry.
I was more than happy.
… … … … … … …
…………………………… … … … … …
………………………………………… … … … … … … …

"You are the sixty-eighth hero." I heard a slightly high-pitched, feminine voice.

I woke up abruptly, immediately overcome by vertigo, nausea, and a pain so sharp it felt like I'd been punched in the head. It was so intense that it took my breath away for a moment. I turned my body in an attempt to escape it, frantically trying to remember what had happened to me.

Who's talking to me? What had I been doing? What is this searing pain?!
"You are the sixty-eighth hero." In the midst of my confusion, I heard the woman's voice again. But I couldn't comprehend the words she was saying, and the voice vanished. For a moment, I thought maybe one of the nurses was talking to me.

But most of all, a pressing question overflowed out of me.

"...Why...am...I...still...a...live?" The words tumbled from my mouth in a voiceless rasp.

Then I opened my eyes here for the first time. I saw my right arm. There was a gleaming, bluish-silver bracelet around my wrist. I moved my head around, trying to grasp my situation while I bore the pain and the nausea.

This was not the room where I had spent my whole life. I had no memory of this place at all.

"Yes, that's right. Shall I explain?" the woman asked calmly; she didn't seem surprised by my reaction.

"......"

As she spoke, the nausea and the pain gradually subsided, and my pulsing heartbeat began to return to normal. I didn't wonder why the pain had stopped or why my confusion had dissipated.

"Brave hero, are you listening?"

I assumed she was addressing me, but I didn't understand why she was calling me that.

"I...I'm not really sure I understand what you're talking about."

"Well, I'd like to explain it to you now. You're feeling fine, yes?"

"Yes. I don't feel nauseous or in pain anymore."

She nodded in response, then calmly explained my situation, the position I was in, and about this country. I detected a hint of contempt in her attitude. With every word she spoke, new questions arose inside me, but for some reason, I couldn't bring myself to ask them. I just quietly listened to her speak.

"Very well, then. I shall show you to your room. I can explain things in more detail there."

I nodded to show that I agreed and unsteadily rose to my feet. She began to slowly walk away, and I tried to follow after her, but my legs would not move. I'd intended to take a step forward, but when my legs didn't cooperate, I lost my balance and collapsed. I felt pain; I must have struck my head on something, because I slowly began to lose consciousness.

The only things I saw as my consciousness slipped away were the woman's cold eyes as she glared at me and the pale blue circle embroidered upon her black robe. For some reason, I noticed that it looked just like a moon hanging in the sky at midnight, then lost consciousness.

I wasn't sure how much time had passed after that, but at some point, I woke up. While taking into consideration my physical condition, she once again explained this world to me.

This was not the world in which I had been born and raised. A different world from the one I'd lived in before...? We called that an isekai in my previous life. And in this other world, I appeared just as I had in Japan: I had black hair and black eyes.

The woman told me I had the qualities of a hero and had been summoned here by a certain kind of magic that could summon a soul that had ended its natural life span. These *heroes from another world* were brought here in order to protect mankind from monsters. Honestly, I wondered why I had been chosen.

Perhaps the concept of a hero was different here, but my younger sister, Kyoka, and I had enjoyed adventure novels like that, so we'd read them often. We should all try to protect our world, but of course, I never expected that role would ever come to me. All those thoughts were running through my head as I listened, and perhaps that was why I wondered why they had to summon heroes to this world.

I asked the woman about this, and she furrowed her brow in response to my question but still answered me. She said the summoning magic granted great physical and magical benefits to the person who was called here. Their body would be revived in its prime and strengthened, then given immense mana.

Therefore, the summoned hero would become an existence far superior to humans in this world and would be able to fight monsters that they were helpless against.

Summoning a soul would revive the physical body? It sounded so far-fetched that I said I couldn't believe her.

"What purpose would there be to summoning a soul without a physical body? Magic is created to serve a specific meaning. That's just how it is," she responded.

But here I was, lying in bed in a white room.

The only thing that had changed was that I felt a little younger—perhaps eighteen. I had my same familiar appearance, and yet my heart whispered that this was *not* me. I had left my life and my body back with my parents and younger sister.

Ever since that day, I lay in bed, lamenting sorrowfully over that fact.

My sickness had not been cured. The only thing that was different was the world I lived in. Nothing had changed about *me*.

Personally, I doubted that I had become physically stronger or been given magical powers. I hadn't even been given the chance to test it out. The benefit I really wished for was to have my illness be cured. I didn't need some superior or special powers.

I had been bestowed the role of a hero, but since I was ill, there was no way for me to carry out my duty. So instead, I stayed in a room that seemed like it was inside a hospital, just as I had in the world I'd been born in. Magic had not cured my illness. There probably wasn't a way to do it in this world, either. They gave me strange medicines as I continued my bedridden life.

To be honest, I wasn't even sure if the medicine was meant for my illness.

Several more days passed. Since I couldn't see what was going on outside, I just had to count the days by the number of sleeps I had. They provided me with food, clothing, and shelter, but I was not allowed to leave the room. I was confined in the name of medical treatment, but perhaps the most accurate way to describe it was that I was being kept under surveillance.

They had selfishly summoned me, deemed me useless, then taken away my freedom. However, I had a feeling that even if they did think I'd be useful, they would not have given me liberty.

I spent most of the day alone, and the number of people who were allowed to approach my room was limited. I figured I would just remain by myself, slowly heading toward death once again. It was all the same as it had been back in Japan.

No, there *was* one thing that was different, in a bad way. This time, I had no family to support me. There wasn't a soul in this world who cared about me. I was completely and utterly alone. And I never thought being alone would cause such anxiety and sorrow. Placed in this situation, it made me realize for the first time just how much my parents and sister had loved me. They had cherished me much more than I had ever thought.

"Since your life ended in your previous world, you cannot return to it." My heart ached when I remembered what the woman told me. I desperately wished I could go back home. But here I was, in a white room that resembled my past one so much.

All I could think about was my family.

One year had passed since I was summoned to this world. I was moved from my original room to another simple room, but I could see the scenery outside from this one. From my view outside the window, I learned that there were seasons in this world, too. I experienced the cold and heat, and once there were more days with a comfortable temperature, I suspected that a year had gone by since I was summoned.

The passing days had brought many changes; surely time was going by in the outside world the way it did in my old world.

Although that had nothing to do with me, since I was not allowed to leave this room. Though I thought that perhaps the calendar year in this world differed from Japan. When I was first summoned, I had counted the days for a while, but my memory became spotty after a certain point. So I decided to give up counting rather than having some messed-up calculation in my head. I realized it was pointless to continue anyway, so I stopped.

The biggest change in the past year was probably when I had been officially deemed to be completely useless. I overheard the soldiers who patrolled outside my room talking and learned that the *69th hero* had been summoned. If that was true, then this situation would probably be coming to an end for me soon. Now that they had their new hero, they no longer had any use for an ill, incompetent one like me. I just wasn't sure if I would die from my sickness in this bleak room or be killed. I knew this kingdom wasn't so kind as to allow someone useless to continue living.

But, more importantly, I'd given up on life. Even if they did let me out of here, I would be completely in the dark about this world. I was sick; there was no way I could survive. Maybe I could if I were healthy, but it would be impossible with this sickly body.

I vacantly stared out the window from my bed. The thing we called a moon on earth shone with a blue light, sadly illuminating my figure. How many times had I wished it was yellow like the one back home?

"Hey, you. Aren't you a hero?" All of a sudden, I heard an unfamiliar voice break the silence in the room. I was supposed to be the only one in here. I tore my gaze away from the blue moon and looked toward the sound of the voice.

I saw a young man standing there, with light-green eyes and golden-brown hair. When I didn't answer, he grew impatient and approached my bed. "Hey. Answer my question."

For a moment, I wondered if he was an assassin, but even if he was, there wasn't any way for me to resist him. I wasn't confident I could

escape in my condition. I'd long thought this would be my fate, and now it had come for me. In that case…

In that case, wouldn't it be all right if I had one last conversation? I really hadn't talked to anyone these past few months.

"Who are you?"

"First, answer my question. Are you a hero?"

"Technically, I am the sixty-eighth hero."

"Wait, the sixty-eighth? You're not the sixty-ninth?"

"I was summoned here a year ago."

"Hmm…" The man pondered this silently.

I gave him a curious look. "Now it's your turn to answer my question. Who are you?"

"Ah, right. I was the twenty-third hero. Before coming here, I lived in Japan. I was summoned in…2015, I believe."

His answer was so completely unexpected that I was rendered speechless. I was not only surprised that another hero had suddenly appeared before me but that he was also Japanese. I couldn't even reply.

It wasn't that I never considered there could be heroes who were Japanese. But the fact that one had appeared before me in this exact moment was nothing short of a miracle to me.

"What about you?"

"I was summoned in 2020…" My heart was pounding so fast that I could barely speak.

"Hmm. Stay still for a second," the self-proclaimed 23rd hero said, placing his hand on my chest. I tensed up for a moment, wondering what he was going to do to me. I felt a brief pulse run through my body, but there was no pain. I understood at once that he had used some kind of magic spell on me.

"I see. So that's why," he muttered, a bitter look of understanding on his face.

I silently gazed at him. He noticed and said without a hint of apology, "Oh. I looked through your memories."

I didn't have any memories I would be particularly embarrassed to have someone see, but shouldn't he have at least asked first? I snorted a bit to express my dismay, and he gave me a serious look. "You know they're gonna kill you, right?"

"Yeah, I know. But it's not like I can do anything about it. Nor am I planning to," I answered calmly.

He stared at me, as if he was peering into the depths of my heart. "If your illness was cured, what would you want to do?"

"Die like the camellias," I answered without hesitation.

He gave a wry smile at my abstract response. Since he had read my memories, I knew he understood what I meant. The slow crawl toward death here in this place, in this white room, was unbearable.

"That's what you want to happen, yes. But I'm asking what you want to *do*."

What do I want to do? There was only one thing that came to mind.

"There's nothing? There must be something, right?"

"If my illness was cured, I'd want to travel around the whole world. I don't want to die here…but in a place that I've chosen." I quietly told him my wish.

As I spoke, he stared at me impassively. "If you want to travel around the world, then I'll give you something you need to be able to do that. I no longer have a reason to continue living in this world anyway… So I'll give you my life." He said it without a hint of sorrow, as if he were talking about giving me his favorite snack or something.

He'd just told me he would give me his life so that I could travel around this world. For a moment, I doubted my ears, but I could tell by his expression that he was serious, and without meaning to, I raised my voice. "I don't want to travel that bad! Not so much that I'd want someone to sacrifice their own life for it!" My body couldn't keep up with my agitated emotions, and I began coughing violently, pain growing in my chest. I clutched my chest and turned away to try to ease the pain. He placed a hand on my back and slowly, sympathetically, rubbed it.

I tilted my head slightly to look up at him, and he had on a conflicted smile. "I worded that wrong, sorry. I'll tell you the whole story, so please just listen. Then you can decide after you've heard everything I have to say. Is that all right with you?"

"If all I have to do is listen."

"Yeah, that's all you have to do for now."

After watching me catch my breath, he pulled his hand away. I panicked slightly as his soothing warmth left my body, but I pushed those feelings deep inside me. I turned my gaze toward him so I could listen. He sat down in a chair and looked at me.

"Where'd you get that chair?" It wasn't in the room before. He hadn't carried it in here, and he had nowhere to hide it, either.

"First, I'll introduce myself." Apparently, he had no intention of answering my question. "I am the twenty-third hero summoned to this kingdom. My name back in Japan was Kanade Tokito. In this world, my name is Kyle. I threw away my Japanese name. So you can call me Kyle." He gave me a pointed look as if to say, *"Now it's time for you to introduce yourself."*

I didn't feel like it was necessary, though, since he had looked through my memories. "I'm Setsuna Sugimoto..."

"What's wrong?"

"Nothing, it's just...I feel like that's the first time I've said my name since I came to this world."

"I guess that makes sense..." Kyle glanced down to the bracelet encircling my right wrist.

"I collapsed before they could tell me many details. They probably decided it wasn't even worth asking my name."

"......" He fell silent, as if he was deep in thought. He didn't tell me why, so I had no idea what was going through his mind.

After our introductions were finished, Kyle began telling me about himself. About when he was summoned, what happened afterward, and what he'd seen during his time here in this Kingdom of Gardir.

People summoned were given the title of hero, but really, they were little more than slaves to the kingdom. Only the royal families and a small group of people in Gardir, and another kingdom named Ellana, knew the truth about the summoned heroes. The value of a human life was very low in this world. Kyle's face was filled with bitterness as he told me about his experiences and knowledge.

We had been called here to be used as tools to fight monsters. I had a sense that the outside world was filled with danger. Kyle had lived in it, so I figured he had gone through tougher times than I could even imagine.

Suddenly, his face brightened. "But then there was someone who rescued me from my life as a hero."

"……"

"The fifth hero saved me."

"The fifth…?"

"That's right."

His face lit up and his voice filled with joy when he spoke of this person. I could tell they were very important to him. And as I listened to him, I realized something. This was the first time I was having a conversation as Setsuna Sugimoto since coming to this world. Very few people ever came to my room, and not one of them ever tried to interact with me.

There were maids who took care of me, but they only spoke the absolute bare minimum.

Because in this world, I wasn't a person. I was a *thing*.

I knew I had to listen to Kyle's story, but I couldn't stop the tears from streaming down my face. He saw me as a person, asked my name, and talked to me. He listened and responded to me. He gave me all the things that were so natural to receive when I was surrounded by my family—the things I had lost since coming to this world.

That was why I felt so happy for this time with Kyle. I realized I had been starving for human contact.

"Stop it. I won't comfort a man who's crying," he said in a somewhat teasing tone, consoling me despite his claims to the contrary. The contrast between his harsh words and gentle touch made me laugh for the first time since I'd come to this world.

He was the first friend I'd made here. Even though we'd just met. I wondered if he would let me call him that, though?

After a while, I regained my composure, and Kyle told me about the 5th hero. The 5th hero had also come from Japan, and his name was Shigeto Hanai. "Meeting him changed my whole life," Kyle said with a smile. From what he told me, I gathered he had been a very honest and steady individual.

"So this is the important part. You know that bracelet on your right arm? It's made of something called bluesilver—a rare metal in this world that is harder than diamonds. Bluesilver isn't necessary to make magical tools, but it's what you use when you make something you don't want broken. A magical tool is an item infused with special magic and powers. That bracelet is one of them, and it transmits your location and vital responses and will continue doing so until you die."

"So that means they'll know where I am and if I'm alive or dead no matter where I go, right?"

"That's right. You can't escape if you keep wearing that. If you try to take it off, it'll inflict physical pain, right up until the moment kills you." Kyle heaved a deep sigh. "In other words, the bracelet can only be removed after you die. And everyone summoned here has one of those put on them. It's called the Hero's Testament."

He stared at my bracelet with irritation, then continued. "Even cutting off your hand won't work. The bracelet will just appear on your other wrist. I had one of those put on me, too. I spent day after day in anxiety, defeating monsters and following the king's orders. That was the only way I could survive."

Since I had never experienced a life-and-death battle with a monster,

I had no idea what to say to comfort him, so all I could do was look at his pained expression in silence.

"They let me eat and dress as I pleased, but…" He looked at me, sadness filling his eyes. "I'd gotten to a point where I just couldn't bear living like that anymore. That's when I met the fifth hero."

"Did Hanai not have the Hero's Testament?"

"He did, because he was a hero, too. But back then, they didn't function as reliably as they do now. He had a tough fight with a monster and was on the verge of death. The bracelet mistakenly diagnosed him as dying, and by the time the old man realized what happened, the Hero's Testament had vanished."

"He was so injured it thought he was dead?"

"Yep. It's a miracle he even survived."

"No kidding."

"He told me once the Hero's Testament disappeared, he decided to start his life over. He never had any hesitations about killing monsters, but he had a rough time not being able to live the way he'd wanted."

Kyle paused for a moment and closed his eyes as if swallowing something down. I had a feeling both he and Hanai had gone through a lot of the same things and suffered greatly. I quietly waited for him to continue.

He opened his eyes and chuckled lightly, telling me not to worry about it, then changed the subject.

"The old man's in this kingdom's history books, you know that?"

"He is?"

"That's right. As a hero who fought bravely five thousand years ago."

I was about to nod when I suddenly realized something. "But that's impossible, isn't it? If Hanai was a hero from five thousand years ago, how could he have met you? That's ridiculous," I said.

A mischievous smile spread across Kyle's face. "Guess how old I am, Setsuna."

"Hmm. You look about twenty-five, but after hearing your story about Hanai, I'm guessing I'm wrong?"

"So then take that into account and guess."

"Hmm… I can't use magic, but if Hanai could, maybe you're about eighty?"

"Wrong. Was that a serious answer? I gave you a hint."

"Yes it was. That you're eighty years old."

Kyle suddenly laughed, then told me his real age. "I've lived here for more than two thousand five hundred years."

"……" I was stunned by the outrageous number. I thought he would tell me he was joking. I waited for him to, but he didn't. My eyes widened when I realized he was telling the truth. He explained life spans in this world to me. The average life span in this kingdom was generally from two hundred to two hundred and fifty years old. Nobles or royals, who could use magic, generally lived to be about three hundred and fifty. Sorcerers lived even longer than that.

There were races that did not have magical abilities, and they had different life spans from humans. All that was to say, I realized that the life spans of the people here in this world were very long. I understood that, but if nobles lived to be three hundred and fifty, how had Kyle lived to be over two thousand five hundred years old? It just seemed impossible.

"The old man, and now me—well, there's no limit to our magical abilities. So for all intents and purposes, I'm functionally immortal," he said with a serious expression. "I inherited that immense magical ability from the old man, along with all his experiences, knowledge, skills, and abilities. He gave all of it to me. He met me at a time when he felt that he had lived enough in this world and was longing for death. He looked at my Hero's Testament and asked—"

Kyle tore his gaze away from me and continued, a slight fondness in his eyes as he spoke. "He asked me, 'If you could take off that bracelet, what would you do in this world?'" It resembled the question Kyle had posed to me. "I told him I wanted to live a life of freedom. Not one full of restrictions, being bound by others. But a life of liberty."

"……"

"After I told him that, the old man said he'd gotten more than enough enjoyment from his life, and if I wanted, he would set me free."

Kyle was telling me this in simple terms, but I had a feeling the conversation between the two of them had been much more complex.

"So the old man ended up giving me my third life. That's why I'm here. If I had never met him, I would've kept hating and cursing this world until I died."

I listened quietly. Even though I thought I knew where he was going with this, I didn't want to interrupt him. He stared straight at me. And I stared straight back at him.

"So this time, I'm going to give you your third chance at life. Cast away that body and put your soul into this one."

I could tell he had chosen his words very carefully.

"To put it simply, your soul will combine with mine. And the old man's soul, too, of course. Now, I say 'combine,' but what that really means is that my soul, and the old man's, will be transformed into *information*. They won't have any influence on your personality."

I couldn't answer.

"Our immense mana, skills, knowledge, experiences, and abilities. They would all become yours. And that would greatly aid you in doing what you want—traveling around the world. The old man was very strong, and so am I. After you inherit those powers, you'll become the most powerful man in this world." Kyle smiled, his eyes glowing with sincerity.

"No…"

I finally met someone. I was all alone in this world, and he found me. I'd finally made a friend who could understand how I felt here. A really good friend I could trust my heart with.

And I didn't want to be alone anymore.

"Setsuna. I've lived for more than two thousand five hundred years. You never accomplished anything, back in Japan or here, right?" Kyle wasn't giving up. "I think you should live. You should go out and see all kinds of things and experience them. Discover the joy of life and reach out and grasp it. Of course, it isn't all sunshine and rainbows. There are many painful things here. This isn't our world. And the values are completely different. Honestly, it's not easy to live here." Kyle was straight-forward and honest with me; he made no attempt to hide his concerns.

"But even then…there is beauty here. Things that will move your heart. And I want you to experience them." He was trying to convince me, but I shook my head.

"N-no."

"Even if you turn down my offer, I'm still planning on leaving this world. I'm satisfied with the way I lived my life, and nothing's going to change my decision."

"What?" Kyle's response to my stubborn refusal was shocking. I could feel the blood draining from my face.

"Setsuna. If you take this body, my sense of self will disappear. But I can still be with you. You'll be able to freely travel around this world and go wherever you want. Accept the testament that the old man and I have lived. Just try to take that one step."

I felt sad and afraid at the thought of being left behind, along with an inexplicable sense of anxiety and loneliness.

Kyle stared at me and calmly said, "I want you to live. I know it's only been a few hours since we met, but don't you want to make your friend happy?"

Tears streamed down my cheeks, falling onto the blanket, when he referred to me as a friend.

"The old man and I were both perfectly trained in swordsmanship and hand-to-hand combat. No one else can beat us when it comes to magic or our abilities, either. And you'll inherit all our knowledge of this world that we've gained. Not only will you be equipped with abilities to protect yourself, but I'll make it so you can also search through the information we leave within you." Even though it was clear to Kyle that I wasn't yet convinced, he continued anyway. "You were never able to go outside in your old world, either, were you?"

"……"

"It would be convenient if you knew everything from the beginning, but I think that would take some of the fun out of traveling. So I'll make it so that the information won't be shared with you unless you specifically search for it. You like reading books, right? Exploring the world won't be exciting if you get spoiled beforehand. I want you to travel around and experience things at your own pace."

My heart wanted to turn down Kyle's offer. But the more I listened to him, the less I felt that way.

"Think of it like looking for something on the internet. It's convenient but also a little inconvenient sometimes."

Kyle sensed my resolve wavering as my eyes darted around. He looked at me and said firmly, "Setsuna. *Live.*"

That made my desire to turn him down weaken even more—now I was leaning toward wanting to live. As Kyle stared at me, I found myself nodding...and that was when I decided to live.

"All right. I'll try. I'll try to do my best. Thank you...Kyle," I murmured.

He lowered his gaze for a moment and then smiled happily at me.

"Once you begin your new life, I think you'll understand this immediately...but the old man's and my abilities will mix with yours. I'm not sure what yours are at this point in time, but as long as you have ours, you won't ever run into any trouble."

After I told Kyle I wanted to live, he didn't seem to be sad at all; in fact, he looked happy. "So it's not a far-fetched dream for you to actually be able to explore the whole world."

I had to chuckle with how spontaneous it all sounded.

"If you get tired of traveling, find a place you like and protect it. Become a demon king. Live the way you want to live. Or you could travel your whole life... Just get out there and interact with people, Setsuna."

At that moment, I felt as if Kyle was more of a family member than just a friend. If I had an older brother, that's what he would be like.

"What about you, Kyle? How did you spend your days for two thousand five hundred years?"

For some reason, his gaze darted back and forth. "Th-that's a secret for now. But I saw your memories, so I'll make it so that you can view my past as well... I'll just lock up two of them, though. Once you fulfill certain requirements throughout the world, they'll unlock. Good luck finding the keys to them!"

Is he really that uncomfortable with me knowing about his past? What in the world have you done here?

There were many things I was curious about, but for the time being, I decided to agree. I suspected he wouldn't answer me even if asked anyway.

We continued talking for a long time. But I knew it would have to end eventually. Kyle closed his eyes, then slowly opened them. He looked at me with a hint of sadness and of lingering reluctance. I had a feeling I knew what he was going to say, and I felt my fingertips growing cold. Even when he looked at me like that, his resolve did not waver.

"Are you ready, Setsuna?"

I didn't think I could ever be ready for something like this. My heart began to fill with sadness. I wanted to scream *"No! I don't want to leave you!"* but something got in the way, and I couldn't utter a sound. Even if I could, I knew he wouldn't change his mind. He wouldn't change... he wouldn't...

That's what his eyes were telling me.

"......"

I looked down briefly, trying to hide my expression.

If you won't change your mind...

...then I promise to go on a journey, since you were so kind to me. You wished for my future and made me believe it was okay for me to wish for it, too. I will never forget my first and final encounter with you.

And so I put on a brave face and gave him these words:

"Farewell, *Kanade*."

All he did was smile and quietly nod.

"See ya, Setsuna. *Live* like the camellias." The corners of his mouth curled up into a smile. He rose to his feet and intoned something, casting a magic spell.

I clenched my fists tightly, fighting against my desire to stop him. I was certain I wasn't the only one feeling conflicted. I watched as Kyle's expression changed many times in that brief moment.

First, he nodded in agreement, then he looked apologetic, happy, and finally a bit troubled as he stretched his hand out to me. The moment his hand touched my forehead...

I lost my bearing, my vision, my weight, my size. I was pulled in by something and sank down in it before I even had time to feel afraid. I was within something I couldn't describe in words. My instincts whispered at me to start kicking my legs before I drowned.

Before the whispering ended, that *something* swallowed me up and flowed into me from all directions. It didn't take long for it to completely settle inside me. Now I knew what Kyle meant when he said I would inherit his and Hanai's life experiences. I took all of it—every last drop.

I slowly opened my eyes.

I was standing beside the bed, looking down at the me who still lay in it—the familiar figure I'd grown accustomed to seeing in the mirror for twenty-four—no, for twenty-five years. The black hair and the black eyes—even though right now they were closed.

When I was summoned here, I was younger than I had been in my previous life, but it was still me.

I just stood there and watched the Hero's Testament slowly fade away from my gaunt right wrist.

And then...the human known as Setsuna Sugimoto died once again, disappearing from this otherworld along with Kanade Tokito.

"I'm going to abandon everything, right here."

My quiet whisper filled the silent room and then vanished.

I wasn't sure how long I lost myself in sorrow after that. But suddenly, I heard a flurry of activity in the distance, which pulled me back to reality. Up until now, I'd never sensed the presence of another human before. The new sensation bewildered me, but I began thinking about how I should escape from this room.

I'm sure they were alerted that I had died. I couldn't afford for them to find me, so I knew I needed to leave. I searched for the way Kyle had entered the room. Everything he had talked to me about before now felt vividly real. It was like some kind of network had been established inside my brain.

At any rate, it seemed he had come here using teleportation magic. I only vaguely understood how he had found me. Perhaps I would understand more later?

I didn't feel any kind of uncertainty about whether I'd be able to use magic; it just felt as if it was naturally flowing through my body.

I didn't feel like myself, but I figured I would get used to it. Then I noticed someone's presence inside the building. I wondered what the sensation was and tried to focus on it. I learned that I could sense very detailed things, such as where people were and how many of them there were. I focused a little harder, sharpening my senses toward the outside of the building, too. There was a place away from here, where a large number of people were gathered.

Was it the castle town?

In my mind's eye, I found a spot away from where anyone else was gathered and used magic for the very first time to teleport myself there. All I had to do was think of the word *Teleport*. At the same time, another spell activated, which would conceal my mana. I wondered if Kyle had cast a spell on this body to make that happen. Perhaps he had done so because he, too, had sensed all those people nearby.

I escaped from the place where I had been both summoned to and imprisoned, and I finally gained freedom.

"Live like the camellias."

I tucked the memories of Kanade inside of my heart, engraving his words upon it. I took the first step of my third life, filled with a mixture of sadness and excitement.

◇Part Two: Kanade Tokito

It was a quiet, still room. The moon hung outside the window, casting its blue light inside. He was alone, sitting up in bed, gazing at it.

The moon here was a completely different size and color from the one on Earth. But I painfully empathized with how he felt as he looked at it. I had done the same thing countless times myself. I wondered how many times I had wished for that moon to be yellow.

I had returned to the continent for the first time in several years. I was having a drink when I overheard a certain rumor. According to "prophesy," the 69th hero had "awakened." The patrons in the bar were all raising a fuss about the hero without knowing any of the facts. I drained my glass so that I could get out of there.

I honed my senses to focus in on the *summoned* hero and came across a very nostalgic presence. Apparently, the victim was from the same country as me. "Wonder what kind of person got summoned this time," I muttered, the noises from the lively city drowning out my voice. "Maybe..."

I strengthened my resolve and used magic to leave the city.

I had entered the room by using magic, not a door, so my compatriot did not notice my presence. I decided to observe him for a while until he did. I couldn't see his face from where I stood, but I was able to see his body. I frowned.

No matter what *actually* transpired behind closed doors, in general, heroes were given nice living arrangements, fine clothes to wear, and good food to eat...

But it was apparent this person had not been given the same. Those summoned here as heroes were supposed to have a healthy constitution, both physically and mentally, yet he...

He was gaunt and hardly had any muscle to speak of. He looked so sickly, it was as if he could pass away at any moment. I felt pity as I watched this man on the brink of death, and at the same time, my heart ached as it reminded me of watching my young daughter suffer from a bad case of the flu.

I could tell they had determined he was too sick to be useful and decided to keep him here until he died. I clenched my fists at the thought.

Then I heaved an inward sigh.

I didn't come here to see my compatriot out of pure curiosity. The clan I was protecting on the other continent was gone now, and along with them, my reason for living. That's what I thought anyway.

I had been swallowed up by the fate of destruction when I first encountered them, as ephemeral as morning dew, and I knew I had to protect them. But in the end, I was powerless against their natural life span. I watched over them, and in a sense, felt satisfied that I had done enough. Of course, there were things I hadn't been able to do, but if I let that affect me, I would never find a place to quit.

That was the decision I had made, absently thinking I should let myself rest in peace...and that's when I heard those rumors.

If I was going to put myself to rest...

I began thinking maybe I should free this guy who had been summoned here, just like the old man had freed me. But if I didn't like him, I'd just ditch him.

After I finished observing him, I called out to the very unlikely hero. "Hey, you. Aren't you a hero?"

The man shifted his gaze toward me without a hint of bewilderment. Wouldn't any ordinary person be surprised when someone showed up in their room and spoke to them out of the blue?

Just as that thought crossed my mind, I looked into his eyes and realized why he hadn't been surprised to see me. I inwardly clicked my tongue.

He was alive, but he was heading toward death. He had the eyes of someone who had given up on everything and accepted his fate.

I repeated my question and listened to his response. I was surprised to hear that he was *not* the 69th hero, but the 68th. Summoning wasn't something that could be done lightly. Direct descendants of the founder of Gardir who possessed strong mana could only do it twice in their lifetime. The fact that they had used up one of those opportunities in just one year meant they were in dire straits indeed...not that I cared about what happened to this kingdom.

But why hadn't I noticed he had been summoned a year ago? I should have been able to sense the presence of someone from my own country, even from the other continent. I was confused as to why this had happened. I thought about it and arrived at one conclusion: I had been too absorbed in protecting the clan at that time.

At that point, I felt it was too much trouble to ask him a bunch of questions, so instead I read his memories in order to learn more about him—about this man named Setsuna.

He was an earnest guy. Almost too earnest. But at the same time, I learned just how much suffering he had gone through in his life. He'd been treated so cruelly that I wanted to end the life of every single person in this castle.

Once Setsuna learned I was also from Japan, he seemed to start feeling things again—the proof of that was when he gave me a dismayed look once he found out I had read his memories. Still, I knew the people here would probably kill him. And when I told him that, he didn't even bat an eye.

I knew the people of this kingdom were so evil that they had driven this kind young man to this point. Violent anger surged within me, but I forced it down. Going off the rails here wouldn't change his future. I let out another inward sigh and asked him a similar question to the one the old man had asked me.

"If your illness was cured, what would you want to do?"

I asked him about his future, yet he responded with "Die like the camellias."

He couldn't bear dying alone. Setsuna told me he wanted to expire with grace, like the flowers.

Camellias had made a very strong impact on him. That promise was his last remaining reason for living.

I chuckled wryly and told him that wasn't what he really wanted to do.

He then very quietly told me that he wished to travel around the world. He said some other things after that, but I decided not to listen. He was a bit angry with what I said, but I soothed him and told him about myself, the old man, heroes, and this world.

As I explained all these things, tears quietly streamed down the young man's face. And when I realized why he was crying, my heart began to ache as well.

He had experienced true loneliness. He hadn't been able to rely on a single person here. He had struggled and suffered, and no one had reached out a hand to him. And he had no one to talk to.

Once I learned that, I knew I couldn't just abandon him. I'd only just met this young man from my own country—a man wildly younger than me, that is—a few hours ago. Yet it felt like I had been friends with him for years. Or perhaps he felt more like a younger brother. Maybe I felt close to him because I had read his memories?

I wasn't sure if it had something to do with Setsuna's personality or if it was because I simply liked him. But for what it was worth, he thought of me as a friend. Was I his first?

If I was, then that would make it harder to convince him...

He didn't seem like a man who would bend his will for anyone. But I had to, no matter what it took. I needed to push past Setsuna's stubbornness and convince him. Because I wanted him to live.

Once he began to change his mind, I started making my preparations before his resolve wavered. I stood up, and the chair returned to the bag automatically. He was so deep in thought that he didn't even see it happening.

It was both his greatest strength and greatest weakness that he struggled so hard to change his mind once it was made up. This time, it was a weakness, and thanks to that, I had plenty of time to prepare.

My mana and abilities were so strong that I usually didn't even have to utter incantations anymore, but this time I wanted to do it properly, with the strongest magic I had.

I added several little *quirks* to the spell, but I don't think he noticed. Hey, could you really blame me? The last friend I made was so sheltered that I wanted to help him out. I needed to make sure he wasn't too sad about my death, too, because knowing him, he'd just sit here stunned for way too long.

Geez, I'll be so worried about him I won't be able to rest in peace. What a pain.

I couldn't believe I'd grown so attached to something in the very last moments of my life. I wished I could have been able to accompany him on his journey.

I gave an inward, wry chuckle. I couldn't help but grin when I thought about Setsuna living his life with a smile on his face. If he found happiness, then my life wouldn't have been in vain…including this past year.

I surrendered myself to that feeling of satisfaction and fell asleep next to him.

Chapter Two
Pincushion Flower ~ Departure from Zero ~

◇Part One: Setsuna Sugimoto

I teleported to a spot away from other people, but to be honest, I was at a complete loss. My illness was suddenly cured, and now I had a body I could actually walk around in without growing short of breath. Apparently, I could also now fight without difficulty and use magic, too. Although, I had to wonder if I'd be mentally capable of squaring off against someone.

At any rate, I decided I needed a place where I could sit and carefully think about things. I didn't even know what I looked like right now or what else I was capable of. I'd chosen to travel around this otherworld, but other than that, I hadn't made any decisions at all.

I didn't get a wink of sleep the previous day, because Kyle and I had stayed up all night talking. And I was hungry for the first time in a long while. I wanted a place where I could get some rest and something to eat.

I'd search for an inn and book a room there, then think about what my next move would be. Suddenly, I realized that I'd need money to stay at an inn. "Money...," I muttered. I'd never had any in this world.

I searched my pockets and realized that a bag was slung over my shoulder. As I stared at it, I remembered Kyle speaking of it with such amusement before he went to rest in peace.

"I'm gonna give you my greatest masterpiece! Take real good care of it. And make sure you thoroughly *check the contents!"*

Was this the bag he was talking about?

I was incredibly curious about what was inside, but right now I needed money. The bag was made from a coffee-colored fabric, and I found a drawstring pouch inside that was the same color. I opened it in search of something that resembled money. Kyle really had left everything to me...

Now that I'd solved that issue, I racked my brain for any mention of money while I looked for an inn.

According to Kyle's memories, the money of this world was organized in this fashion:

10 copper dimes = 1 full copper
5 full coppers = 1 half-silver
2 half-silvers = 1 silver
10 silvers = 1 gold

And if you converted that into yen, then it would be something like this:

1 copper dime = 100 yen
1 full copper = 1000 yen
1 half-silver = 5000 yen
1 silver = 10,000 yen
1 gold = 100,000 yen

That was generally how it was, but occasionally there would be fluctuations in the value of the coins. At any rate, the system of currency was different from the one in my old world, but at least I had a general idea of it.

While I went over all of that in my head, I arrived at a building that looked like an inn. I nervously opened the door and went inside. In my past life, I very rarely had gone anywhere except the hospital. There was a woman sitting at what I assumed was the reception desk, so I approached her.

"I'd like to book a room. Are there any vacancies available?" Even though I was nervous, my voice was even, which made me feel relieved. I had successfully stated my business. But for some reason, she didn't answer me. Puzzled, I repeated myself.

Suddenly she shook her head as if coming back to herself and stared at my face as she answered me. *Do I have something on my face? Now I'm worried.* "Welcome. A single room is four coppers per night. If you'd like dinner, then it'll be a half-silver."

Since I was hungry, I told the woman I wanted a room with dinner included. "I'd like to book a room for three nights."

"A single room with dinner included for three nights, correct? We require payment in advance, so that will be one silver and one half-silver, please."

I took the money out of my pouch and handed it to her. She accepted it with a beautiful smile. "Your room is on the second floor right at the top of the stairs, room 201. Please enjoy your stay." She handed me a key with a broad smile. I thanked her and headed upstairs.

The room was simple, with only a bed, a desk, and a chair, but it was very clean. I sat down on the bed and sighed. I was exhausted, which was to be expected after the dizzying events of the past day. The bed creaked as I looked toward the mirror that was leaning against the wall.

And my reflection surprised me.

Was that really me? My face looked nothing like the old me. But I didn't exactly look like Kyle, either. But strangely, I was able to accept the face I saw as my own. I didn't have black hair and eyes, nor Kyle's golden-brown hair. Instead, it was more of a shiny walnut brown. Kyle's eyes had been light green, but mine were light violet. Walnut-brown hair and violet eyes...

I stared at my reflection and greeted my new self for the first time. Next, I looked down at my body, which was also completely different. Back in Japan, I'd dreamed about having a healthy physique, but this surpassed that—I was muscular from head to toe. I don't mean to boast, but I had the ideal body. A smile crept onto my face.

If my younger sister, Kyoka, could see me now, she would shed tears of joy.

I lay down in bed and fell asleep.

It was dinnertime when I finally woke up; I'd been asleep for almost half the day. I finished eating, then returned to my room. I decided to give in to my curiosity and check the contents of the bag. I opened it up and laughed out loud despite myself.

I felt like a child excited to open a present. I'd long forgotten this feeling.

Following Kyle's instructions, I thoroughly inspected the bag's contents. "Now let's see what's inside…"

I pulled out items one by one. There was a white robe and a black one. Fine clothes that had an air of nobility about them. A cloak… Was there more than just clothes in here? Some looked like things Kyle would wear, but others made me raise a brow, wondering if he had ever put them on at all.

After I'd finished with his wardrobe(?), the next things I pulled out were weapons. A shortsword, a staff, a whip, a bow. And some things I was absolutely sure they wouldn't sell in stores. I didn't know if he obtained them from some kind of ruin or made them himself. I wanted to take my time and appreciate them, but I needed to check my inventory first.

I switched gears and kept pulling out items. Next was a canteen, three pouches filled with money, a chair… Wait, a chair?!

It looked familiar. Ah, that's right—so that's where Kyle had gotten the chair he'd sat on while we talked. Now I understood why he was laughing then. He was imagining my reaction when I plucked this out of the bag. Still, when had he put it away?

After the chair, there was a stuffed animal, another stuffed animal, and then another one… All in all, there were twenty-five in total. Why were there that many in here?! I was a bit frightened of their eyes as they sat all in a row…

Now thoroughly puzzled, I continued digging to find musical instruments next. There were two stringed instruments. One was normal, but

I sensed mana coming from the other one. After those, it was books. Ooh, books! Since I was a bibliophile, my heart filled with expectation as I checked the titles...and my jaw dropped.

Little-Known Date Spots: Your Complete Guide!
Top Inns for Romance
Your First...

I put that one back in the bag before I finished reading its title.

With every item I pulled out of the bag, I felt my doubts about Kyle grow. *Hey, Kyle? Were you* really *an adventurer?*

After that, I pulled out things I couldn't even identify, things I had no idea why he even had them, and magical tools that looked like I'd make a fortune if I sold them.

Next, I found several pieces of notepaper that were folded in half. I unfolded them and saw slightly sloppy Japanese written on them. I absently traced the characters with my finger. They brought back so many memories.

It was a letter addressed to me. When had he had the time to write it? I wondered as I thought back on my time with Kyle. Then I began to read the letter.

Dear Setsuna,
You're probably thinking, "When did he have time to write this letter?" But there's no point in wondering, right? Because by now, you should understand. I created it with my ability Materialize. I'm going to write down all the things I wasn't able to tell you in this letter, so please read it.

I guess I have no choice but to do that, huh, Kyle?

What abilities was he talking about, though? Up until now when he referred to them, I was taking the word literally, but apparently it was a bit different. I tried to unravel the knowledge I had inherited from him for an answer.

Abilities referred to special powers possessed by intelligent creatures in this world. It seemed that there were many cases where they remained dormant. With that in mind, I continued reading.

My abilities are of a rare variety. And the old man's abilities were even rarer. You might have some awaken within you, and those might be uncommon, too.

There are a lot of people who possess abilities, and if the ones that manifest are common, there's no need to be anxious. But I don't think the rarity of an ability has anything to do with whether it should be disclosed. Abilities can be a sort of trump card, so there are a lot of people who choose not to talk about them. That being said, jobs might come your way if people are aware that you have certain abilities. Whether you hide them or not is up to you. Disclosing an ability that's a bit too convenient can be annoying because it tends to attract a lot of people.

In that case, I really had no choice but to keep them a secret.

Well, in my case, I hid mine. Because I have the strongest abilities in the world.

Materialize allowed one to freely create any object they imagined, besides living things, food, or drinks. I suppose that was a pretty strong ability.

That's enough boasting. Knowing your personality, I bet you're going to choose to hide your abilities.

You seem to be the careful type, so I know you'll go down the right path, but I'll still leave you with some words of warning.

You are an anomaly in this world. You understand why, right? Heroes themselves are anomalies. They have perfect bodies and unparalleled mana. They're summoned possessing special abilities. Although you only have the physical body the old man left us, you have the mana and abilities of three people.

I don't know how you'll choose to use what you inherited from us, but don't forget that you have the power to destroy the world with your abilities depending on how you use them.

Honestly, hearing I had the capacity to destroy the world didn't feel real at all.

Oh, and since I'm talking about whether to disclose your powers, you might be wondering if it's all right to tell anyone that you were reborn into someone else's body.

I won't say to never tell anyone else, but please think about it very, very carefully before you do. That's because it's forbidden to use magic on souls in this world. And this reincarnation magic worked by having your soul accept ours. Just be aware that telling someone about this is like dropping a bomb; it will change your environment forever.

I hadn't planned on telling anyone, but I decided to keep all that in mind. Still...

The Kingdom of Gardir is secretly breaking the law by using forbidden magic to create slaves they call "heroes." Don't worry. I know how you feel...

I could tell that Kyle had the same violent anger I felt toward them.

That was the end of the first page. Thinking about both Kyle's thoughtfulness and the contents of the letter summoned all kinds of contradictory emotions in me. I took a deep breath to work through them as I moved on to the second page.

You don't know much about this world, right? So I thought I should give you some advice. Aren't you happy? Well, aren't you?

I suppose it would depend on what he was about to tell me.

First, about what's in the bag... Don't even try to take everything out of it. Why's that, you ask? Well, that's because... At first, I really tried to organize everything neatly. I'm a pretty tidy person. But that bag can hold anything, regardless of size or weight. And it will remain the way it was when you put it into the bag.

After about five hundred years, I stopped keeping track of what was inside...

Hang on a second. That had to be impossible. I re-read the letter and then looked back over at the bag. He hadn't taken an inventory of the contents in two thousand years?!

So that meant the inside was a complete mess!

I looked back down at the letter, feeling a bit irked as I continued reading.

But don't worry! You don't need to organize it! Just think of whatever item you want, and it'll come to you. That's how it was designed to work. So there's no problem, right? Of course, if a certain item isn't in the bag, it won't appear. In that case, you'll just have to give up and buy it or make it yourself.

Um, that sounds like a problem!

I was surprised I was even able to find the letter at all, in that case. I looked up again and gazed into the distance, dissociating for a bit before I continued reading.

I'll answer the question you have in your mind right now. You're probably wondering how you ever found this letter, aren't you? I'll tell you something that'll surprise you. Count the objects you took out from the bag. There are sixty-seven, right? I made it so that the sixty-eighth thing you pulled out would be this letter. Aren't you glad you weren't the five hundredth summoned hero?

Yes, I was definitely glad I was the 68th. At this point, I'd grown to hate that number, but Kyle's prank did get a little chuckle out of me. I continued reading his message, making sarcastic remarks in my head as I went. It felt like my heart was getting a bit lighter.

All right, I digress...

You have enough tools and money so that you'll never have to worry about those. Worst-case scenario, you can use your abilities to make some more cash.

Knowing you, you'll probably want to work to earn it, but I really want you to travel around the world at your leisure and not have to work.

You know what they say, Kyle. A man must work to eat.

I'll go ahead and give you simple explanations of the various tools you'll need on your journey. There's a canteen, right? Well, that canteen doesn't need to be filled. It will refill automatically with water. So you don't have to get your own.

By the way, in my case, I always thought it was a pain to get it out, so I just used magic to create water and drank it that way.

What was the point of having the canteen, then?

As for food, you need to get your own and put it in the bag. There are emergency rations in there, but they're way grosser than the ones back in our world. Part of the joy of traveling is the grub, after all. So make sure you sample all this world has to offer. You can eat monsters here, too, so there's plenty of new dishes for you to experience.

Tonight's dinner was pretty tasty.

I have separate pouches for gold coins, silver coins, and copper coins. I have another for half-silvers and copper dimes.

Go ahead and stay in as many inns as you like. Also, make sure you register with the Adventurers Guild. They'll help you on your journey, and you can make money there. You can learn some helpful information there, too. Register. Got it? Well, that might be it from me.

An adventurers guild... Kyle sounded so enthusiastic talking about it that it got me interested.

Oh, right! When you sign up, make sure to put down what magical attributes you can use. Now, you might not know what I mean by magic attributes, so I'll explain it in simple terms. You can look this all up later if you search through my knowledge, but I might as well tell you. I'm not being overprotective, I promise!

Why did he forget to explain abilities? *Um, Kyle?* I thought.

There are eight different magic attributes in this world. Remember that abilities and magic are separate things.

Uhhh, Kyle? Seriously, aren't you going to explain about abilities?

The more mana you have, the more magic attributes you can use. You can't choose your attributes. Right now, the sorcerers with the most mana can only use three types. You, however, can use all of them. Now do you see how much more powerful we are compared to everyone else?

I mean, I guess. I didn't really get it, so I continued reading.

The order of the attributes from most to least common is as follows: Fire, Water, Earth, Wind. Most people who can use magic will at least have one of those. The less common types are Light, Darkness, Void, and Time. When you register with the guild, I would recommend that you register as a Wind magic user, because that attribute covers healing magic.

I wondered why he recommended that, but the answer was written just below.

You can choose whatever type you want to write down, but healing magic is valued everywhere. There are overwhelmingly fewer Wind magic users than Fire, so a lot of people will depend on you. Then you'll have more chances to interact with others. Also, I kind of think Wind magic suits you.

......

That's all I'll say about this topic, but if you want to learn more, then you can search for it. I only explained magic attributes here, but there are other varieties of magic out there. For example, ancient magic, which is cast by using the ancient language.

I think that should be it for my warnings and explanation about the bag. Ah, speaking of the bag—it'll come back to you no matter where you set it, and you're the only one who can use it. Pretty handy, right? Heh-heh-heh...

It sounded more like it was cursed than handy. And why was he laughing like a villain?

One last thing...

I want you to really prioritize your life. Kill before getting killed. This isn't our old world. You need to accept that this isn't Japan. You'll have it a lot easier here if you cast aside your values from our old world...

I wondered if that was how Kyle had lived.

That's why you should accept quests from the guild for a while, too. It's important to learn the basics. You can choose another occupation if you want, but whatever you choose, I can't recommend that you should live in this kingdom.

He didn't have to worry about that. I had no intention of being buried in this kingdom. Also, I wanted to travel.

All right. That's all for me. See ya later, Setsuna.

"See you later?! What's that supposed to mean?" I blurted out. I wanted to know more about that final sentence and remembered there was a third page.

P.S.

Put your hand inside the bag. Did you take out a small box? There's a ring and earrings inside, right?

The earring on the right is for magical defense, and the one on the left is for physical defense. The ring is to help suppress your mana. Don't take it off until you get used to using magic.

Even though he claimed he wasn't overprotective, it certainly sounded like he was to me. Still, I was touched that he had taken the time to leave me with these magical tools. Kyle was the only one who had ever shown concern for me in this world.

And now he was gone...

Sadness weighed heavy on my chest as I continued reading the postscript.

The book is a compilation of all my experiences in this world. What you need most is...

I put the letter back into the bag without reading the rest of it. The sadness had suddenly turned into a wry chuckle. I didn't need to read Kyle's book right now, and honestly, I wasn't sure if I'd ever need it. I slipped the ring onto the middle finger of my left hand. I picked up the earrings so I could put them on, but the moment I touched them, they automatically moved to my earlobes.

Magic certainly is convenient, I thought as I gazed at the earrings in the mirror. This was my first time ever wearing jewelry, so it felt a little odd. I also felt a little embarrassed wearing it.

I let out a sigh, thinking that I'd just have to get used to it.

I absently pondered the contents of Kyle's letter again and decided I would go to the Adventurers Guild the next day.

Now that I had finished reading Kyle's letter, I cleaned up and had another good night's sleep. I woke up at the crack of dawn the next morning, although it felt like I had slept for a very long time.

You could have breakfast at the inn for an additional fee, so I decided to wait until it was time to eat. I chose some clothes at random from the bag and got dressed, then decided to exercise a bit. The reason why I wanted to do that was because I still wasn't sure what this body was capable of. If I had to compare it to something, I'd say it was like getting a brand-new bicycle with all the bells and whistles but not knowing how to use any of them. It'd be a waste of talent.

I wanted to see how far I could jump, how much force I had to apply to things before they would break, and things like that.

Honestly, I was a little surprised at how well my body cooperated with me when I tried to move it. I'd spent most of my life bedridden, so I'd had very little, if any, muscle tone. I'd never experienced having sharp reflexes, or extreme flexibility, or the strength to lift heavy objects before.

This really was the ideal body.

After a while of doing that, I felt warmed up enough to really start exercising. I thought about it for a while. Honestly, I'd never been that interested in martial arts, so I had never given much thought to training.

I decided to search my mind to find out anything I could about my body. The former hero's body was trained to perfection and would always revert to that state. In other words, I could maintain this condition without having to do a thing.

That made me wonder if Kyle had trained at all, so I looked into his past ventures and found something very interesting. Even if one was well-trained, they were only strong in the generic sense. For example, even if I mastered the spear, my overall strength wouldn't change, and I would still remain a jack-of-all-trades. I would excel at the spear as part of my versatility, but to the same extent, I would also be inferior in another area.

In other words, I could guide my body toward specializing in whatever I wanted. In Kyle's case, he'd decided to focus on the sword and hand-to-hand combat, and so this body right now was best suited for that.

After I learned all that, I decided I would just keep up what Kyle had done and focus on how he had trained.

Since my room was small, I trained without a sword. Next time, I would do it outside. I practiced seriously, thinking that I had to do so in order to protect myself. It was still amazing how I could move so much without being out of breath.

I once again felt a little emotional that I could move exactly as I wanted to. And I discovered that exercise was a pure joy.

I must have been at it for an hour or so when I decided to stop for the day. By then, I was drenched in sweat and wondered what I should do about that. I searched my internal database, wondering if there was some kind of convenient spell I could use to take care of it. To little surprise, I found out I could solve my problem with magic. Once again, I thought how handy magic was as I cast the spell on myself.

I went to the dining hall and ate breakfast, then headed to the Adventurers Guild as planned. I was able to find the guild without much trouble. I was a bit nervous as I opened the door and went inside. The interior was surprisingly spacious. There was a reception desk in the back and a bulletin board on the wall. I went to the reception desk and spoke to the person sitting there.

"I'd like to register, please."

The middle-aged man looked me over carefully. "Fill this out first, please." He handed me a piece of paper, and I began filling it out.

First was my name. I thought for a moment and decided to just write Setsuna. Setsuna Sugimoto had died.

I hadn't lived at all in the year since I'd been summoned to this world.

I had breathed and moved, but nothing more.

I used to be Japanese, but the day before, for the first time, I told a person in this world my name. And that would be the last time I uttered my full name here in this otherworld. Kyle was the only one who knew my past and my full name. He'd gone to sleep inside me, and when I inherited everything from him, I cast aside everything from my old life.

The person standing here right now was no longer Setsuna Sugimoto. He was just Setsuna. Even though I said I cast aside everything, my weakness prevented me from giving myself a new name.

◇Part Two: Setsuna

I let out a little sigh and pulled from the knowledge I had to fill in the blanks on the sheet.

Name: Setsuna
Age: 18
Occupation: Scholar, Sorcerer
Attribute: Wind
Abilities: None
Skills: Herbalism, Pharmacology
Languages: Common Language, Ancient Language, Southern Dialect, Northern Dialect

I decided to write that I was eighteen. In my old world, I was twenty-five, but right now I certainly didn't look it.

I put down scholar as my occupation because it gave me a reason to travel; I wanted to show my curiosity and desire to learn. I hoped I could find something new to research. Since Hanai and Kyle had lived so long, they had extensive knowledge of just about everything. It's not bad to travel to places I already knew about or to walk wherever I felt like.

As for my abilities, I had decided to conceal them. I didn't want to attract all sorts of unsavory individuals like Kyle had mentioned.

For skills, I wrote down what I was interested in. Although my chances of it coming true were low, I had dreamed of becoming a doctor. The moment I found herbology and pharmacology in my internal database, my heart sang with excitement. I was the son of doctors, after all.

I listened to my father and mother and studied medicine in my own way. I wasn't sure whether the knowledge from my past life would come in handy in this world, but at any rate, I decided to choose herbology and pharmacology.

Although neither Kyle nor Hanai seemed to have had a vested interest in either, they had studied the basics of both. So now the rest was up to me.

Finally, I had to write down what languages I could speak. The language mainly used in this world was called the common language. Scholars needed to speak the ancient language in order to understand things found in ruins and such, so I included that as well. Next, the beastfolk who lived in the south widely used the southern dialect, which was sometimes called Beastian. The empire had a strong influence in the northern territories where the northern dialect was spoken, also referred to as Empirean.

Surely I'd be believable as a scholar if I knew this many languages.

I handed the sheet of paper back to the man, who looked bewildered after reading it. I hadn't intended on writing anything so surprising...

"You're a scholar at your young age? Are you a linguist or something?"

"No, I just learned those languages out of curiosity. But books aren't enough, so I'm hoping to learn more through my travels."

"I see. There are a lot of eccentric folk who are scholars. Guess you're one of 'em, hmm?"

"Do I seem weird to you?"

I wasn't sure why that would be the case.

"You're putting your life on the line to satisfy your thirst for knowledge, aren't ya?" he asked.

Only then did I remember that traveling in this world was considered a matter of life and death. Take one step outside the city, and you entered a place where monsters lurked around every corner. No wonder this guy thought I was weird.

The corners of his mouth curved up as he looked at me. It wasn't a patronizing smile, but a sort of fatherly one. "It's not a bad idea to travel around and see all kinds of things while you're young. Life is long, you know? And it seems like you're pretty strong, so get out there and do your best, just as long as you don't overdo it."

"Thanks, I will."

"By the way, my name is Nestor, and I'm the guildmaster here. You can just call me Nes."

"I'm Setsuna. It's nice to meet you."

Nestor gave a satisfied nod. "Want me to tell you about the guild?"

"Yes, please."

"All right, I'll go ahead, then. First of all, there are various quests, from real simple ones to dangerous ones." I nodded to show I understood. "Here at the guild, we recommend quests by rank. When I say recommend, I mean we post 'em over there on the bulletin board." He pointed to the board I'd noticed earlier. "We don't post the black quests there, though, and you have to inquire directly about the white ones."

"Black quests?"

"Yeah, ranks are separated by color. You start out at yellow, then green, blue, purple, red, white, and then the highest rank is black."

"I see."

"......" He gave me a look. "Are you some sheltered boy?"

"Pardon?"

"Well, even kids know about ranks." He seemed disappointed that I didn't know even the most basic knowledge. I regretted not doing some research beforehand.

"Aw, don't give me that look. I won't ask why." Nes gave a wry chuckle when he saw that I was speechless, then continued his explanation as if it was no big deal. "All right, let's get you registered. Put your left hand on this magical tool." He produced an object that I assumed was the magical tool he spoke about. It was about the size of a crystal ball I'd seen fortune tellers use.

I did as instructed and felt a faint jolt of mana. I knew that some kind of magic had just occurred. I was surprised that I could sense such a subtle thing but was even more surprised when I looked at the top of my hand. There was a yellow emblem drawn there of a small bird protecting a camellia.

I was captivated by the image for a while, but Nes's voice pulled me back to reality.

"The mark is different for everyone. The color indicates your rank, and any symbols on your emblem have to do with your occupation. For example, if you're a swordsman, it might be a sword, a sorcerer might have their familiar, a scholar might have a plant. There are loads more. If you're curious, you should look them up in an emblem encyclopedia."

I didn't know there was such a thing. I definitely wanted to read it if I had the time.

"Your emblem is very personal to you and expresses something you hold dear. If you want to learn more about the specifics, you should head to the guild headquarters in Lycia. It's something that's still being researched. I'm sure they'll have the latest information on the subject if you go there."

"You can't tell me here?"

"You're a scholar, aren't you? I don't know enough about it in detail to satisfy an academic."

"Touché."

"Good," Nes said, nodding firmly. "Next, I'll tell you how to take on quests. Go look at the bulletin board, keeping the color of your rank in mind."

Ah, I see. Looking around the room, there were six in total, each one a different color.

"As I'm sure you can guess, you can accept quests based on the corresponding color of your rank. You should carefully select one that's within your abilities."

"Okay."

"If you don't complete it, sometimes you'll get demoted in rank."

I asked what happened if you failed a quest when you were yellow rank.

He frowned and told me they recommend those people find another line of work. "Now, I'm sure you'd like to know how to raise your rank. Well, there are points listed on every quest. Successfully complete one, and you get them. And if you do a really great job, you can be awarded bonus points. Following so far?"

"Yes."

"Bonus points are decided by the client who posted the quest and guild members. Just completing a quest won't get you bonus points. You'll have to show us what you're made of and go above and beyond."

"Okay."

"If you want to know how many points you have currently and how many you have to go until the next rank, you can inquire at the reception desk. We only disclose that information to the person themselves."

"It must be a lot of work dealing with everyone individually."

"Not really. Most get sick of it after a while."

"What do you mean?"

"The points you need to move to the next rank exponentially increase every time. A lot of adventurers get bored along the way. They realize that it's much easier on them mentally to just take things one day at a time and complete their quests instead of caring about a bunch of numbers."

I guess that made sense. Although I liked seeing numbers add up.

"Now, I see you smiling at that yellow mark on your hand, but just so you know, you're gonna get teased until you make it to green."

"Teased?"

"Doesn't matter how much you care about numbers. Until then, you're just a chick with its shell stuck to its butt."

......

"That's all for my explanation. Oh, I almost forgot. This probably goes without saying, but the mark on your hand will change colors when you move up ranks. So good luck with that."

"Thanks." I tried to drill the information he'd given me into my brain.

"Finally, I'm gonna give you ten of a certain magical tool called a Cube. When you defeat a monster, put 'em in there. Just activate it in front of the dead monster, and the monster will be contained inside. You can use every part of a monster without wasting anything. And you can bring 'em here for money and points, so bring me as many as you can."

I thought it was very interesting that the very monsters that attacked people could be so beneficial after they were defeated. I'd read so many stories about dead monsters turning into poison and making the area around them uninhabitable for humans and things like that, after all.

"Anything else you wanna know?" Nes asked. I inquired about several things I was curious about and thanked him with a bow. "Just doing my job!" He laughed, then handed me a booklet with all the guild's rules and regulations.

I put the booklet in my bag, and as I did so, the mark on my left hand caught my eye. The sight of the camellias made my heart ache as I remembered the two promises I'd made. I closed my eyes, trying to tuck those painful feelings away in my chest, then walked over to the bulletin board to choose a quest.

I stood in front of the board. First, I pulled out basic information related to the things written on the board to commit them to memory so that I wouldn't make another mistake like before. Once I was prepared, I searched for a quest I thought I could handle. There were various types posted, such as gathering herbs, slaying monsters, making deliveries, harvesting crops, and helping people pack.

As I looked at the quests, I sorted through the information left behind by Kyle and Hanai. I had a general idea of what they were both good at. After that, from the vast amount of knowledge I gathered, I focused mainly on scholarly pursuits, languages, and herbology, since that was what I had registered with the guild.

There was a ton of knowledge about ancient ruins when I delved into scholarly pursuits. It seemed Kyle had in interest in ruins and liked to thoroughly explore them. I had a feeling most of the odd objects that seemed to be magical in Kyle's messy bag—er, the bag Kyle gave me— were objects he found there.

However, I wasn't able to confirm what his goal had been during his explorations. I wondered if this was what he was talking about when he said I wouldn't be able to see any memories that deeply involved him.

It seemed that Hanai was the one who had been interested in and studied languages. Once you were reincarnated into this world, you automatically learned the common language, but you'd have to study the others on your own. And so Hanai had learned the northern and southern dialects, along with several other regional dialects. Since he had studied magic, he learned the ancient, spirit, and dragon languages (which was also called Dragonian). For that reason, I'd be able to read and write most of the ones used in this world and speak them as well, more or less.

I say more or less because once Kyle inherited Hanai's body, he really hadn't sorted through the dialects. Languages are living creatures, so I didn't know how much they had changed during Kyle's lifetime, and that made me nervous.

Hanai had studied the basics of herbology, and Kyle had filled in the gaps. I didn't know the plants of this world, so it felt strange to see one and immediately recognize it by its shape and color and know what it was used for.

As I searched through my memory banks, I discovered that Hanai, Kyle, and I had several things in common. For example, we were like omnivores when seeking knowledge. We would dig into topics we weren't even that interested in until we understood them to a certain degree. We had an unquenchable thirst for wisdom.

I thought about the reason for that, then realized something else. Our motivations for seeking knowledge were all different. In my case, I was trying to use knowledge to satisfy my desire and hunger for things that could otherwise never be fulfilled. But they did it to protect their freedom as they lived in this world.

"Maybe I'll try gathering medicinal herbs?" I said as I carefully read the descriptions of the quests.

Quest Name: Gathering Medicinal Herbs
Herb Name: Phyllanthus
Gathering Location: Urn Orchid Forest

Deadline: 2nd Silkis 26
Payment: 3 half-silvers
Description: Please gather at least twenty Phyllanthus.
Purpose: Plant research
Warnings: Monsters called metis appear in the area.
Points: 30 points

It seemed the quest was to gather a medicinal herb called Phyllanthus. It grew in sunny locations and was said to be effective against insect bites and cuts. When the leaves were crushed and applied to the affected area, it would draw out the pus inside the wound.

The deadline was 2nd Silkis 26. Today was 2nd Silkis 20, so I had six days. Every month in this world had thirty days, and there were fifteen months in a year. There were four seasons: Spring was Silkis, summer was Salkis, autumn was Manakis, and winter was Wilkis. The seasons seemed to be named after the goddesses that presided over them. Silkis, Salkis, and Wilkis all had four months each. Only Manakis had three. Thus, there were fifteen months in a year. After 4th Silkis 30, it would become 1st Salkis 1, and then a new calendar year would start.

The location of the quest was a place called the Urn Orchid Forest. Where was that? I searched through my internal database for the place. It would take about four hours on foot from the castle town to get there. I was confident this body would allow me to get there and back with no problem.

It seemed as though the monster the post warned about was called a metis, and it commonly appeared in that forest. It was an animal that resembled a rabbit. However, I wasn't quite sure the image of the monster which popped up in my mind *really* looked all that much like a rabbit...

Since I had general knowledge of both herbs and monsters, I decided to choose this quest. I tore the paper off the board and brought it to the reception desk.

"I think I'll take this one."

Nestor took it and filled out the paperwork for me. "The deadline is in six days. It's not a difficult quest, but be careful all the same."

"Thank you."

After that, I felt myself drawn to the corner where books were for sale. I just wanted to touch one, so I picked up an illustrated book about medicinal herbs. Hmm, it was pricey, just as I'd expected. It cost eight silvers. I knew I had plenty of money, but I was still a bit hesitant to buy something so expensive.

I put my hand into my bag, intending to pull out a book about medicinal herbs, but instead there was one gold coin in my hand. I had a feeling Kyle was trying to send me a message—a present telling me to enjoy shopping.

I decided to take him up on his generous offer and bought it, along with a simple map of the region. With the money left over, I bought some food, put all of it in my bag, and went back to the inn.

I decided to set out the next morning. With that in mind, I sat down to slowly read the book.

I was taking the first step of my adventure and the first step of my new life here. I was anxious, of course, but I was also extremely excited.

I left the inn early the next morning. I hesitated about whether I should use teleportation magic to get to the Urn Orchid Forest or walk there, but in the end, I decided to do the latter. I was overjoyed that I could move my body so freely.

The Urn Orchid Forest was a brighter place than I expected. The sunlight filtered through the trees, creating a beautiful scene. Phyllanthus would definitely grow well in a sunny spot like this. I kept an eye out for monsters while I searched for the plant, and I found it more quickly than I expected. Perhaps yellow quests were easy after all.

The forest was huge, and the farther you ventured in, there would be quests of higher ranks.

I picked the phyllanthus carefully so as to keep them intact and counted them as I went. "Eighteen, nineteen, twenty..." After I gathered the necessary amount, I split them into groups of five. While I was here, I picked some phyllanthus for myself, along with some other plants in my medicinal herb book.

Things had gone smoothly so far, with no sign of monsters anywhere. I had safely gathered the herbs, along with some other ones that I thought might be useful. If I went back now, I could reach the castle town by nightfall. I was glad I had set out so early in the morning.

I quickly walked toward the edge of the forest, but then something caught my eye. From what I could make out, it looked like a person. I cautiously approached it and saw it was a man who appeared to be in his thirties. Judging by his clothes and the symbol on his left hand, he was a fellow adventurer. I wondered if he had been attacked by a monster.

I tried to sense if there were any presences around, but I didn't pick up any. At any rate, it didn't seem dangerous, so I called out to him. "Hello? Are you all right?" I spoke to him several times, but he gave no response. He was breathing, and he didn't appear to be in pain. I thought he was merely unconscious, but he looked as if he were just asleep. It didn't seem like he was injured in any way, and he wasn't bleeding. He didn't have any broken bones, either.

According to Hanai's knowledge, there was a way to diagnose internal body conditions with Wind and ancient magic, so I decided to cast the spell. His body glowed blue, and there didn't seem to be any abnormalities. There were flashes of yellow here and there, but those seemed to be minor cuts.

If he was just sleeping, I'd leave him alone. But I was worried he was truly unconscious and that I should help him. Based on the common sense of this world, it seemed unlikely that someone would choose to sleep in a place where monsters ran rampant... Probably. They wouldn't, right?

"I guess I'll just have to wait here until he wakes up," I decided. But since I didn't know when that would happen, I thought I should probably move away from here. Earlier, I'd chosen a place to make camp in case I didn't find the herbs today, so I decided to take the man there. I threw him over my shoulder and carried him to the camp, but he still hadn't woken up.

I stared at the man, who was sleeping so soundly, and I let out a little sigh. It didn't look like I'd be able to go home today after all. Although, with my body, I bet I wouldn't even get tired if I carried him the entire way back. I could use magic, or teleport as well.

I might have if he had a life-threatening injury, but since that didn't seem to be the case, I didn't want to do anything that would stand out too much.

He might have been in the middle of a quest. If the deadline was coming up, he might fail if I brought him back now. I also didn't know whether he was unconscious or just asleep. I knew there were some eccentric people out there, so I couldn't rule it out.

At any rate, I'd decided it was too late to head back, and I started pulling out some necessary items from my bag. I set up a magical tool called a barrier stone to create a barrier around the camp. Kyle had made this one by hand, but they were sold in stores, too. They were quite expensive, but it was an essential item for any adventurer who traveled alone. I thought I would probably be fine without a barrier if it were just me, though.

I'd thoroughly sorted through anything related to magic from the knowledge I'd gained, so I didn't think any monsters from this area would be able to hurt me. The only catch was I hadn't personally seen or fought one yet. I wasn't confident I could guard a person who was incapacitated while fighting at the same time, so I figured I should stick to the basics to be on the safe side.

Speaking of the basics, I couldn't forget about the most fundamental part of camping, which was the campfire. It provided warmth and was necessary for cooking. I'd learned how to make one, so I created a circle with rocks, then filled the space between with fallen leaves and twigs.

I made a small flame with magic, lighting the leaves on fire. Adventurers who couldn't use magic probably used a flint, but I was a sorcerer. I didn't need tools to light a flame. Even though I had said I was sticking to the fundamentals, I was feeling quite elated about using magic to make the fire.

The leaves caught fire, which then spread to the twigs. That's when I breathed a sigh of relief. I wondered if I could have made a barrier using magic instead of a barrier stone.

I stoked the fire, put some water into a pot, and made a simple soup. This was my first time cooking, but thanks to Hanai and Kyle's knowledge, I had no difficulties. Once the water was boiling, I scooped some of it out to make tea from some of the herbs I had gathered. These particular ones had rejuvenating effects. I took a sip, and it wasn't bad.

Tonight's menu was a simple soup with bread that had cheese on top.

Now all I had to do was wait for the man to wake up. I watched over him, feeling anxious that maybe he *wouldn't* wake up, but just then, he began to moan.

"Ngh..."

"Hey? Are you okay?" He seemed to be regaining consciousness, so I called out to him.

"Where am I...?"

"Just outside the Urn Orchid Forest," I said. He looked at me with glassy eyes, as if he was dreaming. Then, after he thought about it for a moment, his eyes snapped wide open, and he bolted upright.

"The Urn Orchid Forest?!"

"That's right. I found you passed out in the forest. Don't you remember?"

"Oh, right... I was huntin' metises," he said, then looked down and fell silent.

"Did one attack you?" I asked.

He then had on a guilty expression. "I couldn't find any. Ran outta food while I was lookin' for 'em..."

There was a heavy feeling in the air between us, so I decided to introduce myself.

"I'm Setsuna. I just became an adventurer, and I came here on a quest."

"I'm Zigel. I should've thanked ya earlier. I really appreciate it."

"It's all right. I'm just glad you're not hurt. I only have a simple soup and some bread. Would you like to eat together?" I asked, knowing full well why he had collapsed. That's why I didn't wait for him to answer before handing him a bowl full of soup and a piece of bread. Zigel thanked me and accepted it, then quietly began eating. I watched him regain some of his energy and started on my own dinner.

After we finished the whole pot of soup, I cleaned up, then handed him a cup of tea I'd made. We sat around the campfire and sipped our drinks while we talked.

I'd had so many firsts today. My first quest, my first journey and adventure, my first time gathering herbs, and my first time finding someone unconscious and taking care of them.

And now this was the first time I shared a meal with someone I'd just met and talked with them while drinking tea.

I felt my heart opening up just a little bit. I took out a bottle of alcohol and shared it with Zigel; this was my first time drinking. You were allowed to once you turned sixteen in this kingdom, although the laws differed elsewhere.

Perhaps it was because we had been drinking, but Zigel became very talkative. Well, it was more like he was complaining? But that was how my long night with a drunk adventurer began.

"Lissen, Setsuna. I useta work fer Killena Co." He stared at his cup of alcohol as he told me about himself.

"Oh, you had a job?"

I wondered if he was like a Japanese salaryman. I sipped my drink and listened to his story.

"I worked day an' night, sweatin' my ass off. I put work first over spendin' time with my wife an' kid."

"Mm-hmm."

"If I made good money, that'd make life easier for my family, an' I could buy my daughter whatever she wanted. An' I thought if I worked harder, Killena Co. would grow even bigger." Zigel sounded so self-assured. I could tell he'd had a lot of confidence in his job.

"But then…but then! One day, they just canned me, outta the blue!"

The light from the campfire illuminated Zigel's face, highlighting his deeply sorrowful expression.

"Did you make some kind of mistake?"

"If I had, then I could've accepted bein' fired. But no. They said they had to cut down on their employees."

So in other words, he'd been laid off.

"I went home after I got fired an' told my wife...and then she left me."

I silently nodded, not having the slightest idea of what to say.

"She took my daughter and went home to live with her parents." Tears started streaming down his face. I realized I was crying, too, and drained the entire contents of my cup.

"Think I can have another?"

I nodded and poured more alcohol into Zigel's cup. He watched me, and once it was full, he began talking again. "I worked for my company, for my family. I worked and worked... I worked so hard. Don't ya think my life's just in the worst shape it could be right now?"

"......"

"After my wife left me, I had an idea. I thought if I worked *that* hard and I still got canned, then I'd get a job where I wouldn't answer to anyone."

"Ah, and that's why you became an adventurer."

"Exactly. I started about a month ago. I knew it was near impossible, but I had a dream, y'know? Of slayin' monsters, completin' quests, becomin' a better man." Zigel wept with a quiet smile. "I'd become a better man and go see my daughter!"

Ah, I see. Now I understood why he was crying. He had been fired for no reason, and on top of that, his wife had left him. That had to be painful. But the most painful thing of all was not being able to see his daughter.

"Yet here I am."

"You just started, though. It's too soon for you to be depressed. If you keep going, surely things will get better." I tried to comfort him, but he shook his head.

"I chose a job I just wasn't cut out for. But now it's too late to go back."

"Don't say that..." I was about to continue but fell silent when he looked at me.

"I don't know what led you to become an adventurer, Setsuna." From his tone, I knew he wasn't trying to pry. "But the start-up cost of becomin' an adventurer cost me three months' salary."

I continued listening.

"It looks to me like you've got all the finest equipment. You're wearing nice clothes, have a nice sword, and they're enchanted with the highest class of magic, aren't they?" He stared intently at my equipment. But I couldn't tell him how I'd gotten all this.

"Are they? Well...I inherited all of this from my older brother."

I had no intention of telling him the specifics about my relationship with Kyle, so I decided to say he was my older brother. Zigel nodded emphatically several times, then smiled.

"Sounds like he cares a lot about you, Setsuna."

"He does." I nodded because it was the truth.

"Once you can tell the type of magic cast on the equipment, you'll get a general idea of how much it would cost. Make sure not to talk about it to just anyone."

"Why is that?"

"Because some folks'll target you for your gear and tools."

"I see." I nodded, and he smiled at me.

"I can tell just from a glance that your clothes alone could feed a family of five for a whole year."

"What?"

I was speechless.

"Most good equipment and weapons are reinforced with some kinda powerful magic and made out of materials that make it easier to move. There are all types of weapons, but when they're enchanted, their price skyrockets," he explained when he saw my surprise. "It seems like you're a bit ignorant about the price of things."

"What make you say that?" I inwardly began to sweat, wondering if I'd made some grave mistake.

"I'm not criticizin' you. When you're young, that's how you should live your life. You shouldn't worry so much. But the sooner you learn the value of money, the better."

"I'll be—"

"I'm gonna teach ya right now."

"Okay..."

I was about to tell him I'd be careful, but he interrupted me. Apparently, I was about to get a lesson on money. I was planning on telling him he should get some sleep, because I could tell he was drunk. But it didn't seem like that would work. I couldn't put a damper on him. His eyes were completely glazed over.

"One day, you're gonna have a family. And since I'm older than you, I can teach ya a few things about it," he said, then gave me a lesson about life.

"Listen. For one family of five to live comfortably, you'll need three gold per month."

So you needed a monthly salary of about three hundred thousand yen per month.

"That means you need to make at least one silver a day. Every job's different, but most job postings you see 'round here will have a monthly salary of two gold and six silvers. And since that's less than three gold, it'll be up to your wife to see how comfortable you can manage."

He smirked, then wet his whistle.

"To give ya an example, my salary last month was four gold and five silvers. From everything I've heard at the guild and taverns, I was pretty lucky when it came to money. But adventurers who mainly slay monsters or have some kind of specialized knowledge can make even more than that."

"So you make two gold more than someone who has a regular job? People who can fight are just better off becoming adventurers, as they can make more money, right?" I asked, but Zigel shook his head.

"If you just take it at face value, the adventurer's salary does seem exceptional. But you gotta take into account that it's not stable income."

"I see..."

"And it ain't as easy as you think to become an adventurer."

"It's not?" I just thought as long as you had the ability to complete quests, anyone could become one. So that's why I hadn't really understood what Zigel meant.

If you couldn't complete a quest, not only did you not get paid, but your rank could also drop. Was he talking about that? I had been able to finish mine, but there might be times when I couldn't. But if someone asked if I would stop being an adventurer because of that, I'd have to say no. And I'm sure the others would say the same.

I still didn't understand why it wasn't easy to become an adventurer, so I waited for him to continue. And so he told me about the reality of how life was for an adventurer.

"The quest I took was worth one silver and one half-silver."

"So was mine."

"That's about how much all the yellow quests outside the castle town are worth."

"One silver and one half-silver. You think that's a lot of money?" Zigel asked, and I nodded.

I'd never had a part-time job in my old world. But Kyoka did, and she made one thousand yen an hour. When she worked an eight-hour shift, she'd bring home eight thousand yen a day. On the other hand, this quest was an eight-hour round trip. It was an easy task—gathering herbs. So I thought it was a lot of money taking everything into consideration.

"Where do you sleep in the castle town, Setsuna? Do you camp outside?"

"I stay at an inn."

"And how much does your room at the inn cost per night?"

"It costs four copper. A half-silver if you want dinner included."

"And that's the difference between adventurers and people who work in a shop. Some adventurers have a base, but most of 'em stay at inns or places of lodging run by the guild."

I nodded, showing him I understood.

"Now, I'm talking about you here."

"Okay."

"You'll earn one silver and one half-silver from this quest. So if you subtract the price of your room at the inn, you have one silver left over."

So my daily wage was fifteen thousand yen. Lodging was five thousand. So I had ten thousand left...

I couldn't help but convert it to yen in my head.

"So you have one silver. Let's think about what else you need. You gotta eat breakfast and lunch, right? Five copper dimes is plenty for breakfast. Then eight copper dimes for lunch. So let's say you need one half-silver, one copper, and three copper dimes to get by comfortably every day."

Breakfast and lunch together was one thousand three hundred yen. Combine that with price of lodging, and it was six thousand three hundred yen. So I'd have eight thousand seven hundred yen left over...

"Now you have one half-silver, three coppers, and seven copper dimes remaining. For an adventurer just starting out, if you earned that much, you could save a little for the days you didn't earn as much. Have a drink every night at the tavern, maybe even have a good time with a pretty lady, yeah?"

I nodded again, ignoring that last part. Anyway, it seemed like I'd have enough money that even if I ate an expensive breakfast and lunch, I'd still have change left over.

Zigel dropped his gaze and stared at his cup, then spoke in a quiet voice. "That's what I thought at first. I thought I'd just borrow my start-up costs from the guild, pay it back right away, and then live a life of freedom."

"You borrowed money from the guild?" I asked, and he nodded.

"You need armor and a sword to be an adventurer. Like I told you before, it costs about three months' salary to have all the equipment you need. That's about nine gold."

I was surprised to hear that. Zigel looked at me and chuckled wryly. "See? That's a lotta money, ain't it? And that's just the bare minimum."

Nine gold would be nine hundred thousand yen...

He rattled off the list of equipment he'd bought and their prices.

A sword was two gold.

A shield was one gold, five silvers.

Protective gear was four gold, five silvers. He bought gauntlets, boots, and body armor.

And then he'd spent one gold on tools.

"Some people take on temporary jobs just so they can afford to become adventurers. But most of 'em are like me and borrow money from the guild to get the necessary equipment. And there are those like you, too."

I listened to him speak without interrupting.

"When you borrow from the guild, they charge you twenty percent interest for it on the thirtieth of each month. Some people prepare a down payment and borrow it, but that depends on the individual. In my case, I borrowed the whole nine pieces of gold. I was naive," he said, looking tired. "In the case of no down payment, if you eat dinner, breakfast, and lunch at the inn, you'll have one half-silver, three copper, and seven copper dimes, just as you calculated earlier. So if you paid it all off..." Zigel paused, then let out a heavy sigh. "Generally... I mean generally, it'll take ya a hundred and forty-two days to pay it all back. And if you skip breakfast and lunch, it'll take ya a hundred and fifteen days."

"Okay."

"Now, it'd be best if you paid back the same exact amount every single day, but things don't always go that smoothly, ya know?"

"Mm-hmm."

"Why, you ask? Well, because that figure ain't taking miscellaneous expenses into account."

"......"

"People say if you're yellow rank, it'll take you at least five months to pay off the loan. Three months if you're real talented."

"......"

"But sometimes your weapons or armor break during your journey, right? So you gotta buy new ones, and..."

I never imagined that becoming an adventurer would be so tough. I had just assumed getting weapons and armor was simple, that anyone could freely become an adventurer. But I guess those items were consumable goods. Since they protected your life, you had to maintain them, and sometimes they just got worn out. Then you would have to spend more money.

Thinking about it now, it seemed so obvious. The reason the pay was so good was because you had to put your life and body on the line. You had to come face-to-face with danger and death. So obviously, you had to spend money on the items that protected you. And that money didn't just fall from the sky. You had to work to earn it.

It was only when Zigel explained all this to me that I finally understood this wasn't some fictional world.

Zigel looked a bit down, so I poured more alcohol into both our cups. I stared into my cup and murmured to no one in particular, "My older brother gave me weapons and armor and enough money to get by. I'm very blessed."

In my other world, it was my parents who took care of me. In this one, it had been Kyle who gave me the means to live.

"And living...I mean, making a living...really is hard work," I said quietly.

Zigel chuckled wryly and answered, "Damn right it is! But I got a daughter who I love! So I can't give up now, because I'm gonna go see her again someday!"

He wasn't necessarily saying it to me but to himself. Encouraging himself. Putting his desires into words.

◇Part Three: Setsuna

That night, after Zigel told me he was going to go see his daughter again, he told me about how much he loved her. I remember him also half-boasting and half-complaining about how scary his wife could be.

He told me that his family was his reason for living, and he swore to work harder for them. He seemed so strong when he said that. And he still had that strength.

That talk with Zigel was the first time that I viscerally understood this world, and it taught me about what it was like to live on your own.

◇Part Four: Zigel

I heard somebody's voice and slowly opened my eyes to find a pair of light-violet eyes staring at me with concern. It was a young man so unusually handsome that I thought he might be an angel. I thought about asking him where I was, but the words wouldn't come out.

"Where am I…?"

I thought I was by the shore of some calm body of water. But the angel told me I was somewhere else, somewhere I knew well. "Just outside the Urn Orchid Forest," he said.

Apparently, he rescued me after I'd collapsed. When I told him the reason why, the mood got a bit awkward. Perhaps he picked up on the fact that I was feeling quite pathetic and embarrassed.

But he was considerate and changed the subject by introducing himself. His name was Setsuna, and to be honest with ya, he didn't look like an adventurer. But when I glanced down at his left hand, sure enough, there was a yellow mark. Adventurers had their own way of calling themselves adventurers, but I guess Setsuna didn't know that. I decided to tell him that later, but for right now, I told him my name and thanked him.

Afterward, he gave me the first meal I'd had in two days, and it was delicious! Now that I felt more comfortable, I decided to observe young Setsuna a bit. I prided myself on my observation skills due to my old job, but no matter how I cut it, he just didn't seem like an adventurer.

For a guy who said he'd just started, he had some really expensive equipment. Not only that, he had cooking utensils, a barrier stone, and all sorts of tools the average novice adventurer wouldn't use. I found it was strange, but I decided not to let him know I thought that. I had my reasons for becoming an adventurer, and I'm sure he did, too.

I drank the tea he made and asked him a little more about himself. He told me he'd gone on his very first quest today. And he'd only become an adventurer the day before. In that case, shouldn't he have mentioned that instead of saying he became one recently?

It seemed Setsuna was in high spirits from being on his first adventure. Then, all of a sudden, he pulled out a bottle of booze from his bag and invited me to have a drink with him. "This is my first time having alcohol," he said. I was surprised to hear that.

"You sure you wanna drink with a depressing old man like me?" It seemed he didn't understand what I meant by that, because he gave me a puzzled look. I told him under normal circumstances, a man would have his first drink on the day he came of age. He'd have a birthday party with his parents, relatives, and friends, and they'd all celebrate together. Setsuna nodded once, with a gentle smile.

"It's all right. If you don't mind, I'd be happy to drink with you." He had on a somewhat sad look, and I don't think it was just my imagination, either.

I decided not to pry and enjoyed a drink with him. But once I got some liquor in me, I started telling him about myself. I had a lot bottled up inside, and I wanted to tell someone else, y'know? I'm not proud to admit I was venting to a young man at my ripe old age, but there you have it. Those were the thoughts that were running through my mind at the time.

As we talked about this and that, I began to worry about Setsuna. His values were a little...no, very...warped. I may not have looked it now, but I worked for a famous company. I'd seen all kinds of people in my day. And that was how I knew this guy wasn't rooted in reality. So wouldn't you think it was my duty as a father figure to guide this young man on the right path?

Even though I was drunk, I began talking to him like it was my duty. Setsuna didn't seem to think I was meddling, either. No, he listened to me with a serious expression. Someday, he'd have a pretty wife and live with her and their beautiful children. So that was why I thought it was necessary to teach him about money. I didn't want him to turn out like me. My wife always held me by the purse strings, and to make matters worse, she left me! I made sure to warn him about that. I meant it as a lesson for Setsuna, but at the end, I felt like I was delivering the final blow to myself.

Then young Setsuna said in a thoughtful voice, as if etching it upon his heart, "And living...I mean, making a living...really is hard work."

Now, I don't know what was going through his mind when he said that. But it gave me the courage to keep on going. Living was hard. Most of the time, things didn't work out the way you think they would. But you still had to keep moving forward.

I realized I was the one who'd forgotten that. And that's also when I realized Setsuna was serious about living, too.

There were a lot of people who were serious about their dreams.

There were a lot of people who were serious about things they should protect.

And a lot who were serious about their work.

But surprisingly, there were few people who thought seriously about living.

Because you didn't have to think that hard about it to continue with your life.

Is it just me, or did I just get real philosophical?

Anyway, I didn't know what Setsuna's circumstances were, but something about him just didn't match up. Yet here he was, listening to an old man cry and complain while drinking without even batting an eye. In my heart, I prayed to the gods that the light would always shine at the feet of this gentle and upright young man.

I couldn't remember what happened after that. Probably because I was so happy, I immediately fell asleep.

*   *   *

The next day, Setsuna helped me with my quest, which was to defeat five metises and put them in a Cube, then bring them back to the guild. Setsuna said he'd never seen a monster before, so we hunted them together. I suppose if he'd spent all his time in the city, it made sense that he had never encountered one.

"So why did you go to the Urn Orchid Forest, Zigel? You can find metises in other places, right?"

"That's right. But the other places are pretty tough to do solo."

"Solo?"

"Ah, that's just what us adventurers call those who hunt alone."

"Oh…"

"This is the easiest place to do that. And when I say easy, I mean…"

"There are fewer monsters here?"

"That's right. Metises are popular because they're delicious roasted with a bit of salt sprinkled on their skin."

"…Are they?"

"They're a little pricey, but you should try it sometime."

"Okay."

We cautiously walked around looking for them, taking the occasional break and chatting. That's when I learned Setsuna was a scholar, which made sense to me. He definitely didn't seem like he was accustomed to violence. He told me he became an adventurer because he wanted to see the world.

After a while, we found some metises, and they noticed us. There were three of 'em. I immediately gripped my sword, but they all charged at me at the same time. I wasn't sure if I could take care of three at once.

But I was nervous to up and let Setsuna take over the battle when this was his first time seeing a monster. This was my quest, after all, so I prepared myself to defeat them.

However, at that exact moment, Setsuna captured two out of the three with Wind magic. So he was a sorcerer, too. I thought he just fought with a sword. I regretted not talking this over with him before we set out.

I'd spent four days looking for metises with no luck, yet that day I was able to slay five and put 'em in my Cube. And with that, both Setsuna and I had finished our quests.

When I told him my luck definitely increased after meeting him, he gave me a soft smile. Both of us were in high spirits as we walked along, making our way back to the guild. We reported to Nes that we'd completed our quests.

I handed him my Cube and got my reward.

Setsuna handed over his herbs. I was impressed when I saw them. He'd washed all the soil off them and put them into five little neat stacks. I had a feeling he'd done his research before going into the forest.

Most of the time, young men like him would come across herbs on their way to slay monsters and pull them roughly out of the ground. They'd bring 'em home just like that. Every time they did and came to hand them in, Nes'd yell at 'em. *"It's a waste to pull them like that! Don't ever do that again, dammit!"*

Every young man Nes lectured would carefully pick the herbs after that. Of course, there were young folks who did their research beforehand like Setsuna. But men in their teens and twenties…even mid-thirties, tended to be a little hot-blooded. Especially those who chose to become adventurers.

There were a lot of young men who rushed headlong into the world, thinkin' they were gonna strike it rich. They were the kind who were driven by a burning passion. They weren't rooted in reality for a different reason than Setsuna. Most of them weren't smart enough to listen to warnings from their elders.

Yet Setsuna had been nothing but calm since I first met him. Guess it was a little late for me to be realizing that, but it was true.

"Hey, that's pretty good!" I heard Nes say. I looked over to the reception desk and saw him complimenting Setsuna, who had on a shy smile. You know, when I saw him smiling like that, I felt happy, too. I was sure he'd get bonus points.

After I submitted my Cube, I thanked Setsuna. I wanted to give him half my reward money, since he had saved me and helped with my quest. But he refused.

"Helping you was payment for the life lessons you gave me," he said with a mischievous grin.

"It wasn't that big of a deal."

"It was to me. The time I spent with you was very important." His grin vanished, replaced by that earnest look again.

I gratefully accepted his feelings. But I really wished I could have thanked him for saving my life.

It was time to say good-bye. "Zigel, please have another drink with me one day after you become a famous adventurer." I was overjoyed by his words.

They filled up my heart. I had a feeling that one day, Setsuna would leave this kingdom. But he promised that someday, we'd share a drink together again.

Reality hadn't changed at all. Even so, I met Setsuna, and he saved my life. I completed my quest. I felt like that was enough for me to take one steady step forward, and I was optimistic now. One day, I'd become famous and see my daughter again. And I'd have another drink with Setsuna. Having that second goal encouraged me to keep on living.

Chapter Three
Coriander ~ Hidden Worth ~

◇Part One: Setsuna

Two months had passed since the day I'd gone on my first quest. Today was 4th Silkis 20. The day after I met Zigel was the first time I slayed a monster. I didn't feel much guilt or unpleasant feelings when I took their lives.

I thought that probably had to do with Kyle and Hanai's experiences influencing me. I didn't enjoy killing, of course, but I would take a monster's life without hesitation if it meant I was protecting myself.

I'd experienced a lot of firsts during these past two months, but I was still confused about a lot of things. There was so much I didn't know and so much I needed to learn that sometimes, I couldn't help but sigh.

But in the end, I just had to do what I could. The first step was to internalize what Zigel had taught me and live off the money I earned as much as possible. This might be obvious, but after talking to him, I realized I had been somewhat naive.

However, I would gratefully use all the items inside the bag besides the money. After all, Kyle left those things because he cared for me, so I wanted to honor his feelings. I thought that was the right thing to do.

*   *   *

I'd left the first inn I had stayed at and was now living in a dormitory run by the Adventurers Guild. That was because with my current daily salary, I couldn't quite afford the half-silver-per-night fee that the other inn had charged. It might have been fine if I wanted to stay in Gardir forever, but my goal was to see the whole world. For that reason, I needed to save up enough money to travel.

By the way, any adventurer could stay at the guild's dormitory for three coppers a night, and it included breakfast.

For the past few months, I had been taking on quests like translating, moving packages, and occasionally slaying monsters. I'd learned more about the guild, too. For example, there were certain levels you had to progress through before you could reach the next colored rank.

There were three levels from yellow to green, three from green to blue, five from blue to purple, five from purple to red, ten from red to white, ten from white to black, and then finally ten more levels to reach the highest rank of black.

Right now, I was at green level two, so the emblem on my hand had changed to that color. When I reached level three, the color would begin to change to a greenish-blue. It went without saying that I was always surprised when the mark on my hand changed colors. After all, there was nothing like it in my previous world.

My schedule was typically pretty regular. I worked five days and took the next one off. I'd rested the previous day, so I was eager to start another quest. I did my morning training like I always did and left the dormitory.

"What kind of quest should I do today?" I mused.

Two days ago, I had helped someone carry supplies, so I thought I might slay some monsters this time.

Those thoughts ran through my head as I opened the door to the guild. As soon as I stepped inside, I immediately realized something was different in the air. I looked around, trying to see what was going on, and noticed everyone was looking at the reception desk. I followed their gazes and saw that Nes was speaking with an adventurer who had a somewhat dignified appearance.

The other adventurers carefully whispered to each other so they wouldn't disturb the two, and I strained my ears to hear those conversations. I learned that the person talking to Nes was someone with a black emblem. That was a symbol of the guild's highest rank, what most guild members aimed for.

Everyone was staring at him, but he didn't seem to care. Meanwhile, I slipped past them and made my way over to the bulletin board.

"So? Why'd you call me here today?"

"Gardir has requested a joint survey of the ruins."

"From me? If it's ruins, why don't you ask *him*?"

"He's currently surveying a different one. And the request was for it to be done as soon as possible."

"I don't understand. Could it be...?" Then, suddenly, the man lowered his voice. "Did an adventurer discover new ruins?"

"Bingo," Nes replied.

The two were talking in fairly low voices, but there were some adventurers who had the ability to hear them. Their expressions visibly changed when they heard that a new ruin had been discovered. I wondered how the kingdom was related when it was an adventurer who found it, so I searched my internal database for the answer.

It turned out there was a specific protocol in place between the guild and the kingdom about ruin excavation.

For example, let's say an adventurer found previously undiscovered ruins, like what had happened here. Once word got out, both the kingdom and the guild would do a joint survey of the area. The kingdom would consider the ruins part of its territory, so by extension, it would also claim ownership over the treasures within it. On the other hand, the adventurers would think the ruins belonged to no one, and so they would claim that the treasures were the property the person who found them.

Because of this difference in opinion, horrific incidents would occur in the kingdom every time new ruins were discovered. After many twists and turns, the guild began acting as an intermediary in these situations, helping the kingdom and the discoverer reach an agreement about the status of ruins and their contents. It was decided that each side would have witnesses for the joint survey. The witness for the kingdom's side would be a general or higher in rank, and the guild's would be an adventurer of black rank or a top guild official. That was why the black-ranked man had been called here.

By the way, any item found in the ruins after the joint investigation was generally considered the property of the person who discovered it. Although, the kingdom would sometimes lodge a complaint if a rare magical tool was discovered.

I found other bits of information, but those were the important points.

That meant Kyle had been flouting all those rules when he went to those sites. The contents of my bag told me as much. I had a feeling he'd say, *"When it comes to ruins, it's finders keepers!"* No, he definitely would say that. I'm sure of it.

"Does that mean their witness is waiting nearby?"

"Well, about that… They said they're going to leave the survey of the ruins to the guild."

"I don't understand." The black-rank adventurer frowned.

"A large group of giant monsters appeared near the northwestern border of Gardir and Ellana."

The mood in the room instantly changed. More people reacted to that revelation than the story about the ruins. If that many people perked up, it must mean it was a dangerous situation. I tried searching for information on giant monsters, but all I could find from Kyle was that they were slightly stronger than average. *Just how strong were you, Kyle?* I had to stifle a laugh.

In contrast, the other adventurers, the black-ranked fellow included, all wore very serious expressions.

"Are you sure I should go on the survey?"

"The Gardir and Ellana armies are fighting the monsters together right now."

"......"

"I heard the sixty-ninth summoned hero is participating in the battle, too."

"I see. Then they won't need us."

"Right."

I felt my heart skip a beat when he mentioned the 69th hero. That was the hero who had been summoned because I had been useless. If they were going to be nothing but a casualty and had been summoned to replace me, then I could never meet with them face-to-face.

I had considered going to find them to apologize, but I felt like that was wrong.

Even if I could apologize, it wasn't like I could do anything to change things. I had no way to solve the situation. The magic Kyle had used on me could only be used on a compatriot.

So I decided not to go see the hero until I had come up with a way to free them.

I had no idea how to get there, though. There wasn't any sort of record about it inside of me.

I felt like I heard a scream inside my heart, but I decided to ignore it.

"The kingdom is busy defeating the monsters, so they contacted me and asked if we could do the survey of the ruins ourselves."

"And they won't come complaining about it later?"

"I'm not sure. It's required to put on the magical tools that Gardir has prepared for you before entering the ruins and to record everything inside. Also, if you find ancient magical tools or treasures, you must set up a barrier stone to keep people away. They gave me the barrier stone. And the magical tool for recording has been enchanted with Mana Detection."

"Sounds like you're saying they'll complain later."

"Also, I'm sorry to say, but they want you to take those magical tools and report to Gardir's general afterward."

"I'm not interested in doing a survey, though."

The black-rank adventurer seemed to think it was a huge pain in the neck. Just before he was about to say no, Nes continued without letting him finish. "I'm not expecting you to do that. All you have to do is make a lap around the ruins, that's it."

"You make it sound so simple."

"The adventurer who found it says it's not very big."

"All right."

"So will you do it?"

The man had a look in his eyes that said, *"As if you're giving me a choice."*

"Tell me more about these ruins," he said with a sigh.

Nes told him everything he knew.

"A Wind portal?" the man murmured. I didn't recognize the term, so I did a search. It was a door protected by Wind magic. You could only open them by using Wind attribute magic.

"You have Saara in your party, don't you?"

"Saara's doing a different quest right now."

At this, Nes manipulated some kind of magical tool, then nodded.

"I came here because I heard it was urgent."

"Are things okay on your side?"

"Chris and the others can take care of that kind of quest."

"That's true."

"So the only one who can help right now is Beet," the black-rank adventurer said, glancing at a young man who stood behind him to the left. But the man was clearly trying to avoid making eye contact with him.

"Gardir was going to dispatch the general and his staff officer, a Windmaster sorcerer."

"And now they can't."

"Since the hero is fighting in the battle, they can't afford to lose. National prestige is on the line."

"There's no way to do the survey if we don't have a Wind sorcerer." I didn't think it was my imagination that the black-rank adventurer looked a bit happy about this.

"True..."

Both of them looked troubled, and Nes began to look around the room. For some reason, his gaze settled on me. The moment I saw his smirk, I knew there was no escape.

"Hey, kid. You lookin' for another quest today?" he called out to me. Suddenly, every person in the room turned my way. *Please stop*, I thought. I didn't want to stand out. I also wished Nes wouldn't call me kid. Couldn't he have used my name? Although, I supposed I could understand why.

I was a novice adventurer and pretty much a child in this world, both in age and experience. I might even have less experience than one. So it was frustrating that I couldn't complain...

Still, it didn't sound like he was calling me that in a patronizing way. I knew he meant it affectionately. That was partly why it was so unfair of him.

I heaved an inward sigh and returned Nes's greeting, which had become somewhat of a daily ritual. "Good morning, Nes. You know, I have a name, and it's Setsuna."

We had this same exchange every time except on my days off.

Nes snorted. "*Kid*'s just fine for a baby chick like you."

I sighed again as he replied just as he always did.

I kept telling him I didn't like it, but he ignored me with a cool expression.

"Nestor?" The black-rank adventurer had been watching our exchange with a mystified look.

"He's the guild's only solo Windmaster right now."

"Oh?" The man looked me up and down.

My old Japanese habits surfaced, and I bowed the moment our eyes met. "Good morning."

He seemed to be taken aback by that but smiled and returned the greeting. "Morning. You're awfully polite for an adventurer," he commented.

Nes interjected. "Isn't he? Pretty rare for a kid these days. He speaks politely and does all his quests carefully, but he's still a fledgling."

That last part wasn't necessary, I thought.

Nes ignored my reaction and continued. "As I was saying, he's the only solo Windmaster here."

"I see..." The man thought for a moment as he stared at me, then nodded. "I'm Agito, the leader of team Moonlight. I'm a swordsman. My guild rank is black. I'd appreciate it if you remembered that."

He spoke in a very humble manner, but he was oozing with strength. Was there anyone who would forget an adventurer like him? Having the strongest member of the guild introduce himself to me made me feel a little shy.

But now it was my turn. Zigel had taught me the proper way to introduce myself to someone in the guild. First, you said your name, the party you belonged to (if you were part of one), then your occupation and guild rank.

"I'm Setsuna. I'm a scholar. My guild rank is green, and I can use Wind attribute magic."

"A scholar? Not a sorcerer?"

I hesitated for a moment, unsure of how to answer that. "I think the way I live my life right now is closer to the former. That was why I registered as such at the guild."

Nes looked at Agito. "Strange kid, right? Normally, someone wouldn't hesitate to put down Windmaster first."

"Ah, so that's why he's solo."

"Yep. That's why he's solo."

I got the gist of what they were trying to say.

In general, the more dangerous a quest was, the higher the reward. But those were riskier to do alone. That was why most people formed teams or parties to do them. A team was a group of adventurers who were only recognized as one after applying and registering with the guild, while a party was only assembled temporarily to carry out a quest.

The guild usually refrained from intervening in problems that occurred within parties. But when they assembled one, they would often act as a mediator. And to form a party and team, you needed people, so for that reason, there was a guild register.

Anyone was free to browse the register, but only a person's name and occupation were disclosed. If you wanted to know more personal information, you had to go through the guild.

Even novice sorcerers would be recruited by teams. That was because not everyone could use magic, and if you didn't have the talent, you couldn't become a sorcerer, so they were quite rare.

Of course, forming a team or party had many merits for the sorcerer as well.

First of all, the amount of mana you had was limited, and so you had to conserve it.

Also, using magic required concentration. For example, the power of magic was determined by the amount of mana one expended for the spell. If you used magic without focusing, you ran the risk of losing control of your spell. Even if it didn't backfire, it still wouldn't have power.

So in order to overcome those disadvantages, many sorcerers would participate in teams or parties.

That was only a guess, though, because it didn't apply to me.

There were few Windmasters, and Nes told me it was rare to find any who were solo, although they did exist. The reason I hadn't been recruited was because I'd written *scholar* as my occupation instead of *sorcerer*.

Nes had tried to introduce me to teams before, but I turned down the offer because I didn't feel the need to join one. There weren't really any advantages to me being in a team, after all. I had an endless amount of mana. I was working on my concentration, but in a different sense than most sorcerers; I had to be careful that I didn't focus so much mana into a spell that I blew the whole place up.

Since I had inherited Hanai and Kyle's abilities, there was no need for me to intone spells. They both had a mixed fighting style of using the sword, martial arts, and magic. I had inherited that same style, of course.

At first, I was skeptical about my body, and it felt uncomfortable. But in these past two months, I had become more familiar with using magic, and I'd expanded the types I was able to use. I practiced it along with my swordsmanship and martial arts every morning. So now I no longer felt uncomfortable with either form of combat.

Ultimately, I could fight just fine on my own, and I had every type of magic at my disposal. If I joined a team or party, there was a possibility that they might find out my secret, so I figured it would be easier to remain teamless.

I gazed at Nes and Agito, waiting for their decision. Honestly, it felt as if everyone in the guild was staring daggers at me, so I wished they would get it over with.

"The kid *is* a Windmaster, but he's only been with the guild for two months. And he's only taken solo quests," Nes said, trying to encourage Agito, who still hadn't answered.

"I see."

"But he can slay monsters. He also completed healing quests using Wind magic without issue. As long as he stays outside the ruins, he'll be able to protect himself just fine. But if you plan on taking him inside with you—"

"All right." Agito interrupted Nes, sounding like he agreed. Apparently, that meant he would take responsibility for my safety.

"This might be the first time he'll be traveling this far, though. Keep that in mind if you plan on asking him for help with the quest."

"Huh? I thought you were gonna prepare horses for us? Isn't this urgent?"

"Sorry. All the horses are taken right now. I tried contacting the farmers, but bandits have been rampant, and I couldn't find anything suitable."

"I see. Well, I suppose there's not much we can do about that."

"If you happen to see any bandits on the way, feel free to get rid of them."

"If they're on the way," Agito answered Nes with a grin, then looked at me. It seemed like he'd made his decision. "Setsuna, right? Would you help me with my quest?"

I didn't really have a reason to say no. Plus, I was interested in the ruins. I knew why he needed me, but just as I was about to ask for more specifics, I heard someone yell from behind me.

"Dad! Why the hell are you letting a little chick who's gonna get in our way come along?!"

"Beet."

"I'm against it! Even though he can use magic, he's a coward who registered as a scholar. What can he do?!"

That was pretty sharp criticism, but it didn't bother me. I slowly turned toward the voice.

I turned around and saw the young man named Beet with his arms crossed, glaring at me. He called Agito "Dad," so I guessed they were family.

"Is it fair to call someone you don't even know a coward, Beet?" Agito chided him, but the young man didn't seem to care.

Not only did he not seem to care, he also snorted with laughter as he kept going. "What's wrong with telling it like it is? He wrote down *scholar* because he's not confident in his magic skills. And we don't need a scholar on our team!"

I was a little impressed with just how off the mark he was. But it seemed like the people around us had similar opinions, and I saw some nodding.

"The fact that I said all this and he didn't say a word in response proves it! There's no reason for us to bring someone who'll be useless in an emergency! That's what I'm trying to say!"

"So does that mean you can open the Wind portal, Beet?" Agito asked.

Beet's voice dropped. "Well… We just have to find someone else to do it."

"Did you even listen to what Nestor said?"

"……"

"It's true that this quest might be tough on a novice. And I'd prefer a Windmaster with more experience."

"Well, then—!"

"But Setsuna is the only solo Windmaster available at the guild right now. That's what Nestor said, remember?"

Beet still didn't look convinced.

"If he doesn't have experience, then we'll just have to protect him. Or maybe you're not sure you have what it takes to protect a single sorcerer?" Agito asked, prompting Beet to glare back at him. That didn't seem to bother Agito, whose arms were crossed as he provoked the young man. That gesture rather suited him and looked like something out of a movie. "Also…"

Once the adventurers heard the tone of Agito's voice, they all took a step backward. He had the same smile as before, but I could feel him radiating anger. "People are free to choose whatever occupation they please when they register for the guild. It shouldn't be something that's forced."

Beet began to look a little pale.

"Do you have a complaint with the guild's policies?"

"No!" Beet immediately denied it.

Other adventurers averted their eyes from Agito and started shaking their heads.

"Just as you chose the sword, he chose to pursue the path of knowledge. That's all it is, right?"

Ah, I see. Agito was doing this so that the rest of the guild members didn't shun me.

"It's not for *you* to say," Agito said, staring right at Beet; then he turned to me. "Setsuna. I'm sorry my son was rude to you." The other adventurers whispered among themselves when he apologized to me.

"It's fine. It didn't bother me."

Beet's face went totally blank when he heard me say that, like I'd just poured oil onto an open flame…

Meanwhile, Agito gave me an amused look.

"Fine! Do whatever you want!" Beet yelled angrily, and he ran out of the guild.

"Oh, I'm sorry…" I'd clearly said something wrong.

He looked even more amused. "There's no reason for you to apologize, Setsuna. I wouldn't blame you if you were angry."

"He didn't really say anything that would make me angry."

Agito thought for a moment and said, "Are you really eighteen? Normally, a novice adventurer would blow his top after being called a coward."

"Really?"

"Yep. Not all of them, of course. But most of them."

Nes let out a deep chuckle in response. "My son would still get mad if someone called him that."

I thought that was an astute thing to say to someone who doubted my age.

"There are certain words I don't like, too. But he didn't call me any of those this time."

"I see. Well, if you say so. So what'll it be, Setsuna? Will you come along with me on this quest?"

"You mean to survey the ruins?"

"Pretty much. It'll take three days to get to where the newly discovered ruins are. I just need you to open the portal."

I nodded.

"We'll be the ones inspecting the inside. But if I decide we'll need your help once I see what's in there, you might need to enter, too. If that happens, you'll get paid extra."

"When you say 'newly discovered ruins,' does that mean no one has surveyed them before?" I asked, and Agito nodded with a serious expression.

"That's right. So it might be dangerous for a novice like you."

Ruins that were once cities or villages in the distant past were relatively safe, but there were some that had deadly traps or guardians because valuable treasures were hidden there. Since this one was protected by a barrier, it was highly probable that it was the latter type.

"I've never joined a party before. Can't you work together with another team?"

"When you accept a quest from the kingdom, all teams have to be approved beforehand."

"Oh, I see."

"And even if we applied for approval now, they're busy fighting giant monsters, so they wouldn't see it in time."

"Are you really sure you want me to come with you?"

"The kingdom knows we need to have a Windmaster with us. And they say this is urgent. That basically implies we can add one to our party without their permission." Agito answered all my questions carefully. "Our goal is to record the interior of the ruins and, if necessary, place a barrier stone to keep people out."

"All right."

Agito stroked his chin with his left hand as he spoke. As he did that, the mark on his left hand caught my eye. His emblem was a two-handed sword with thorns wrapped around it.

"Even though it's just a survey, we're still entering the ruins, so there's no telling what could happen."

I nodded.

"I'm a beginner at all of this, but I'll accept the quest. I'm looking forward to working with you."

"Same here. Thanks," he said and smiled at me.

Now that things were settled, we officially accepted the quest. I heard adventurers around me talking about it enviously. I couldn't blame them, since they all dreamed about becoming black-ranked adventurers themselves.

Agito told me we would leave the next morning, and we agreed to meet in front of the guild.

There were several ways of checking the time in this world. First, there was the sound of the bells that the kingdom rang on an hourly basis. There was also something called a color clock that changed color over time. In Lycia, where the guild headquarters was located, they sold pocket watches. I already had a handmade one.

After I parted ways with Agito, I decided I didn't need to take on another quest, because I needed to prepare for the next day. He had told me about everything I would need for the quest, so I figured I should go buy those things now.

* * *

I left the guild to go shopping. It would be a round trip of six days, plus two days to survey the ruins. I needed enough food and water to last the whole time. I had a canteen, so I didn't need to get any water. Agito had given me one, along with several aqua magical tools.

When you put one of those tools in a canteen, it would give you about ten liters of water. You had to use a special kind of bottle for them to work, though. But once you had it, you never had to worry about having enough water.

Once he explained it to me, I understood it was a very valuable item, so I planned to turn down his offer. But Agito and Nes both told me it was an essential provision for a black-rank quest, so I accepted it.

Now I had to bring clothes and medicine. I needed salve, medicine for stomachaches and headaches, antibiotic ointment, and antidotes. Then I tried to make a barrier stone on my own. I did my best, but it was difficult.

That was how I prepared for my first long trip—even if it was just with a temporary party.

I prepared carefully, because I didn't want to cause anyone trouble.

Honestly, as long as I had some food, I probably had all the necessary equipment in my bag already. If there was something I needed, I could just use Kyle's ability to create it. However, Kyle said that no matter what, the basics were important. That was why I'd decided to prepare for the journey using the money I'd made myself.

Plus, I'd finally gotten the hang of haggling recently. I wasn't as good at it as the older ladies who went to the market, though. But for some reason, they also bargained for me, which helped me out a lot.

After I finished shopping, I went back to the dormitory and decided to spend the rest of my time reading up on the medicinal herbs found in the area where we were headed.

I woke up the next morning and did my usual training, then changed clothes. I went with a white shirt and navy-blue leather plants. Then I put on a dark blue coat that reached my knees. It didn't look much different from my normal attire, but this was my combat uniform.

Most sorcerers wore robes. But I chose to wear something else because of my personal preferences.

I was about to put on my scabbard so that I could wear a sword at my hip, but then I stopped. I was acting as a sorcerer today. I put my sword away and took out a shortsword, a weapon more befitting of my supporting role.

I had it equipped to slip into the back of my belt, so I went ahead and attached it. A small pouch hung from my belt so that I could place magical tools inside and easily access them.

I thought it might seem suspicious to Agito and the others if I didn't wear a ring, as sorcerers usually wore them in order to cast magic, along with a staff, so I went to fish one out of my bag, but then I remembered I was already wearing one to control my mana. That would do.

I looked at the mark on my left hand and suddenly thought about the color of Agito's emblem. It was a very deep black. Once you achieved the highest black level, your emblem would begin to take on a slightly golden tone. I wondered how many quests he had undertaken, how many monsters he had slain to become a black-rank adventurer...

Not that I was particularly concerned with ranks.

But it was the first time I'd met a top-ranked person in the guild. He had something about him that drew you in. You couldn't help but admire him. Kyle had told me that he and Hanai had been the strongest men in the world, which meant I was, too. But it still didn't feel like it.

I looked away from my emblem, put on my black leather fingerless gloves, and left the dormitory. As soon as the guild came into view, I saw Agito and Beet standing outside, waiting for me. I quickened my pace.

"Good morning. I'm looking forward to starting our quest together," I said.

Agito turned toward me. "Morning. So am I. Beet," he said, nudging his son, who reluctantly introduced himself.

"I'm Beet. I'm also a member of Moonlight. I'm a swordsman. My rank is blue. And I don't think you belong here."

"Beet!"

After that one-sided introduction, he started walking without so much as a glance toward me. Agito called his name sharply, but he didn't turn around.

"I'm sorry."

"It's fine. Please don't worry about it."

"Beet is just about a mid-level adventurer, but he's got a lot to learn when it comes to swordsmanship. He's more of an apprentice. And he's around the same age as you, so there's no need to be formal with him."

"Apprentice? I didn't know that was an option," I said, putting the matter of being formal aside.

"Yeah. Beet's my apprentice," he said with a small smile.

I realized the meaning behind it and told him earnestly, "He's very lucky."

Agito nodded, his expression not one of a black-rank adventurer but of a father. I felt a little envious seeing that, because he was protecting his son, as both a father and a mentor.

"Well, let's get going," he urged, and we began to walk. As I watched his back from behind, I thought about Beet and came to a conclusion. He was working hard to gain his father's approval, which must have been very tough.

We'd been walking for about two hours after we departed from the castle town when the scenery began to change.

The road disappeared, and we started to walk through grassy meadows, with trees growing here and there. I had a feeling the farther we went, the more trees we'd see.

Those thoughts ran through my head, and I wondered if I looked tired.

Agito glanced at me with concern. "Are you tired, Setsuna?"

I'd just looked at my pocket watch; we'd been walking for three hours. But ever since I inherited this body, I no longer felt fatigued. I had so much stamina that I could probably take on a quest from the guild every day. But I took a day off because I wanted to learn more common knowledge and study magic. There were other things I wanted to do as well.

"I'm fine, thank you."

"All right, but don't hesitate to tell me if you do. I don't want you to be so exhausted that you can't fight."

"Okay." I took his warning to heart.

Agito had been talking to me along the way, so I wasn't bored. On the other hand, Beet walked silently ahead of us. It seemed he had decided to ignore me completely.

Since we began our journey, I hadn't sensed any monsters around. The Gardir army had apparently slain them all on their way through here.

"Can I ask you something, Setsuna?" Agito inquired. I nodded. "Will you tell me why you're carrying so little?"

I looked at his back and at Beet's, and I realized they had fairly large knapsacks.

"Since you're an adventurer, I'm sure you're prepared, but..." His comment seemed to come from genuine interest rather than judgment. I wondered if the thorns on his emblem symbolized his thirst for knowledge.

I asked him what he had in his bag, and he readily answered me. He had the bare minimum of provisions. I inquired if he'd brought a change of clothes, and he said he used a magical tool that was capable of cleaning his clothes and body. Speaking of which, I remembered seeing it sold at the shop in the guild. I'd never really paid much attention to it, since I had magic that did the same thing.

He said he usually traveled by carriage, so he only needed to carry rations, a canteen, and magical tools.

"How heavy is your bag?" I asked.

He chuckled and let me put it on. I thought it would be heavy, but it was actually pretty light. I imagined that was so he could easily counterattack in case he had to fight monsters.

"It's enchanted with high-level magic to make it light."

"There are so many handy spells, aren't there?"

"There truly are. Enchanted items are pricey, but it's worth reducing the burden on you."

"I feel the same way."

Agito put his bag back on. We walked side by side, and this time we talked about mine.

"This bag is an ancient magical tool," I said. It wasn't a lie. After all, it had been made two thousand five hundred years ago.

"Huh?" He looked genuinely surprised. I even saw Beet's shoulders jerk a bit.

"Its function sort of resembles a Cube's." The magical workings of Cubes were confidential and not publicly disclosed. So there were rumors that it wasn't actually magic but a product of someone's abilities.

"It can fit anything inside of it, regardless of weight, quantity, or size."

"You're lying, right?"

I shook my head. I wasn't lying.

"Time is frozen inside, so you can pack food and it won't rot."

Agito's eyes grew round at my explanation, and he stared at my bag. "Can I take a look at it?"

"Sure." I took it off my shoulder and handed it to him.

"Setsuna. I'm glad you trust me, but you shouldn't hand over an ancient magical tool to just anyone. I really don't approve of that," he cautioned me in a serious voice.

"Don't worry. If the bag gets a certain distance away from me, it'll automatically come back. Plus, I'm the only one who can take items out of it."

For a moment, Agito's hand froze as he reached out toward the bag. "That's...amazing." He took the bag from me and looked it all over. "Can I open it?" His eyes were filled with curiosity.

"Go ahead."

On the outside, it appeared to be nothing more than a coffee-colored, tattered old bag, but there were no buttons on it. It was just shaped like a simple pouch with the top third of it folded over. I could easily unfold it, but Agito couldn't.

"That's amazing. Truly stunning." He seemed truly impressed as he returned it to me.

I thought Kyle had probably made it out of fun and curiosity. He must have often lost it, considering how he made sure it always came back to him. He seemed like the type to forget something important at the store.

I responded to Agito as those thoughts ran through my head. "It's such a nice bag I almost feel like it's wasted on me." It was certainly stuffed so full of items that most of them *would* be wasted.

"Are you a son of some noble?"

"Pardon?" I stared at him, not understanding what he meant.

"No, it's just...the way you speak, your knowledge, the way you behave, the equipment you have...it's just so different from the average person."

I wasn't sure how to answer that. I had a feeling he'd be able to tell if I lied...

"I don't know any nobles," I answered with a smile as I told him about myself. "I'm not the son of an aristocrat. I'm an orphan." I had no family in this world. "I did have someone who I thought of as an older brother, but we weren't related by blood. And he taught me all sorts of things."

Our relationship had only lasted for one day, though.

"I inherited this bag and all my equipment from him." Along with his body, his experiences, and all his knowledge.

"Is your brother an adventurer?"

"Yes, he was."

"Was?"

"Two months ago, he departed for the Waterside." In this world, people thought you went to a place called the Waterside after you passed away. But actually, he was sleeping inside me.

"So the reason you became an adventurer..." Agito trailed off.

I finished his thought for him. "Yes. My brother encouraged me to go see the world."

He quietly listened to my story. Beet seemed to be listening in as well.

"I'm well aware that I don't have the ability to use most of the items in my possession yet."

"Setsuna."

"But my brother left them behind for me. I wanted to honor his feelings, so..."

That's right. He left them behind for me.

"I'm sorry I pried." It looked like Agito realized he'd touched on an inconvenient truth.

"No, it's fine. Anyone's curious when they see something unusual," I said cheerfully, trying to change the subject.

Agito chuckled. "You sure don't seem like you're eighteen," he said, glancing at his son. I was sure Beet sensed his gaze, but he didn't turn around.

The sun was just about to set. "Let's make camp here for the night," Agito said. "I thought it would take three days to get to the ruins, but I think we can make it there tomorrow."

Even though Agito and I had chatted a lot on the way, we'd made really good time.

"So we've walked halfway there?"

"Yep, just about. You've got a lot more stamina than I thought you would, Setsuna. Honestly, I'm surprised."

Now I understood—he'd said three days because he thought I would have to rest more.

Each of us began to prepare the campsite. Beet cut grass and dug a hole for the fire so that it wouldn't spread to the meadow. Agito began to build the fire.

I took out the magical tool I'd made from my pouch. It was a triangular pyramid-shaped silver needle about the length of my middle finger. I stuck it into the ground, and the magic immediately activated. A barrier with a diameter of five meters appeared, with the needle at the center. I'd made it from a barrier stone.

"What's that?" Agito looked down at the silver object, interested because he'd never seen one before.

"A magical tool used in place of a barrier stone."

"Is that an ancient magical tool, too?"

"No, I made it. Monsters won't be able to enter the area within a five-mer radius of that needle, and no one will be able to hear our voices outside of it, either."

A mer was a unit of measurement in this world. One mer equaled one meter. Perfect, in my opinion. It made things very easy for me.

"Why don't you use a barrier stone?" Beet blurted out.

"Because they are consumable items. I could create a barrier directly, but I thought it would be a good idea to put my surplus mana into this magical tool before I went to bed."

Honestly, I didn't make it to preserve my mana. I thought the stones were a waste because they were disposable, but I couldn't tell them that, as I didn't think they'd understand.

"You can use that multiple times? That's a pretty good magical tool. Won't take up much space in a bag, either."

"Thank you."

"But sorcerers often conserve mana at night when they're on a quest."

That was true. Unlike me, other sorcerers' mana was limited, so they always had to be prepared for an emergency.

"And that's why they use barrier stones?"

"That's right." Agito gave me a concerned look.

"Agito?"

"Ah, it's nothing. I hope I didn't offend you."

I shook my head. "No, I'm grateful that you're teaching me the correct things."

"Oh?"

"Also, if I should conserve my mana while on a quest..."

"Setsuna?"

I decided to reassemble the magic construction formula, which was an arrangement of symbols that could change mana into matter. Once the mana took form, it was called a magic circle, and the manifestation after the flow of mana was called magic.

Magic itself was very interesting, as it didn't exist in my old world, so I had been studying it for the past few months. As part of my studies, I'd made this barrier needle, but after listening to Agito's feedback, I felt that it needed to be improved.

I took out a triangular pyramid-shaped silver needle from my bag and chanted a short spell to enchant it with magic.

"This might be better. I've made it so that it can replenish my mana five times over."

"What do you mean?"

"I can restore my mana on the days I don't plan on using magic."

"I see."

"Although, I think it can still be improved in many ways."

Agito looked stunned for moment, then burst out laughing. I didn't understand what was so funny, so I just had to wait until he was done. "Ah, sorry. I just remembered a sorcerer who did the same thing, a long time ago." His shoulders were still shaking with laughter. "Although his motivation for making improvements was different from yours..." He let out a little sigh and looked at me and nodded. "It's a good magical tool. It won't be a burden to Windmasters."

"Thank you." I was genuinely happy that he approved of something I'd made.

"Maybe you should quit being an adventurer and just make a living selling those things."

"Beet." Agito said his son's name in a warning tone. For a moment, they glared at each other until Beet snorted and returned to making the fire. "Should I strangle him...?" Agito muttered in a deep voice. I looked at him, and he seemed serious, so I decided to stop him. He was a little scary...

"Please don't worry about it."

"Are you sure?"

"Yes."

"I'll overlook it this time, then." He gave me a wry smile and patted me on the arm before returning to his task.

It was really reassuring to have someone like him as my party leader. I went back to working as well.

We sat around the campfire and took out the food we had prepared. When you were in a team or party, it was common for people to eat the same thing in order to lighten the luggage. But this time, we had agreed to all bring our own food.

While we ate, Agito and Beet kept arguing back and forth, although I was sure they would say they were just debating.

"You only brought meat *again*?"

"Shut up. Who cares what I eat?"

"Adventurers rely on their bodies. How many times do I have to tell you that?"

"Just shut up and eat!"

"Don't you wanna be healthy?"

"I never said I didn't!"

"I'll give you some of my food. Just eat some vegetables."

"I'm not a kid anymore!!"

I had to stifle my laughter as I watched them. Agito was right, but he had a harsh way of putting things. He seemed like an ordinary concerned parent.

Their conversation reminded me of my own father. He used to say the same kind of things that Agito said.

"Come on, Setsuna. You won't get better if you don't eat properly."
"Don't worry. I'm eating."
"You didn't finish all of it. Don't be picky. Just eat."
I didn't leave behind food because I was picky. Dad knew that, but...
"I'm not a kid anymore."
I was hit with a pang of nostalgia, and at the same time, my heart ached a little...

I wondered how my dad was doing. I hoped he was all right.

"...suna. ...Setsuna?"

I heard someone calling my name and looked up with a gasp. I'd been so absorbed in my memories that I hadn't noticed Agito was speaking to me.

"Ah, yes? What is it?"

"Nothing. Just felt like you were off somewhere else."

"I was just thinking of something silly," I said with a smile. Then he asked what I'd been thinking about. "I was wondering why you become an adult at age sixteen...," I blurted out.

"What?" Agito gave me a puzzled look. Beet was quietly eating, but he hadn't touched his vegetables.

It was strange for me to ponder such a thing as they were arguing. But I couldn't tell them what I'd actually been thinking about. I didn't want to, either. I had a feeling Agito knew I was lying, but he went along with it anyway.

"If people can live to be two hundred fifty years old, don't you think sixteen is a little too soon to be called an adult?"

"That's true. It's an artifact of the past."

"The past?"

"I'm not sure if it's true or not, but it seems that life expectancy back then was around one hundred twenty years old."

I wondered what kind of advancements led to people living until they were two hundred fifty.

"It's said the reason our life span has gotten longer is because the gods have bestowed their blessings on us."

Suspicious, I thought as I listened to Agito. Still, since I'd never heard this before, I found it very interesting. It was something I just randomly brought up to change the subject. But he was seriously answering me. I felt a little guilty, but I tucked those feelings away inside my heart.

Even after we finished eating and cleaned up, Agito and I continued chatting. The stories he told me about the monsters he had slain were extremely fascinating. He asked me questions about myself, and I told him I was good at making medicine. When I mentioned I was making changes to my dispensing process, he asked me to give him some. I told him once the quest was over, I'd make a new batch. He told me to just leave it at the guild for him.

I didn't sense the presence of any monsters. After we enjoyed a peaceful evening, I decided to go to sleep to rest up for the next day. I settled in under my thin blanket and looked up at the starry sky. As I stared up at the beautiful twinkling stars, I fell asleep at some point...

*   *   *

But no matter how deep of a sleep I was in, I would always wake up when I sensed monsters nearby. It was something I'd realized when I'd gone on a quest to slay a monster, but it must have been a quality from inheriting Kyle's body.

And right now, I could tell by the slight vibrations of the ground and the flow of the wind that they were nearby.

"Four... No, maybe six," I murmured as I opened my eyes, confirming my hunch. It might be more than I could handle right now.

"I'm surprised." Agito woke up at the same moment beside me. For an instant, I thought perhaps I'd made a mistake by saying it out loud. But since I wouldn't be able to take care of them by myself, it was perfect. "You can tell?"

I understood right away that he wasn't asking me because he didn't know how many there were. An adventurer of his caliber would obviously have the same sharpness I had.

"Yes. I cast a Wind magic spell before I went to sleep." I understood he was wondering how a novice like me could know, so I thought about that answer for a while. I couldn't tell him about my natural detection ability without telling him about Kyle. It was a lie, but it couldn't be helped.

"Detection magic?"

"That's right."

"Got it." He seemed to accept my explanation, so he turned his gaze toward the group of monsters. "Think they'll come this way?" he asked. He didn't have to, because he knew the answer. I thought maybe he was trying to test how strong I was.

"I think they'll be close enough for us to see in ten minutes. But they won't come this way. They'll pass by us."

Agito nodded.

"They might change directions if they smell us, though," I said.

"True. But this barrier's strong, so I don't think they will. I've used my fair share of sorcerers' barrier stones, so I can say it with certainty. You've got a lot to be proud of."

I was thrilled by his compliment, but that wasn't the point. "I think I should dissolve the barrier."

He looked at me, and his lips curled slightly into a smile.

"Because if the monsters pass by us, they might invade the castle town. I'm sure they could probably handle it, but I can't guarantee there won't be casualties. I don't want to see regular citizens die, and part of an adventurer's job is to protect the common people."

Agito nodded. "So in other words, we'll act as bait and fight them? Don't you think that's a little reckless, not knowing how strong they are?" he asked.

This time, he was definitely testing me. I told him to wait a bit. I could only gauge the strength of monsters because of Kyle's ability. I used magic to investigate them.

"I used Wind magic to find out their size and shape. Without a doubt, they're corvasals."

Corvasals were a midsize monster, about five mers long. They resembled a giant rhinoceros with armadillo scales. The reason I didn't explain that to him was because he was a black-rank adventurer, so he already knew what they were.

"Corvasals…" Once you got to purple rank, you would often slay those monsters, so Agito would have no problem exterminating them.

"I'll kill them." Beet woke up in the middle of our conversation. He could probably take care of them if he had Agito's help. I wasn't sure about myself, though. It didn't matter what my actual ability was. Right now, I was only a green-rank adventurer. That was a clear downgrade. It wasn't my place to participate in this battle.

Agito nodded at Beet and turned toward me. "We're gonna fight. That okay with you?"

Within me, Kyle's experiences seemed to be saying, *"This'll be a piece of cake for you, Setsuna!"* but I put a lid on it. I didn't want to lie and let other people take care of it, but I couldn't tell them about Kyle. So I had to. I inwardly apologized to both of them.

"Once I dissolve the barrier, I'll cast support magic on you, then put the barrier back up again and wait inside."

"Good decision." Agito patted me on the shoulder and nodded with a serious expression. Beet glared at me like he wanted to say something, but even he was hesitant in this kind of situation, so he kept his mouth shut.

I gave the signal, then took the barrier pin out of the ground. Agito put out the fire and closed his eyes. Beet did the same thing. It was so they could quickly adjust their eyes to the darkness.

I cast Wind magic to raise their agility. I wished them good luck, and they left.

The wind changed directions, and I felt it come toward me, so I put the barrier back up. The ground rumbled, and the moment the monsters came into sight, Agito and Beet slowly opened their eyes.

Agito ordered Beet to go to the left. The corvasal in front chased after Beet, and two others followed. The remaining monsters closed in on Agito.

They weren't that fast, and there was no danger of them catching up to Beet, since I'd cast support magic on him. I thought maybe Agito would wait for the corvasals to come to him, but surprisingly, he charged toward the monsters.

Just when I thought he was going to run right into them, he twisted his body and leaped to the side of the one in the lead. It couldn't react in time and kept moving forward due to inertia, allowing Agito to smash its legs from the side with his greatsword.

The monster fell over with a thunderous *thump*, and Agito crushed the second and third ones in the same way. I was surprised at not only Agito's agility, but also that his sword was durable enough to remain functional after it had been used to strike down three monsters with such tough skin.

Once he saw the corvasals lying on the ground were powerless, he put off killing them and chased after Beet.

I used Wind magic to create a net to contain the three downed monsters just in case and watched Agito. Beet was taking a big detour but was heading this way, panting.

Aside from the two monsters that were chasing him, there were three more lying in wait that suddenly charged at him from the side. I thought if he didn't get out of the way, they'd run right into him.

I was about to throw away everything and cast advanced Wind magic toward Beet. But I didn't get the chance to.

Agito's speed suddenly increased as he charged toward the corvasal and stabbed his blade into its side. The monster was blown away by that momentum, and Agito stood still on the spot.

The giant monster's body, which was as tough as steel, rolled on the ground and stopped. It had a wound where the greatsword had stabbed it.

No way, I thought. How could he have defeated a monster five mers long with one hit? It just didn't make sense to me. On one hand, I'd been told I was the strongest in the world, yet I could only watch as Agito killed the other two.

"Great job. I'm glad you don't seem to be injured," I said as I walked over to the two of them. They were putting the corvasals into the Cube.

"I guess the monster slayer unit missed these ones." Agito turned toward me as he put the first one into the Cube. "Taking them down was a breeze thanks to your support magic, though."

I told him I didn't do much, and Beet piped up from beside us. "Don't go getting a big head. He's just being polite."

"All you did was run around, Beet. Like you're one to talk. Plus, weren't you only able to outrun the monsters because of Setsuna's magic?"

"......!"

Agito ignored his son, who couldn't argue back. "Not only that, but you immobilized the first three corvasals. I think you probably should have conserved your mana in case you needed to cast recovery magic on the team afterward, but you probably made that decision because you were with a high-ranking party member. That was the right call."

"I'm glad to hear you say that."

"Plus, the fact that we knew it was corvasals made it easier for me to make a plan of attack. You definitely were the most valuable player in this battle, Setsuna."

"Oh, no, that's not true. I wasn't risking my life out there like you two."

Agito glanced at Beet, then looked at me and laughed. "You really don't act your age. It's refreshing. I think you should have one of the corvasals. You earned it."

"Dad!" Beet protested, but Agito glared at him to shut him up.

"Thank you, but I have no right to the spoils… Although, this is my first time seeing a corvasal, so I'd like to get a closer look."

I was trying to be considerate of Beet, but I was also really curious about the giant monster that was lying on the ground, and not just the image I had of it in my head. Beet seemed mystified, and Agito burst out laughing again.

I woke up at the same time like I always did. I moved quietly so as not to wake the other two. I did some simple stretches and began to move my body. It was finally starting to feel like my thoughts were lining up more with Kyle and Hanai's thoughts and experiences.

Perhaps if I had been someone who was used to exercising and moving my body, I might have been able to use their abilities more smoothly. But I had spent most of my life ill, unable to move very much, and I thought that was why it was taking more time for me. I just had to make up for it with hard work.

Plus, after witnessing the way Agito moved last night, I found myself wanting to be like him. Finally, I took some deep breaths to cool down and get my heart rate back to normal. After that, I used magic to clean my body and clothes and walked back to camp. As I walked, I looked up at the sky and told myself I would do my best today, too.

When I returned, the two of them were already awake and training. For some reason, Beet looked run-down. I wondered why. Agito had on his usual smile, so I thought this was just how they were in the morning.

I greeted them, and after we ate breakfast, we gathered our things and headed toward the Wind ruins. Meanwhile, Beet was acting how he usually did. He didn't seem tired, so I figured he must train a lot every day.

Agito paused and looked at the map. I stopped walking, too. "The corvasals from last night aren't from around these parts. They're outside of the ordinary. In other words, this is when the quest really starts to get serious. There are more regular reports of monsters appearing starting from this spot. They probably won't be as strong as corvasals, but just be on your guard."

This was probably the branching point; the Gardir army had headed toward the Ellana Kingdom, and we were going in the opposite direction, toward the Kingdom of Kutt. I nodded obediently at Agito's warning, and although Beet groused about it, he became more vigilant, too.

We arrived at the ruins a little past lunchtime. Agito took out the recording device, which was shaped like a monocle, held it in front of his face, then activated it. Mana spread throughout the monocle, then it began to float on its own and stopped in front of Agito's eye. Rather than staying in a fixed position, it automatically moved to remain in front of his eye.

"Using this magical tool, I will now begin recording everything in my vision, the sounds, the smells, and the mana in the area. I swear on my honor as a black-rank adventurer that we have never come near these ruins before this survey." He paused and looked at us. We both nodded to express our understanding. "Next, I'll introduce the members of the survey team." He grabbed the monocle and handed it to Beet. It tried to travel back to Agito, but Beet took it firmly in his grasp and stood still in front of his father, who introduced himself.

"Next..." Agito trailed off and told Beet to let go of the monocle. He waited for it to return to its position in front of his eye, then looked at Beet, who introduced himself. Finally, it was my turn.

"My name is Setsuna. I am a scholar. My guild rank is green, and I can use Wind magic. I'm participating in the survey because they needed a Windmaster."

Now that the introductions were over, the three of us carefully walked around the exterior of the ruins. From the outside, it looked like a one-story palace with only a single entrance and exit, so it wasn't very large. After checking the surroundings, the next step was to go inside the ruins. We stood in front of the Wind portal to inspect it. Ancient characters were written all around the door.

Agito's monocle reacted to the door's mana, and I saw some kind of blue text appear on the lens. From my perspective, it was backward, so it was hard to make it out, but I could tell it was written in ancient script.

Agito took out an old leatherbound notebook and compared it to the writing by the door. It seemed like he was checking the characters.

"Are you looking for something?" I asked, and he looked up from the notebook.

"Yeah, a certain cocky sorcerer warned me to steer clear of ruins with the text written on this page outside them," he replied, showing me the page.

In extremely precise handwriting, symbols that would warn someone of danger or the existence of dangerous magic were listed. "This was written by someone who knows the ancient language well." It was explained in such detail that anyone could understand it.

"Can you read ancient script?"

"Yes. I am a scholar, after all."

"Ah, right. At first glance, there don't seem to be any warnings written around here."

"It's instructions on how to open the door."

"Oh yeah? Do you know what the monocle says, too?" He closed the notebook and put it back in his pocket. He grasped the monocle with his hand and showed it to me.

"It says 'Wind Magic Detected.'"

"Thanks." Agito let go of the monocle and continued. "Will you open the door for us, then?"

"Sure," I responded.

I placed my hand on the door and activated my Wind magic. The magical tool set in the center of the door absorbed my mana and glowed white.

At the same time, a strong blast of wind burst forth in all directions from the magical tool. Pushed open by the powerful gust, the door split in the middle, sliding into the ceiling and floor below. The tool stuck to the door below, its hemispherical surface protruding from the floor. I'd never seen anything like this before, so I was absolutely captivated. Just then, I heard a voice.

"Setsuna. I want you to wait here," Agito said. I thought for a moment and used detection magic to search the interior of the ruins, running a simple check inside. I confirmed that there was no sign of large monsters or other living creatures within. I decided my magic was not necessary, so I nodded. The only problem was that there was a suspicious, unmoving presence hiding itself inside.

"There aren't any monsters around the ruins, but stay alert," he said.

"I will."

"If Beet and I don't return by tomorrow morning, I want you to go back to town and let Nestor know."

"Okay."

"And don't try to come in and save us, either. Got it?"

"...Yes." Agito gave me a look that said he wanted a better assurance than that. "I understand. Please be careful, you two."

He nodded in response and opened his mouth to say something, but Beet interrupted with, "You really are such a coward."

"Beet! Knock it off!"

"But it's true! He's got no attack power, and you told him to stay here and he just agrees because he can't even argue with that!" He glared at me. "Anyone with guts would say, 'Bring me with you!' If you don't have that kind of courage, you shouldn't be an adventurer in the first place! What's wrong with callin' a coward a coward?!"

Before Agito could say anything, I spoke up first. "My job was to open the door."

"You're a scholar, aren't you? These are completely unexplored ruins! Who would just listen to my dad and nod instead of wanting to come along? Only a hoity-toity scholar would make excuses like that. You should've just introduced yourself and said, 'Hi, I'm a coward!'"

It's true that an academic would want to go inside and check it out.

I was interested, too. When I didn't say anything in response, Beet wore a triumphant look, as if my silence confirmed his suspicions. I stared back at him unblinkingly, without averting my eyes, and told him how I felt.

"It's true that I am one, and as such I'd like to investigate the ruins. But the job I'm here for right now isn't as a scholar. I was asked to come along on this quest by Agito as a sorcerer." I continued before he could say anything else. "Agito hired me, so I'm going to follow his instructions."

Beet was surprised by my response, and so was Agito. Beet stopped glaring at me and instead stepped inside the ruins, looking irritated. Agito, who was some distance away from me, waited. "Your job, hmm? So you noticed, too, huh? I'd considered leaving Beet out here, but he didn't realize it. You can use a sword, can't you?"

Now it was my turn to be surprised. I stared at Agito. He chuckled. "You were practicing your swordsmanship and martial arts this morning, weren't you? I can tell from the way you move your body that you're a swordsman."

I had no idea he had watched me train this morning. I hadn't sensed his presence.

"You seem like you'll be vulnerable, but you're not. And sorcerers who can keep up with our speed are rare. Normally, they wouldn't be able to come this far in a day and a half."

It looked like I needed to be more aware of my surroundings. I'd thought he'd been asleep... But the fact that I hadn't known he was watching me until he told me was a problem.

"It wasn't that you weren't quiet enough. The only thing you're lacking is experience," he said reassuringly, as if reading my thoughts. "I wish I could say it was because of my rank, but I'll spoil it for you—I woke up before you did. Next time, try paying closer attention to people who are sleeping and those who are pretending to be asleep."

I nodded, wondering how I would be able to do that. "Thank you. I'll be more careful going forward."

I probably wouldn't have realized it unless he had told me. After I answered him earnestly, Agito gave me a kind look and said, "There's no need to rush. You've got plenty of time."

Was I in a hurry? Was I rushing? Perhaps I was. I wanted to quickly put all the lessons I'd learned from them into use.

"How long are you gonna stand there flappin' your jaws? C'mon, Dad!" Beet lost his patience and came back to the entrance.

Agito glanced toward him, then looked back at me. He patted me on the shoulder and began walking toward the ruins. He turned around and said, "You take care of things here, Setsuna." Then he vanished inside.

I watched him until his back disappeared, thinking, *Leave it to me.*

After I watched the two of them head inside the ruins, I pulled out my pocket watch and checked the time. I didn't sense any monsters nearby. But there was a group of people watching my movements. Assuming they would fail, I put up a strong magical barrier so that no one could pass through to the ruins. Agito had left me in charge, so it was time to get to work.

I sensed a group of ten people from here. Among them was a sorcerer who could use Fire magic. They had yet to realize I had already noticed their presence. Sorcerers were able to sense mana, and their sensitivity heightened the stronger their magic became, to the point where they could grasp exactly how much mana someone possessed. Although, that didn't work on people like me, who concealed their magical abilities.

At any rate, I used magic to figure out what they were doing, and I decided to listen in on them. It seemed that Wind magic was often used to pick up voices from a distance. But I didn't want their sorcerer knowing I was aware of their presence. So I concealed my magic spell that I used to pick up their voices.

There was magic that could block such spells, but when the two were up against each other, the sorcerer who was more powerful would win out. I didn't want to risk the chance that he could sense just how much magical ability I had. That being said, he probably wouldn't be able to block that spell because he wasn't a Windmaster.

The fact that he didn't react even after I cast the spell meant he didn't notice. I breathed a sigh of relief and strained my ears. Agito and Beet had just entered the ruins, so the group was still making plans. To sum it up, I figured they planned to kill and rob me, enter the ruins, then ambush Agito and Beet. Since they intended on harming us, I decided to fight.

I picked up on a horse on the other side of the ruins. Were these the bandits that Nes had mentioned? In that case, this might be counted as part of the quest to slay them.

Having made up my mind to take care of the bandits who were targeting my life and my possessions, I made my move. Usually, you could only cast sleep magic on a small area, but since I'd inherited Kyle's powers, I could expand the range and put ten people to sleep at once. I activated the spell, and a wind that invited them to slumber blew through the trees.

"What the...?" The group seemed suspicious of the sudden gust of wind blowing at them, but they quickly shook it off and resumed their discussions.

"All right, everyone stick to the plan! Let's go!" urged a man who looked like the leader of the group. Everyone nodded, but the moment they went to carry out their orders...they could no longer stand and crumpled to the ground. Completely unaware of what was going on, they exchanged looks of confusion until they fell into a pleasant sleep.

"Hmm, it seems to take longer with this amount of magic. Maybe I need to put more mana into it." I was just thinking about my strategy when I remembered something important that I needed to do first. "Ah, that's right. I should tie all of them up." It was a bit annoying since there were ten of them, but I took out some rope from my bag and walked over to the bandits. This was my first time fighting against humans, but I didn't feel any sort of guilt hurting them, just like with monsters. Perhaps that was also because I was settling into Kyle and Hanai's body more.

Or perhaps it didn't feel real because it had all gone so smoothly? Or because it was the rational choice, as my own life had been threatened? However, I think the reason I didn't want to finish them off was because I didn't feel like I was fighting. This didn't seem like much of a battle compared to the fight I'd seen last night.

While pondering this, I disarmed them and tied them up one by one, but in the end, I couldn't come up with an answer. After all, no one had ever tried to kill me in my previous life. Anyway, it wasn't my job to punish these people. That was up to the Kingdom of Gardir.

I put a barrier over the bandits to prevent monsters from attacking them and returned to the ruins. I felt thirsty, so I took my canteen out of my bag. This canteen wasn't for water, but fruit juice. Kyle had made it so that the contents would stay cold...

I sat down on the steps of the ruins and slowly drank the juice.

◇Part Two: Beet

"Dammit," I muttered with frustration. Not only did my dad treat me like a kid, but so did my older brother, who was the second-in-command of the team.

"You don't get what it means to have a job," he'd said to me. Just thinking about it pissed me off. I *did* understand. I was completing quests from the guild and leveling up in rank.

"What's their problem anyway?!" Lately, I'd been filled with nothing but anger.

I should have been with my brother's party right now, hunting mikrazirs. They were said to be the pinnacle of medium-sized monsters.

Mikrazirs walked the earth on four legs with a giant seven-mer-long body. The great wings that supported their bodies were like those of an eagle, and they could fly as fast as them, too.

Aside from its normal face, a mikrazir's neck had protrusions from both its left and right flanks, and a tail extended from its rump, each with a face at the end. Those four faces were all in the shape of a dragon. There were no blind spots on all four sides, and they could breathe fire.

Monsters generally didn't grow, but mikrazirs were special. They could grow to be as large as twelve mers long. Once one got that big, it gained the ability to breathe ice, making it even more difficult to slay.

Because of their strength and peculiarity, every male adventurer had to defeat one of those monsters, and I was no exception. So I was thrilled when my older brother finally gave me permission to come hunting with him. But then, last night, my plans were changed unwillingly.

"Beet, you need to go to the guild with the leader tomorrow."

"Huh?! I'm gonna be in your party when you go hunting for mikrazirs, aren't I?!"

My brother suddenly announced a change of plans, but there was no way I could give up on hunting mikrazirs when this had been my goal for ages!

"He needs more people."

"Why me? Make Elio go!"

"You're his apprentice. You have to go with him. It's an apprentice's job to help his mentor."

"I don't want to!"

"You're the only one who's free."

"I'm *not* free! I'm going hunting for mikrazirs!"

"You're the least powerful person in that party."

I clenched my fists. "What's that supposed to mean?"

"I'm saying we don't need you in it."

"Are you trying to say I'm weak?"

"I didn't say that. The only reason I agreed was because the leader said he'd provide backup."

"I don't need it! I can fight without Dad backing me up!"

"Beet, this is an order. You'll accompany the leader to the guild. Understood?"

"I don't want to!"

My brother let out another sigh. "You don't get what it means to have a job. That's why you're still half-rate," he said, walking away from me.

My brother's and Dad's orders were absolute, so I reluctantly had to go. It was an urgent request, but it was up to Dad whether he accepted the quest. Maybe if he turned it down, I could join up with my brother and the rest of the party. I held on to that tiny bit of hope.

Dad and I headed to the guild together, and he went to talk with the guildmaster. I listened to them while I looked over toward the bulletin board. As I scanned the postings, I thought my brother and his party must have been hunting mikrazirs right about now. That got me pissed all over again. I couldn't stop wondering, *Why me?!*

I looked around, and the guild door opened. A super weak-looking guy walked in, but several people turned to gaze at him, probably because he was handsome. But he was looking at Dad and Nes, so he didn't realize people were staring.

After that, everyone's attention went back to my Dad and Nes. Dad had a pretty commanding voice, after all.

I learned that they were in need of a Windmaster, so I thought they just had to go find one. I could go join up with my brother, and once we were done with that quest, we could bring Mom along with us, because she could use Wind magic.

I kept them in my peripheral vision, praying for them to hurry up already. Then I saw Nes smirk, and I had a bad feeling.

"Hey, kid. You lookin' for another quest today?" he said with a smile, calling out to the weakling I saw earlier.

Even though Nes had just called him a kid, the guy didn't look angry or irritated. He just told the guildmaster his name. "Good morning, Nes. You know, I have a name, and it's Setsuna."

After I heard his response, I decided I was gonna stay far away from him. I didn't like the way he talked, or his hoity-toity behavior, either. But the thing I hated most was that he didn't get mad when he got called a kid. I quietly listened to his conversation with Dad and Nes and learned that he was a scholar.

If he was registered as an adventurer in the guild, why would he say he was a scholar instead of a sorcerer? Maybe it was expressing his desire to be protected instead of protecting others? Guess he was just one of those guys who wanted the money but none of the danger. Which made him a coward. That must've been why he didn't get mad when Nes called him a kid. It all made sense.

After reaching that conclusion, I figured I'd never have the occasion to form a party with this coward. Dad was pretty strict, after all. It didn't matter if this guy was a Windmaster; if he'd registered as a scholar, Dad would never accept someone who posed as an adventurer.

"Setsuna, right? Would you help me with my quest?"

I couldn't believe my ears, so I yelled out in frustration. Dad scolded me, but I wasn't gonna listen to him. I was right, no matter what.

But then Dad said something that annoyed me even more. "If he doesn't have experience, then we'll just have to protect him. Or maybe you don't have the confidence to protect one sorcerer?" He said it with this cool look on his face, even though he knew I was mad. The moment the other adventurers started insulting the guy like I had, Dad gave off an angry, intimidating aura. Uh-oh. I'd really pissed him off. The other guys slowly backed away from him.

"Do you have a complaint with the guild's policies?" Dad's eyes and voice were dark. If I answered wrong, that would be the end of my career as an adventurer. I told him no. "Just as you chose the sword, he chose to pursue the path of knowledge. That's all it is, right?" I could tell by his tone that he intended on dealing with me later. "It's not for *you* to say."

I could've said the wrong thing and made others ostracize the scholar. This was a place where adventurers gathered, and I shouldn't have said that. I felt guilty, but then what the guy said next erased those feelings. He said it didn't *bother* him! Even though I had bad-mouthed him! So he didn't care that I criticized him? That was the same as saying everything I'd said was worthless! I mean, it was true that he didn't *have* to listen to my complaints. *But!* It still pissed me off!

Dad gave me an icy glare, unbeknownst to the coward. That made me even more irritated. So I decided to blow off some steam outside and left the guild.

The next day, that guy ended up joining our party to explore the ruins. I'd been against it the whole time, but Dad wouldn't budge. He just told me to protect him. I didn't like it and expressed my opinion, but he just sighed.

We waited for the guy, and he showed up looking like some poser adventurer. I had a lot of comments to make about his getup, but I decided to ignore him, so I didn't say anything.

He called himself an adventurer, but he must have gotten his dad to buy that equipment for him. I bet he was a spoiled rich kid. Even I could tell his equipment was hard to come by. Especially for a novice.

Dad gave me a look, telling me to introduce myself as a member of Moonlight. The leader's orders were absolute. So I had no choice but to introduce myself, though I didn't forget to throw in one last dig. "And I don't think you belong here!"

Dad said something to me, but I ignored him and started walking.

The journey to the ruins was so boring. Normally, I'd pass the time chatting with someone from our team. But Dad was talking to the coward, and I didn't feel like joining in on their conversation.

But I listened as I walked. Dad must have wondered about it, too, because he asked the guy why he wasn't carrying much. We were both surprised by his response. "I'm not the son of an aristocrat. I'm an orphan."

An unpleasant feeling spread inside me when I heard that. Because I'd thought he was some spoiled rich kid whose dad had bought all his stuff for him.

I thought it would take more than three days to get to the ruins. And so had Dad. I was secretly impressed when we got there in half the time. Neither Dad nor I thought the guy would be able to keep up with our pace.

He also wasn't *that* useless in the fight we had partway there. I started to think maybe he had some guts after all? But then...

Dad ordered him to open the portal in the ruins and to stay put, and he didn't even argue back! I despised his decision to blindly obey. Wasn't he a scholar? Didn't he register as an adventurer? So then show some damn guts!

And what about Dad? Why would he leave him here when he knew he was interested in the ruins?

I didn't like Dad's behavior, and I didn't like the guy's, either. I couldn't hide my irritation, so I let him know how I felt. Dad narrowed his eyes at my attitude and was about to say something, but then the guy spoke up first.

"My job was to open the door."

"You're a scholar, aren't you? These are completely unexplored ruins! Who would just listen to my dad and nod instead of wanting to come along? Only a hoity-toity scholar would make excuses like that. You should've just introduced yourself and said, 'Hi, I'm a coward!'"

I didn't wanna hear excuses! Then, when he fell silent, I thought I must've hit the nail on the head, and I felt satisfied. But he looked me straight in the eyes and said, "It's true that I am one, and as such I'd like to investigate the ruins. But the job I'm here for right now isn't as a scholar. I was asked to come along on this quest by Agito as a sorcerer."

He was basically announcing his convictions. Before I could respond, he continued, "The person who hired me is Agito; therefore, I'm going to follow his instructions."

"You don't get what it means to have a job."

The words my brother said to me before flashed through my mind. The conversation we had and the one I just had with this guy.

They were about the same thing.

I was trying to put my feelings first over a job. But he was putting his job first over his feelings. He and I were totally different. The moment I understood that, I suddenly felt embarrassed by my immaturity and naïveté. His words made me realize that.

Quests weren't time to play. They were time to work. My emotions had no place on the job. I couldn't say anything else after that. So I rushed into the ruins alone. From a short distance away, I decided to wait for Dad.

And so I stood there, looking at them both...

◇Part Three: Agito

"Hey, Dad?" My son had been awfully quiet since his conversation with Setsuna, but now he spoke up.

"What is it?" I glanced over at Beet as we walked through the ruins. I knew he'd been in a bad mood lately because of an argument he'd had with my oldest son. But I didn't meddle, because it wasn't important enough for me to get involved. However, I never expected him to direct his frustrations toward a novice adventurer.

I tried to work him hard during this morning's training so that he wouldn't let it interfere with the quest, but apparently it hadn't been enough. Once the quest was over, I had intended on teaching him a lesson, but I felt like that wasn't necessary anymore.

I looked at my son, who seemed to be debating whether he should bring it up with me. I didn't force him; I decided to wait until he was ready.

Inside the ruins, there were areas that resembled rooms, but no doors. A quick survey told me there weren't any magical tools, either. The magical tool Gardir gave us that sensed the presence of mana wasn't reacting. The interior of the ruins seemed just as large as they looked on the outside. A few hours would be plenty of time to make a lap around it.

I took a recording using the monocle as we walked all the paths inside. There were no stairs leading underground. It seemed to be just one floor, with some kind of altar at the center of it.

That wasn't enough to tell me why these ruins had been built, though.

Maybe the person who'd forced me to take this notebook could've figured it out. But personally, I didn't sense a need to put down a magical tool that would keep people out of here. I turned back the way we came, feeling a bit disappointed.

Although I was being careful of my surroundings, my mind was on Beet, who still seemed to be deep in thought. I wondered how the young Windmaster was doing.

He'd been polite ever since Nestor introduced us.

But I felt like I'd met him somewhere before... He was so handsome that there was no way I could have forgotten his face. I thought it was just my imagination, but I continued to observe him.

The way he dressed, acted, and spoke was refined. I could easily imagine he was well educated.

Even when Nestor called him a kid, he just politely stated his name. Most guys around his age would've complained, but he just sighed and calmly told him he didn't like to be called that.

That must have been when Beet had decided he was useless.

Honestly, my first impression was that I wouldn't be able to take him anywhere dangerous. Then, when I heard his occupation, that hunch should've turned into certainty. He had registered as a scholar instead of a sorcerer, which meant he wasn't suited for battle. In that case, I didn't want him to get hurt, so I couldn't bring him along on this quest.

But things just weren't adding up.

If all that were true, why would Nestor introduce him to me? There was something off about all of this. *But what is it?* I'd wondered as I continued talking with Nestor.

"The kid *is* a Windmaster, but he's only been with the guild for two months and taken only solo quests."

Two months? He had made it all the way to the second level of rank green in that short amount of time? I hid my surprise and looked over at Nestor, who nodded. So that's what had been bothering me...

Nestor had called him a novice and a little chick. Most of the time, you were a novice in the guild for about six months. The reason was because it often took that long before you progressed from rank yellow to green.

Once an adventurer reached rank green, Nestor started referring to them by their first name. Of course, there were adventurers who raced through the yellow levels. But aside from extreme exceptions, it would still take four months. Out of everyone I knew, the only one I knew who'd reached green right at the four-month mark was a sorcerer named Spuna from the team Thousand Blades. That team was no longer around, though. It was disappointing, because people had been talking about them making black rank.

So with that in mind, achieving level two of green rank in just two months was astounding.

If Nestor had given him that rank, then there was no doubt about it. This young man was extremely talented.

If he was the apprentice of a black- or white-rank adventurer and was already quite capable, it would still be possible, but it would have been a huge topic of discussion. But this was the first time I'd heard of the kid. If none of the other black-rank adventurers were talking about him, then the chances of him having a famous mentor were slim to none.

The fact that Nestor hadn't ceased calling him a chick just made the kid more mysterious. I became curious about him. In the end, since Nestor recommended him and we didn't have much time left, plus my curiosity, I decided he was the best person for the job.

But Beet's mood only worsened when I asked Setsuna to come along with us on the quest. He tore into him and didn't hold back voicing his opinions, and he dragged the other adventurers into it.

It seemed there were many adventurers who were envious of both Setsuna's looks and equipment. I was sure that up until now, Nestor had been keeping them in check. But if things continued like this, I thought it would be dangerous, so I decided to nip it in the bud. After all, my son was the one who'd started it.

Setsuna said the insults didn't bother him, which sent Beet into a rage, and he ran out of the guild.

Although, I had to give him credit for keeping his mouth shut.

I let out an inward sigh at the fact my son had let someone younger than him bother him so much.

Once Beet was gone, Setsuna and I had a little meeting. After we finished, I asked him what his plans were for the rest of the day, and he said he was going to prepare for the next day and left the guild.

I had a feeling he was a bit too serious, but that wasn't entirely a bad thing.

However...

As I glanced over at the door, Nestor lowered his voice. "It makes me nervous to watch Setsuna sometimes. He seems like he's in a rush to grow up."

"And that's why you still call him a chick?"

Nestor nodded.

"And you want me to protect him?" I asked jokingly, but when I looked over at him, he had a somber expression.

"I won't ask you to do that... But just teach the kid to relax a little," he said.

That surprised me. I'd known him for a very long time, and he'd never asked me to do something like that before. "That's unusual. You like him that much, huh?" He *was* a nice young man, but...

"I like kids who work that hard," he said in a gruff voice, then waved his hand at me in a shooing motion.

I took that as my cue to leave the guild. At that time, I had definitely taken notice of Setsuna.

"Hey."

"What?" I answered my son, keeping my guard up as we walked along.

"Why'd you decide to bring him along with us?"

"You're not satisfied with the answer that it's because he's a Windmaster?"

"You could've found someone else." He took a deep breath then said in a low voice, "I thought you hated cowards?"

I had to laugh at his stubbornness in this matter. "I never thought he was a coward."

"He's a Windmaster, but he registered as a scholar. Normally, you'd avoid guys like that!"

I understood why he thought so. I knew I was strict. But I was also aware that not all scholars were like that. That being said, a lot of them flaunted their intelligence, didn't do anything, and put their thirst for knowledge first. In other words, there were plenty of them whom I wouldn't want to work with on a quest.

It wasn't that I disliked scholars as a whole, but I'd never actively wanted one in my party. They had a place in the world... It just wasn't on my team.

"If he was a scholar who only cared about satisfying his lust for knowledge, then I would've found someone else."

I was surprised when Beet quietly listened to me. Normally, he'd be too busy stating his own opinion. Maybe my answer actually satisfied him?

I might have doted on him more than my first and second sons because he was the third one born. And maybe that's why he was a bit selfish and just couldn't shake off that spoiled attitude.

But now he was acting differently. I looked at Beet and told him about Setsuna.

"Two months?" he repeated.

"That's right," I said.

"No way...," he murmured.

"I thought so, too. But I understood he had that much natural talent after I saw him in action."

"On what basis?"

"The fact that he kept up with our speed on the way to the ruins."

Beet shifted uncomfortably.

Setsuna hadn't shown the least bit of fatigue as he kept pace with us. Normally, sorcerers would take a break once every three hours. Even when I got concerned and checked on him, he told me he was fine. I thought maybe he was pushing himself, but he didn't seem tired.

So I stopped telling Beet to slow down and asked Setsuna more about himself. The way he answered my questions so pleasantly made me like him even more.

We talked about many things, and I began to learn more about the kind of person he was. I found out he had no parents, and the person whom he trusted most had passed away. No matter the reason, it must have been hard for a young man like him to live all alone.

Nestor said he felt like Setsuna was in a hurry to grow up. Now I understood why. He also said he felt anxious watching him sometimes. I felt that, too. But neither Nestor nor I could figure out why...

"You were taking your frustration out on him, weren't you?" I asked, and Beet fell silent. "Because he didn't talk back. Because he's a novice and a scholar. Like I told you before, everyone is free to choose their occupation. And all adventurers start out as novices. It seems like you were blaming him for irrational reasons."

Beet stopped and looked down. I continued. "But Setsuna never spoke ill of you, did he?"

"No."

"What did you say to him after he made such a wonderful magical tool to help us? If you were in his position, what would you have done?"

"I would've punched him."

"Exactly. But he just quietly listened to you. Why do you think that is?" I urged him to keep walking. "I wouldn't actively choose to put a scholar on my team. But that just goes to show you how rare it is to find scholars like him."

"......"

"Do you still think it's right to blame someone like that for senseless reasons?"

"No."

"I think the reason why he didn't let what you said get to him is because he's got strong convictions."

Beet stopped again.

"And when you're working hard to better yourself, trivial things others say don't bother you. That shows mental toughness."

Once we turned the corner, the exit would be just up ahead. We'd get there faster than I thought. I turned toward my son and made eye contact with him. "He's still eighteen, Beet. He's only been an adult for two years. But he's in a hurry to grow up. You've got people like that in your circle of friends, don't you?" My son's eyes wavered for a moment. "He doesn't have anyone else he can count on, so his convictions are all he's got to support himself. He's gritting his teeth to survive."

I remembered the sad way he had gazed at me and Beet at dinner the night before. I had a feeling his mind was elsewhere, thinking about someone else.

"So then why didn't you ask him to come inside the ruins?"

"You heard what he said. He did his job."

"Why couldn't I have waited outside?"

I smiled wryly at him. "If he had said he wanted to come inside, would you have offered to wait?"

"No. There's not really a reason for anyone to wait out there, right?"

Deep down, I knew he was kind, but I couldn't applaud him for that stubbornness. I let out a sigh.

"Normally, you would've picked up on it."

"On what?"

"There were bandits following us. About ten of 'em."

Beet clenched his fist and glared at me. "And you left him out there knowing that?!"

"He noticed them, too." It was just a hunch, but I had a feeling that Setsuna had used magic to check the interior of the ruins and decided he didn't need to participate in the survey because there were no monsters inside. Since there was no use for him inside the ruins, he chose to wait outside.

"So his job..."

"Is to provide support on our quest. And in this case, it's stopping the bandits."

It might have looked like I'd asked him to do that, but he'd made the call himself. You didn't see many novices with the ability to act that decisively. And on top of that...

"He's stronger than you." Beet opened his mouth to argue back, but I continued before he could speak. "He's stronger than me, too." Then he closed his mouth and stared at me, a serious look in his eyes.

"That's impossible."

"Right now, I have the upper hand. But in six months, I don't know if I'd be able to beat him."

"What are you basing that on?"

"I watched him practice his swordsmanship and martial arts this morning. Did you notice that he was up early?"

"No."

"His stealth abilities are very refined. If I hadn't already been awake, I don't think I ever would've heard him."

His swordsmanship was first-class as well. If we crossed blades today, I would win only because I had more experience. It was hard for me to tell how strong he was at magic, but I had a feeling he would be able to hold his own against any member of Moonlight.

Yet he did not register as a swordsman or sorcerer, but as a scholar. He was truly interesting.

"He can use a sword? I thought he was a sorcerer?"

"Setsuna's strong. He could make a living with his blade, too." I knew because I'd seen him train. He did it so intently and earnestly, as if trying to make everything his own as soon as he possibly could. I felt like I caught a glimpse of what Nestor was talking about when I saw him swinging his sword.

There was an intense darkness in his eyes when he practiced.

I didn't know what had driven him to that point.

I couldn't help but mention to him that I'd seen him train before I went into the ruins. I hadn't intended on telling him, but since Nestor had asked me to help him relax more, I thought it would be better to say something. But what came out of my mouth was something different than I had intended.

"There's no need to rush. You've got plenty of time."

Black-rank adventurers would tell the young ones that time and time again. Setsuna just nodded silently to my words of advice.

* * *

Beet was walking quickly ahead of me, but all of a sudden, he stopped in his tracks. I went up to stand beside him.

Music...? I heard someone singing from outside the door. It was a melody I'd never heard before.

"What a sad song...," Beet murmured.

I wondered if those lyrics expressed Setsuna's feelings. His soft, gentle singing voice reached us. It was so good that I felt entranced. If Saara were here, she would have loved it.

The song was in the language of a kingdom I didn't recognize. I'd never heard it before, so I didn't know what the words meant. But I could tell they were filled with such sorrow that it made my heart ache.

Beet slowly began walking. He kept his back turned to me and said in a clear voice, "I'm going to get stronger. So I can do my job well."

As I watched him from behind, I suddenly felt like my son had grown up a bit, or perhaps it was just wishful thinking on the part of his father.

I wasn't sure which was true, but...I hoped it was both.

I thanked the gods that I was able to witness Beet's growth.

◇Part Four: Setsuna

It was close to sunset. I was sitting alone in front of the Wind ruins. I didn't have anything else to do, so I was fiddling with the barrier needle to see how I could improve it. I fixed what I could, and when I finally looked up, the sun was slowly sinking into the horizon.

For some reason, I began humming a song my younger sister, Kyoka, liked. All sorts of memories I shared with my family came flooding back. I looked away from the sunset, trying to force those thoughts away.

That sky did not extend to anywhere familiar to me. No matter where I went in this world, I wouldn't find a place I knew.

* * *

Those thoughts were on my mind as I hummed. Just then, Agito and Beet came back. I hadn't expected them this soon. For a moment, I was afraid they'd heard me singing, but they didn't say anything, so I figured they hadn't.

"Are you done with the quest?"

"On our side, yeah. It was so easy, it made me a little suspicious," Agito said with a laugh.

Beet went over to the bandits I'd tied up and poked one of them with the tip of his shoe.

"You're not hurt, Setsuna?" Agito looked me over to check.

"No, I'm fine."

Agito glanced at the bandits, looking as if he was ruminating about something. "Did you use magic to defeat them?"

Ah, that's right. Since he saw me practicing swordsmanship, he's wondering if I took them down with the sword. But I had accompanied him today as a sorcerer.

"Yes. There's a spell I've been wanting to try out, so I used that on them."

"Which spell?"

I thought for a moment and said, "It's a secret." In this world, magic was a sorcerer's meal ticket. So it was better for me not to discuss it with others.

"Well, I guess there's nothing I can say to that." He looked a bit disappointed but shrugged with a smile. That gesture suited him.

Just then, Beet looked at me with a puzzled expression. "It was sleep magic, wasn't it? I just don't know how he can cast it on so many people." I thought he was directing that toward me, but his tone was different from before.

"I know that. I was just hoping he'd answer us and tell us how he did it."

"Oh."

For some reason, it felt like Beet wasn't as annoyed with me as before. Bewildered, I looked at him. He saw me staring at him and fidgeted a bit. Then he averted his eyes and muttered, "I'm sorry." It was almost a whisper, but I still heard it.

I couldn't hide my surprise at receiving an apology from him. He'd hated me so much…

Beet saw my reaction and shrugged. "Even I can apologize when I'm wrong." That was all he said before looking off in another direction. At any rate, I told him it was fine, and he nodded. He changed the subject and asked how I had defeated them. "So? How'd you do it?"

Before I could repeat what I stated earlier, Agito responded. "You shouldn't ask sorcerers to reveal their secrets."

"As if you're one to talk, Dad."

Agito didn't say anything after that. But I had a feeling he did it on purpose. He wanted to keep the light mood in the air. I stared at him, and as he smiled at me, his eyes softened.

After our quest from the guild was finished, Agito bound up the bandits with a magical tool designed for criminals. I had a feeling that the more they looked into these guys, the more crimes they would find out they'd committed. At first, the bandits had an attitude, but they shut up quickly once they saw the color of Agito's emblem. It turned out to be quite easy to take them along with us.

It was actually more difficult taking the horses home with us. There were six of them that they'd stolen from the guild or farmers, and Beet and I were in charge of three each on the road back.

I'd never even seen a horse in person in my past life, so I couldn't say they were exactly what we would call a horse in this world. But from what I could tell, they were quite gentle for animals of their size. I found myself grinning as I stroked their manes.

Every time I did, Beet and Agito teased me that I should quit being an adventurer and open up a farm instead. But I could tell they didn't mean any harm.

I'd never ridden a horse before and was very tempted to try, but they didn't belong to me, and I didn't want to risk injuring them. I could probably heal their injuries with Wind magic, but putting them in danger so that they could be hurt in the first place didn't seem right.

Seeing my reaction, Agito told me he'd borrow a horse once we got back to the guild so that I could try riding it, then smiled at me again.

There were several horses that had been wounded while they were with the bandits. After I used Wind magic to heal them, they grew quite fond of me.

We arrived at the castle town without any trouble, turned in the bandits and horses to the authorities, then went to the guild to give our reports.

I entered the guild with Agito and Beet, and all the adventurers inside immediately turned to look at Agito.

"Hey, little chick. Did you finish your job?" Nes called out to me, ignoring the atmosphere in the room.

"I have a name, and it's Setsuna, Nes," I responded like I always did. Beside me, Beet sighed, then laughed.

"From the looks of it, things went well, then?"

"He did his job without a single complaint," Agito said as he approached the counter. Beet and I followed. Agito signed both of our quest forms and handed them in to Nes.

"Oh, you caught the bandits, too?"

Once the paperwork was done, Agito gave Nes the document we'd received from the police that acknowledged our capture of the bandits. Stamped with the official seal of the kingdom, it listed the number we'd caught in addition to the horses we'd recovered.

"That was all thanks to Setsuna. We weren't involved in any way, so I want you to give him all the points for it. Gardir will take care of finding the horses' owners."

Nes looked taken aback for a moment, then confirmed it with Agito. "Oh? The kid caught the bandits?"

"That's right. We were inside the ruins at the time. Although, I'm curious to know how he did it."

"Well, a sorcerer doesn't part with their secrets so easily...," Nes said, glancing at me. "Actually, I haven't finished writing up the paperwork for that quest."

At first, I didn't completely understand what he meant, but Beet immediately latched on to it.

"Hey, that's not right. You asked Dad to kill 'em."

"Oh, I didn't mean it. I certainly didn't think you'd come across them. It's true that you don't always need to fill out paperwork when asking a black-rank adventurer to do a quest, but I'd never ask one to do something as small as take care of bandits anyway."

I looked over at Agito, who seemed to understand the situation, but his face was tense. "I see. Since the guild's assets were involved, they had to coordinate the reward with Lycia headquarters in order to create the request form. I didn't think it was a serious request anyway."

"The reward was supposed to be officially decided tomorrow. And I was going to post the quest afterward."

"So what about his reward, then? Don't tell me you're gonna make him work for free?"

Nes didn't say anything. I was curious about what Beet said, so I searched Kyle and Hanai's memories. It seemed like the eradication of bandits was usually left up to the kingdom that protected those lands.

But of course, the kingdom couldn't cover everything, so they set aside payment and asked the guild so that the job could be done by the guild's adventurers.

In that case, the quest would be given out immediately, but since horses that the guild had borrowed were stolen, the guild headquarters in Lycia had to sort things out, which took time.

"Hey, Nestor. Judging by the strength of the bandits and the damage they did, I think the points should be enough to get him to level three," Agito said, his eyes darting around a bit.

"Didn't you just say you were curious about how he caught them? Plus, a black-rank adventurer can't just decide the payments of these things. You know that. Or do you not care what the payment is?" Nes gave Agito a suspicious look.

He averted his eyes, a guilty look on his face. "I know. I was just joking," he said, before he muttered, "you ol' hardhead."

I thought the mood couldn't get any more awkward, so I went ahead and said, "If paying me is going to cause some kind of trouble, please don't worry about it." I really meant that. Whatever it was, I could earn it back anytime.

But Beet immediately objected. "No way! An adventurer's body is his life! You don't know when you won't be able to work again. So if there's a reward that belongs to you, then you should accept it. And, Nes, I dunno if you *were* joking or what, but not only did you ask us to slay the bandits, it was a quest. You're the one who said it, and he did it, so he should be the one to get paid. Isn't that right, Dad?!"

Agito seemed surprised and nodded. "Beet's right. If you don't pay Setsuna right here, then people will start to lose trust in the guild."

"Listen, I want to do something about it, too."

"Then say that I officially accepted a black-level quest. We can use the deferred rate system, and once the amount is decided tomorrow, I'll take it."

Beet explained to me quietly that the deferred rate system was used in cases where it was difficult to determine the level of the quest beforehand, so the payment was decided afterward; it was a special privilege of black-rank adventurers.

"There's no problem with the paperwork, but the kid still doesn't get paid," Nes said, seemingly unconvinced of how this was a good idea as he looked at Agito.

"The way I explained it was bad. I accepted the quest not as a team of black rank but as a temporary party. So the party will receive the payment. And the leader is responsible for divvying out the money. I'll use that special privilege and give Setsuna all of it. There should be no problem with that, right?"

Nes nodded.

"But his payment will be a day late. That okay with you?" Beet asked considerately, since I was being left out of the conversation.

"Yes, that's fine. I'm just grateful you thought of me in the first place."

"Well, if it's okay with you, then I won't object, either. Dad, Nes— I'm counting on you."

I was surprised that Beet felt that close to me now. Agito must've felt the same way, because I could tell he was holding back a smile.

After Nes was done filling out paperwork with Agito, he finally took a break and called out to me. "Sorry about all that. You should really take a break tomorrow. Got it?"

"Yes, I'll do that. Thank you again for recommending me for this job. I learned a lot." Nes looked satisfied with my reply and nodded. I shifted my gaze to Agito and Beet and bowed. "I know our time together was brief, but thank you so much for letting me into your party."

I learned a lot of very important things. Agito had left me with some words of wisdom. *"There's no need to rush. You've got plenty of time."* He was right; my life in this world had only just begun.

"You're so...polite. I guess that's just how you are. I wish you could give half of those manners to Beet."

"It'd be creepy if I acted like Setsuna," Beet said with a sour look. "Anyway, I'm glad you were in our party, too."

"Thanks."

"See ya later, Setsuna."

"You too, Beet."

He lifted his right hand, then left the guild. I watched him leave, and just as I thought about returning to the dormitory, Agito called out to me. "Setsuna?"

"Yes?"

"What do you think about joining my team?"

I wasn't the only one surprised by Agito's invitation; the whole guild started buzzing.

"You want me to join your team?"

"Yeah. I've currently got twelve members."

"I see."

"We don't have a scholar, and we only have one Windmaster. I'd love it if you joined us. And I'm not trying to flatter you. I mean it."

Honestly, I was bewildered by the unexpected invitation. And I was flattered. But...I already knew my answer; I didn't need to think about it.

"Thank you."

"You'll join us?"

"No, I'm sorry." I could hear the murmurs of disbelief from the other adventurers.

"Can I ask why?"

I thought about it a little and decided to be honest about my feelings. "Your invitation is very attractive. But right now, I still want to try to make my way on my own."

"......"

"I want to see the world. I want to learn things I don't know, see things I've never seen."

"Honestly, it's not easy to live here. But even then...there is beauty here. Things that will move your heart."

......

Kyle's voice resounded inside my head.

"I think I'd still be able to see the world if I joined your team, but I..."

I don't want to be tied down by the restrictions of being on a team. I want to travel around freely. Before I could finish my sentence, Agito patted me on the shoulder, as if to tell me I didn't need to say it.

"I figured you'd say no. I don't hold it against you." He didn't seem offended. In fact, he smiled at me gently. "Traveling around the world solo until you get sick of it isn't a bad idea."

"Yeah." I nodded.

Agito turned a serious gaze toward me. "Setsuna. If at any time during your travels you're worried about something, find yourself in trouble, or come across some kind of problem you can't solve alone, I don't want you to hesitate to rely on me. I promise I'll help you," he said and took a card from his pocket. "My name, emblem, and team name are engraved on this."

I wondered if it was something like a business card. I took the card, but he didn't let go of it. I didn't understand what he was getting at, so I gave him a puzzled look, and he added, "Just put your finger on the emblem here and say your name."

"Okay." I did just as instructed, and suddenly, my name appeared on the card. Apparently, it was some kind of magical tool.

Agito laughed, amused by my reaction, and explained. "It proves that you're a friend of mine."

The nature of one's mana differed, so putting both of our mana into this card was probably a way of preventing counterfeits.

"When you give the card to a guildmaster, the mana registered on the card will be compared with yours, so even if the card gets lost, a third party can't use it."

"Okay."

"So if you ever have a problem somewhere, show this to the closest guildmaster. The guild will then contact me. And I'll be able to get in touch with you, too."

I wondered if he was worried about me because I'd told him how I didn't have a single relative, and no one to depend on. He'd only spent a few days with me, yet he cared about me so much that he gave me this card...

"Okay...I got it. Thank you." I appreciated the thought so much that my heart felt warm. I didn't want him to notice, so I continued before he could reply. "Where do they make these cards? Can you get them easily?"

"They cost money, but the guild can make them for you. And you can get them right away."

"Agito, are you free right now?"

"Yeah, I got some time."

"Could you wait for a moment?"

Agito suppressed a chuckle and nodded. Nes had been listening in on our conversation. I had him make a card for me with my name and emblem engraved on it, paid for it, then handed the newly minted card to Agito.

"If you ever need a scholar or a Windmaster, I'd love to do another quest with you sometime."

Agito grinned and took the card, then placed his finger on the emblem. The gesture seemed easy and fluid, as if he was used to such a thing. "I'll be calling you," he told me. I stared at him as he put the card away.

I had been all alone, but now I'd met someone who cared about me. And he wasn't the only one; Nes did, too. That made me really happy... but at the same time, it was a bit painful. I wondered why, and I searched for the answer within myself but couldn't find any.

* * *

"Setsuna." Agito's voice pulled me from my reverie. "Are you all right?"

I guess I was spacing out a bit. "I'm fine. Agito?"

"Hmm?"

"Will you take this?" I took two silver pins from my pocket and handed them to him.

"Are these barrier needles?"

"Yes."

They were the ones I'd improved in front of the ruins. These would create the strongest barrier possible and could be used anywhere from five to ten times each. The silver needles were shaped like a pyramid with a display on the front that showed how many uses they had left. These were much easier to use than the first versions I'd made.

"......"

"This is all I have to repay you with right now." I wanted to give something back to Agito for his kindness—and not just with words, but something that contained my feelings.

He didn't reach for the needles, and at first, I thought I might have made him uncomfortable, so I was about to put them away when he suddenly placed his hand on top of my head and roughly tousled my hair.

"Wah!" I looked at him in surprise and saw his eyes were tinged with sadness. I had a feeling that although he was looking at me, he was seeing someone else in his mind.

"I'll gratefully accept these," he said with a smile, and he pulled his hand away from my head. By the time he took the barrier needles from me, he was back to his old self again.

After I told him about the medicine I'd promised to explain to him back at camp, I bid farewell to Agito and Nes and left the guild, closing the curtain on my first quest I'd gone on in a party.

Chapter Four
Crimson Clover ~ Brighten My Heart ~

◇Part One: Setsuna

Time certainly went by quickly. The seasons had changed from spring, also known as Silkis, to Salkis, which was summer. One month had passed since I had completed the quest with Agito and Beet, and three months had passed since I'd become an adventurer.

I'd been regularly completing quests since then and was now level one out of five in rank blue. Now that my rank had gone up, so had my rewards, and I'd saved up enough money to head to the next kingdom.

All I had to do was complete a few more quests, and I'd be ready to leave Gardir.

With that in mind, I had completed a monster-slaying quest today for the guild and was walking on the path toward the castle town. I could return more easily if I used Teleport, but as usual I loved the exercise, so I'd chosen to walk.

Under normal circumstances, I would have reached the castle town by now, but I'd taken a detour after finding a patch of medicinal herbs on the way home. The village was just down the road, but for some reason I didn't feel like going home. I debated whether to teleport back and finally decided to search for a place to set up camp for the night.

* * *

The sun was starting to set...

I walked toward the castle town, searching for a place to make camp. However, I couldn't find a good spot. I was annoyed, so I began to think I should just walk home, when I suddenly heard a faint voice.

The sound of it drew me in, growing louder and louder. Someone was angrily shouting. All I could hear were voices.

"I wonder if someone's being attacked by bandits?" I concealed my presence cautiously and quickened my pace, then used Wind magic to eavesdrop on the conversation up ahead.

"Stop disobeying me, ya brat! You got a collar on your neck, and you still don't understand you can't run away? You won't be able to escape with that leg anyway!"

From the shouts, I could tell that a man was punching someone. And from the conversation, I gathered it was most likely a child. A collar... Was the child a slave?

In this world, some nations recognized slaves as personal property, and Gardir was among them. As long as humans kept fighting with each other, the fights between other races wouldn't stop, either.

Some people believed that if you won a war, you had the right to take someone as a slave because they couldn't pay back their debts or because they were of a different race.

I had a lot of thoughts about slavery. But if I were to start raising objections based on the common sense I'd learned or my idea of human rights, I would be seen as a heretic. Of course, there were some people who objected to slavery, too, but they were outnumbered by those who thought of slaves as convenient tools.

There were also countries who had abolished slavery and countries who had made alliances with nations whose citizens were of a different race. I couldn't help but wish every country could be like that.

The voice I picked up using Wind magic was becoming more and more agitated. What should I do? I couldn't just stand there and turn a blind eye if a child was being abused by an adult. Still, I couldn't very well punch out the man and rescue the child, either. If he was the owner, I would be the one at fault here. I'd be punished under Gardir's laws, and in the worst-case scenario, be executed.

Even if I saved the child from the man's violence here, nothing would fundamentally change. Yet still I found myself approaching them, even as I began to feel powerless at my lack of options.

Now I could hear the man clearly, without the help of Wind magic.

"I finally sold you, but then you got returned! You're ruining my business! Even the food I give you costs money!" The man was shouting furiously. "If you would've just behaved, you could have been doted on as a pet! But now I can only sell you as a lab rat!"

"......"

The child lying on the ground was a slave to be sold, and the man was a slave trader... In that case, I could potentially protect the child if I bought them as a slave. Of course, I didn't think buying a person was the right thing to do, but... I pushed aside my conflicting feelings. I didn't have any other choice right now.

"I sold all the others in the castle town! And now I'm saddled with this useless brat..." When I heard the slave trader's tone, I knew I didn't have time to go back and forth about this. "What?! Why are you looking at me with those disrespectful eyes?! I'm the one keeping you alive!"

The child was in danger, and I was about to say something—but the man's anger must've gotten the best of him, because he kicked the child as hard as he could. They went flying and slammed hard into a tree. The impact must've damaged an organ, because I heard a sickening sound and saw blood spraying from their mouth...

As I stared at the child, who was unmoving, I was consumed with guilt at the thought that I hadn't acted in time.

The slave trader stared at the child as if he was looking at garbage. "Now I can't sell you anymore at all." He scoffed, then reached for the sword on his belt. "I'm not keepin' something I can't sell! Now I can finally stop carrying around this piece of filth!" There was hatred in the man's eyes. "I've been waiting for this day! Farewell, ya little brat!"

the man shouted, and he brandished his sword without hesitation. The child must have been unconscious, as they didn't move.

But before the slave trader could lower his sword, I stepped in between them.

"Huh?" The man froze, surprised by my sudden appearance.

I looked at him and said slowly, "If you're just going to kill the kid, will you give him to me instead?" I glanced at the child, who was completely unconscious and in real danger. If too much time passed, it would be too late. Unbeknownst to the slave trader, I created a barrier and froze time within it. It put the subject in a temporary state of presumed death, but at least it would prevent the child from losing any more blood.

"What're you gonna do with a kid who's practically dead? What is it you're doing this out of? Pity? Sadness? This kid's put me through the ringer. If I can't sell 'em, I'll kill 'em..." The slave trader glared at me and clenched the hilt of his sword.

"I'll pay you. The only reason this child survived was because you took care of them, right?"

Maybe the child wouldn't want me to save them, but...

"Heh. So you're a reasonable man, eh? But what you do plan on doing with the brat?"

"I think they'll be helpful with my magical experiments."

"Oh? You're a sorcerer?"

"That's right. And I'd rather have a live subject for my research."

The slave trader gave me an unpleasant smile and nodded several times. "I see, I see. Everyone has one or two experiments they wanna keep secret, yeah?"

The reason he believed me so easily was because of a group of sorcerers who operated in Gardir. They believed magic was a weapon to fight monsters and a means to kill people. So it was normal for them to want to increase their powers to harm others. I had no intention of speaking against them. I was also always trying to strengthen my powers every day.

But this group of sorcerers bought slaves for experimental purposes. They used them as guinea pigs to perfect their spells. I was angry that the slave trader thought I was someone like that, but I suppressed my emotions and continued my negotiations with him.

He must've been satisfied with my answer, because he gave me a friendly look. His previous demonic expression disappeared. "The kid might be half-dead, but I fed the brat myself. I can't live unless I get that much money back."

I felt an intense disgust for this man, who had been on the verge of killing a child.

"Plus, this kid is beastfolk. A very rare commodity. Normally, they go for twenty gold. But I'll let you have 'em for ten."

I hated myself for negotiating with a slave trader, and I began to feel nauseous, but I managed to maintain my composure.

"Well?"

"All right." I took ten gold out of my bag and handed it to him. That meant I'd be forking over more than half the money I'd saved up to go to the next kingdom, but I had no regrets. "Here's ten gold. You can check it yourself."

If I hadn't been able to pay that amount, he probably would've continued negotiating with me. No ordinary person would pay ten gold for a child on the verge of death. But...I couldn't put a price on a child's life. This man was trading a person's life for a mere ten gold. I clenched my fist tightly.

The slave trader looked surprised and opened his mouth but ended up saying nothing. He probably didn't want to say the wrong thing and risk ruining the deal. He quietly accepted the gold.

He cautiously used a magical tool to check the authenticity of the gold, then put it in his pocket. He took out some other kind of magical tool and handed it to me. "This is the key to the brat's collar. If you think it's gonna disobey, all you gotta do is add some mana to it and the collar will tighten."

"...I understand." I suppressed the urge to throw it away right then and there and nodded. Then I put the magical tool away in my bag and took out some powdered medicine contained in a round barrier like a marble. I hid it in my hand so that he wouldn't notice it.

I picked up the child and said to the slave trader, "May you have the Wind's protection." I smiled pleasantly at him and cast Wind magic on him. A gentle breeze blew softly around the man. It was a spell Windmasters often used that took away physical fatigue.

"Oh! Thanks! Lemme know if you ever need another slave!"

I never wanted to see him again.

"I'm at the slave market in the castle town once every two months!" He climbed onto his carriage and went back the way I'd come. He was probably going to rent a room at the inn in the village. There was a magical tool that warded off monsters on the horse and carriage. I took this road often, and it was relatively safe. A magical tool of that level would be plenty useful out here.

So I thought about walking back home, but...

I turned toward the slave trader, who was nearly out of sight, and murmured, "The medicine will kick in after about a day..."

When I'd cast Wind magic on him, I'd also thrown the powdered medicine I'd concealed in my hand. It was tasteless and odorless. It would enter the slave trader's mouth and nose. He'd be plagued with a terrible stomachache about a day from now. I hadn't been planning on using it, but I'd seen it in a book and was practicing my pharmacy skills.

No matter how I felt, I couldn't interfere with a legal business. Still, I had to do something, or I wouldn't be satisfied. He'd almost killed a kid. It was a small punishment compared to the physical and mental damage he'd inflicted on the child.

I looked down at the child in my arms, who was covered in wounds, and sighed.

I decided I couldn't just go home, so I searched for a place where I could tend to their injuries. They were still unconscious in my arms and felt so light that I could barely feel the sensation of carrying them. I didn't want to think about the reason behind it.

I found a place where I could make camp and put up a barrier. I made it so no one would be able to see us from the outside. We were away from the main road, so I didn't think anyone would pass by anyway, but it was just a precaution.

I took a blanket from my bag and laid it out on the ground, then placed the child down on it. I wanted to prepare the camp before the sun went down completely, so I built a fire and used Light magic to illuminate the interior of the barrier.

Then I carefully examined the beastfolk child who lay on the blanket. I could already tell from how light they were, but the child was very thin. Their right wrist was bent and fixed like that, and their right leg was also twisted and unmoving. I wondered if the slave trader had broken the bones and left them like that.

It must have been incredibly painful for the child to walk. There was no way they could've run. They couldn't have held anything in their right hand, either.

The child was still so young. How could anyone do something so cruel?

I was overwhelmed by anger and sadness. I sighed, letting out my emotions.

I removed the child's blood-soaked clothing to identify the locations of their injuries. They were so thin that their bones protruded. I cast magic on the child's body.

The recovery magic in this world fell under the Wind attribute, but it wasn't all-powerful. Its effectiveness depended greatly on the amount of mana each Windmaster possessed, along with their magic construction formula and ability to control their own magic. It all varied, but... there was a limit to how much it could heal.

For example, for an injury, the magic could close wounds and stop the bleeding. But it couldn't create more blood, and it was difficult to erase the scars of a wound that had closed up.

In the case of a broken bone, magic could make it go back to normal if it was treated right away. But if the wound festered, or if the bone had fused together again in that broken angle, it wouldn't do anything.

The usual treatment for illnesses was increasing one's natural healing powers. You could use magic to recover stamina and physical strength, so it was possible to cure a certain measure of illnesses... But if it couldn't be cured by Wind magic, the goal was to treat it with a combination of magic and medicine.

There were bruises all over the child's body, along with countless marks that looked like they'd come from a whip.

"That must have hurt..." My quiet murmur evaporated into the silence. I shook my head, thinking how people could treat someone like this, just because they were a different race. They could feel pain just like humans could, yet were treated like research subjects.

People threw away their conscience so easily if there was something to gain—no, even if there wasn't.

"......" I lost myself in my thoughts as I stared at the child, then switched gears. The first thing I needed to do was heal their wounds. Treat whatever injuries I could and heal them as much as I could.

I tried a general healing spell, but I could only do so much. I removed the Time magic I'd cast earlier and made them come back from the suspended death state. The child's breathing became regular, and they seemed stable for now. I placed the blanket over them so they didn't get cold.

Now, what should I do?

I'd love to return the child to their parents if possible. But in order to do that, I needed to figure out how the child became a slave. Where had they been kidnapped from? Where did their parents live?

"I'm sorry... I need to look through your memories."

I remembered how Kyle had looked through mine and used a combination of Time and Dark magic.

I placed my hand on the child's forehead and cast the spell. Every time I fell deeper and deeper into their memories, I furrowed my brow.

This child's parents were a human couple, but the boy himself had been born with beastfolk characteristics. One of the parents must have had beastfolk blood. Since they didn't understand genetics, they didn't recognize the child as their own. The father blamed the mother, and the mother was disgusted with her child and left.

The father treated the child like cattle and locked him up in a room. He did not pick the child up or show him love. He raised the child the same way one would raise cows or horses. No—livestock owners probably showed more care to their animals than that. The one good thing—and I wasn't even sure if I could call it such—was that the father was never physically violent with him.

But the child never learned of the outside world and was never given enough food to eat. Every day was a day spent being allowed to live, and that was all.

Even though this child's world was so small, and even though he didn't know the man was his father, the child loved him.

Their life went on like that until one day, he was let out of his room.

At first, the child was scared. But once he saw the place was filled with light, his eyes began to sparkle ever so slightly, like other children I'd seen before. It was the first moment the child had seen the outside world. Although it was a dingy place, the little boy smiled…

"Five gold."

"Twelve. I kept him this whole time so I could sell him for money."

"Seven."

"Ten. I won't go any lower. If you can't pay it, I'll sell him to someone else."

"Fine… I'll give you ten."

The person took the gold coins from his leather pouch and handed them to the young boy's father. The boy stared at him. His father said one word—"Toalga"—then went back inside the house.

After that, the boy's life was… Well, the only word I can think of to describe it is *cruel*. When he tried to escape, he was punched and kicked, had his collar tightened, and was abused. If he showed the slightest disobedience to his master, he was abused.

But no matter how much he was beat up for rebelling, the boy wouldn't stop trying to escape. His master began to grow frightened of him. He was so enraged that it was a wonder he didn't end up killing the little boy. But he returned him to the slave trader alive. Not out of remorse but simply to recover the compensation and the purchase price. Beastfolk boys could be sold at a high price. Even if they were almost dead, they could go for ten gold. More than twice that if they were healthy.

And so the young boy spent his time in that vicious cycle of being abused, returned, and sold again, with the hope that someday, his father would come back and get him.

So that's why he kept trying to escape and didn't back down even when he was hurt. He learned how to speak from another beastfolk slave, and that's when he realized the person who had sold him was his father... But even after learning that, and the meaning of the last word his father had said to him, the boy had still believed in him and waited.

I stopped looking into the boy's memories. That was enough. The current situation he was in was the result of all that.

"......"

I was an outsider, so maybe I didn't have the right to be angry. I wasn't from this world, so perhaps that's why I didn't understand. But still, I felt anger rise up inside my chest. Children were innocent. They couldn't decide how they looked when they were born. They didn't know what kind of situation they would be born into.

I bit my lip so hard that the skin ripped, and the taste of blood spread throughout my mouth.

As I looked at the boy's wrist, which was unnaturally bent, I wished from the bottom of my heart that I could mend it.

Only the boy could heal the wounds in his own heart. But at the very least...I wanted to give him a healthy body back. I wanted him to be able to hold things, to grasp them—without any limitations—and to be able to walk without pain. Even though he'd gone through so much mental anguish, the least I could do was ensure he would be physically free.

I wished for the power to heal his body with all my heart.

Perhaps I saw myself in him, how I had been in the past, unable to live life freely, the way I wanted.

"Heal...," I murmured without realizing it. As though being guided by some invisible force, I placed my hand on the boy's chest. It didn't feel like I was following the flow of mana. I didn't know what it was. If I had to describe it, it was like a ball of energy…of life force. That energy combined with my mana and transformed into what I desired.

The boy's body began to glow with a pale light. He was enveloped in it for a moment. *I will get the results I wish for, the results I want. There is no other possible outcome.* Those arrogant thoughts crossed my mind, and at that moment—my ability blossomed.

"My ability…is the power to heal."

I couldn't think of anything else that suited me better. It was the power to completely heal injuries, illnesses, and all other physical ailments.

The moment my ability blossomed, I instantly understood how to use my power. I naturally grasped the things I could and couldn't do.

The young boy was still asleep, but his arms and legs had totally healed. The countless bruises and wounds that had marked his body were gone. *This is an all-powerful ability*, I thought. I knew if some powerful person were to find out about my ability, they would try to use me for their own agenda.

I felt my back break out in cold sweat when I thought about my life before I met Kyle. I never, ever wanted to be held captive in a place like that again.

I let out a deep breath to try to release all my anxiety and fear. I was fine now. If someone tried to take away my freedom, I had the power to fight back against them, I told myself.

I looked at the young boy and tried to push those unpleasant thoughts out of my mind.

He didn't seem like he would wake up anytime soon, so I thought about what I should do next.

"Hmm… Maybe feed him first? I bet he's starving."

Since his injuries were treated, I thought it would be okay to give him something to eat. But I should still go by the book and give him something easy to digest. But what could that be…? I could make some kind

of stew... I thought about the things inside my bag and realized I didn't have enough ingredients.

The boy would need new clothes, so I decided to head back to the castle town. I wasn't sure if any shops would still be open, but I was sure I could manage.

I thought about where I could let the boy rest. I was staying at a room in the guild's dormitory, so only people registered with the guild could live there. I could use Teleport to bring him back with me, but I'd have a hard time explaining myself if we got caught.

There was no other choice. I'd have to go buy the necessary items and camp here for the night.

I made a mental shopping list and made sure I wasn't forgetting anything.

I strengthened the barrier and made it so that I was the only one who could enter and leave, then used magic to teleport.

I found a shop that was just about to close—I asked the owner to keep it open for just a bit and bought some clothing. After that, I purchased some food and other necessities and teleported back to where the boy was.

But when I returned from the castle town, the young boy (who should have been asleep) wasn't there...

He couldn't leave the barrier, so I knew he hadn't been attacked by a monster. I thought he was probably all right. I concentrated and used magic to look for him. I picked up his presence immediately and walked toward him. He was frantically scratching at the invisible barrier. He was probably trying to escape.

I approached him, making sure my footsteps were audible. The boy noticed me and jumped back from the wall, assuming a fighting stance as he glared at me. The ears on his head and the fur on his tail stood straight up as he tried his best to look threatening.

The eyes that stared back were two different colors. His right eye was a pale blue, while his left eye was a pale violet. I remembered from his memories that his right eye was white; perhaps he had lost his sight from some kind of illness or disease, and I'd healed it with my powers, restoring it to its natural color. I wasn't sure what kind of disease it would have been, though.

He was more cute than handsome.

It was hard to believe he had been on the verge of death before. But he was still very thin and malnourished and unsteady on his feet. He was frantically trying to maintain his fighting stance, but his legs were trembling.

I wasn't sure what I should say to him. Just then, with narrowed eyes, he began to speak.

"You...buy...me?" He spoke to me in a broken sentence. It seemed he was still cautious of me. At any rate, I was relieved we could communicate.

I wondered why he wasn't speaking fluently, though. In his memories, I saw he had been able to communicate fine with the person who had taught him the language. It wasn't the common language, though, so was it Beastian? No, it wasn't that... Maybe it had been a mistake to stop looking at his memories so soon...

"Do you have trouble with the common tongue? I can speak other languages." I hoped he had learned Beastian after the point at which I'd stopped looking at his memories.

"Only...speak...this."

He didn't know any other language...

I tried to figure out why he spoke in broken fragments and came to a conclusion. That's right... You had to keep using language, or else you'd forget it.

Kyle had cast a spell on me so that I wouldn't forget the language of our homeland. He had etched it deep, deep inside me. Or perhaps Hanai had done it before him.

But at any rate, I'd inherited that magic.

Not being able to connect with others was a very lonely feeling. My heart began to sink into darkness.

Since I fell silent, the boy began to panic. Perhaps I'd given him the wrong idea. Suddenly, he started speaking in a rush of broken sentences.

I cast a spell on him so that I would be able to understand his words. It was a temporary spell called Telepathy, which would allow me to hear his thoughts.

"I...strange?"
Am I really that strange just because I'm not a human?
"Didn't...want...born."
It's not like I wanted to be born looking like this!
"Not...fault."
It's not my fault!
"Who...made...like...this?"
Who made me like this?!
"Who...hate?"
Who should I hate?
"Mom?"
My mom, who gave birth to me?!
"Dad?"
Or my dad, who sold me?!
"Humans...hate...me!"
Or the humans who hate me?!

I listened to his lamentations. The boy was not crying. But behind the broken words, I could tell he was weeping on the inside.
It hurts, I'm lonely, I'm scared, I'm frustrated, help me, help me, somebody help me!
His heart was covered in wounds. Every time he cried out, it was like the boy's heart was shedding tears of blood...
Although he was born from two humans, he had beastfolk blood. He hated himself, he hated people, and he wanted to know who had made him like this, the object of people's hatred. He'd wondered that in his heart for so long, wondered why it had to be him.

It wasn't something he could change, and there was nothing he could do about it. But I'd experienced anger over something I had no control over before, too.

145

"Why did you have to be born like this?" A relative had said thoughtlessly when I was a child, and it had hurt me very deeply.

"It's not like I chose to be born like this!" I'd balled up my fist and screamed. What had my mother said to me then?

I took a step closer to the boy. He took that as his signal to strike. Even though he was frail and weak, he moved at a surprising speed. I didn't dodge him. I took the attack, but it didn't hurt. I grabbed the boy's arm and didn't let go. He forgot about trying to escape and stared at me, stunned.

His eyes were wide open, full of fear as he looked at me. Up until now, had been able to injure every other human he'd met with his sharp claws.

The only pain I felt was from his anger and fear.

But he didn't know that, and he was overwhelmed with terror. He trembled and fell to his knees. Perhaps his heart had finally broken when he realized I was someone who he couldn't lay a finger on.

He couldn't stop shaking. He just sat there, like he'd given up on escaping—and living, too.

"…me," he murmured.

"…ll me…"

I strained to hear him.

"Kill me!"

I was speechless. I stared at him in shock, still holding on to his arm. His heart was frozen with hopelessness and terror, and he was in a state of panic. He just kept repeating "Kill me!" over and over again.

He reminded me so much of myself as a child.

No matter what I said, it didn't get through to him.

He'd given up on everything and couldn't find the light.

"Setsuna."

Suddenly, I felt like my mother was calling me.

That's right. Back then, she hadn't said anything. She'd just held me in her arms as I sobbed. She had stayed by my side. She stayed the whole time, until my pain and sadness had passed.

I let go of the boy's arm and knelt in front of him as he continued muttering, "Kill me, kill me." Then I slowly embraced this young boy who had given up on everything. Just like my mother had done for me when I was a child. I remembered what it was like to be hugged so tenderly like that.

The boy trembled violently as I hugged him, and his entire body tensed up.

I slowly rubbed his back, trying to release the tension inside him. Slowly, slowly...trying to calm him down. Until he didn't feel scared, until he stopped shaking.

I didn't know how long or short it took, but eventually, he stopped trembling and began to fidget a bit. I saw that as a sign to let him go. I looked into his eyes and said quietly, "Do you feel better now?"

He stared at me but didn't answer. It seemed he was still cautious of every gesture I made. He was probably confused now. But I think he no longer saw me as an enemy.

I answered the questions his tiny body had screamed out before. I hoped I could at least loosen the shackles around his heart.

"I don't know who made you like that."

His body tensed up, and he averted his gaze by looking down.

"I don't know, but...I don't think you look strange."

Hearing this, he looked up at me in surprise.

"You might hate your appearance."

"......"

"But I think you're cute. I don't hate the way you look at all."

There was confusion in his eyes. He made eye contact with me, then quickly looked away. With his head facing down, he nervously began to speak.

"My...eyes...different. Not...gross?"

Oh, he was worried about his different-colored eyes.

It seemed my Telepathy spell had worn off. Since I was able to understand him for now, I thought we could keep communicating like this.

Somebody must have told him that his different-colored eyes were disgusting.

The boy wouldn't look at me, but I kept my eyes on him as I answered.

"I think your blue and violet eyes are very pretty. Your left eye is the same color as mine."

He hesitantly raised his head. He stared at my eyes, trying to see if I was telling the truth. It seemed he was conflicted about whether I was lying or whether he should extend his hand. Doubt, distrust, and a little bit of hope shined in his eyes.

This child knew he could not live alone in this world full of absurdity and irrationality.

Perhaps he also knew that it would have been easier for him to obey and flatter people.

Still, that's not what he chose. Because he had dignity. And he maintained that dignity even when he was almost at death's door.

But right now, he knew he had no choice. That's why he was looking at me, sizing me up, trying to search for a reason why it was okay for him to compromise. In order to live...

I quietly waited for him to make his decision. I was going to wait until he made one he was comfortable with.

But he was staring at me so intently that I couldn't help but let out a wry chuckle. I wondered what he thought of my expression. His eyes widened in surprise and blinked a few times. The next moment, the boy's blue and violet eyes wavered, and tears began to fall from them, one after another...

That must have been the trigger, because he burst into tears, as if the thread that had been holding him tight had broken.

He let out all his emotions.

Even when the slave trader had punched or kicked him, he hadn't made a sound. He'd tried to escape until the very end. He had a strong will and never gave up on living.

Once again, I embraced the child as he desperately sobbed.

After sobbing out every last tear he could, he seemed to calm down a little. He must have been done crying, because he pulled away and looked up at me. There was no longer caution or fear in his eyes. It seemed he had come to a compromise within himself.

"What...happen...me?"

He was asking what would happen to him now, and I wasn't sure how to answer that. Then I thought perhaps I should leave him in the custody of a shelter. They were places that took in and gave refuge to children of other races. There were shelters like that in Gardir, but were the ones in this kingdom safe?

Slavery was legal in Gardir, so it was inhospitable to beastfolk. I could certainly take him to a shelter here, but I wasn't sure I could place my confidence in them. I hated Gardir from the bottom of my heart, and I didn't trust them. So I thought about taking him to one in a different kingdom. I decided I would ask Nes where the best place would be.

"Well, there are places that protect children like you. Shelters. But I don't trust this kingdom, so I'll..."

I was about to say that I would take him to a different kingdom, but he shouted, interrupting me. "No!" He grabbed my arm and pleaded with me. "I...want...stay...with...you!"

He seemed surprised by his own actions and let go of my arm, looking frightened. He fidgeted uncomfortably, then touched the collar around his neck. His eyes widened as he looked at me. "I...work...as... your...slave." He looked at me with such certainty, like he wouldn't take no for an answer. Now it was my turn to be shocked.

Until just a few moments ago, he'd been afraid of me and thought I was his enemy—I'd assumed he only let down his guard because he believed he had no other choice. I thought he was crying because he was feeling anguished.

So I never considered he would say he wanted to be with me or be my slave. I was so taken aback that I blurted out thoughtlessly, "I don't need a slave."

The boy's hand dropped from his neck. Tears filled his eyes, and he clenched his fists. He looked devastated, and I realized I shouldn't have said it like that. But I didn't understand why he was so fond of me.

The boy looked down, his face pale. He was standing there, frozen. He didn't move a muscle—it was like everything would come crashing down if he moved.

I thought about his determination and let out a little sigh.

That's right. He was the same as me.

Despite the fact he hated humans, this boy's heart was filled with so much loneliness that he wanted to be with me.

He was all alone in the world, without anyone on his side. I knew how that felt better than anyone.

He'd meant it when he said he wanted to stay with me. It wasn't out of doubt, distrust, dignity, survival instincts, or because he thought he didn't have a choice. He genuinely wanted to be with me, because I understood his loneliness. I saw the boy for who he was. Because I smiled at him.

I knew exactly how happy that could make someone. And once you met someone like that, obviously you wanted to stay with them. I understood that more than anyone.

But...

Honestly, I wasn't sure if I was satisfied with myself right now. I'd managed to make a living for myself, but I was still in the middle of securing a livelihood. Was I at a point where I could protect and raise a child on my own?

As I asked myself those questions, I heard a faint voice in my ear.

"Don't...leave...me..."

The voice was so quiet that I barely heard it. I lifted my head in response to his plea, which sounded like a prayer. The ground at his feet was wet with tears. How much courage had it taken for him to say those words?

I just couldn't do it. I couldn't let go of this boy's hand. Our circumstances were just too similar. I couldn't abandon him, even though I knew it was out of pity and hypocrisy.

But right now, my hand was the only one he could grasp. He wished to hold it.

Couldn't I do it, too? Couldn't I be a beacon of light for this young boy, like Kyle, who had given me life?

"I don't need a slave."

His body trembled the second time I said it, and he couldn't look up. When I saw him like this, I strengthened my resolve.

I would take care of him and raise him. I wouldn't do it half-heartedly, either. I would protect and raise this boy until he became an adult who could live on his own. That's what I decided.

Now that my mind was made up...

"I don't need a slave, but I am looking for an assistant who can help me with my magic research."

His ears perked up a bit, and he turned toward me.

"That's right, I'm looking for an apprentice. If only there was a child with cute ears and a cute tail who would be willing to do that..."

The moment he understood what I meant, he quickly lifted his face. His ears were moving around enthusiastically, and his tail began to wag.

"Me! I'll...do!" He stared straight at me with a determined gaze. "I'll...help!" He held my arm even tighter than before, frantically telling me he would help me. "You...my...maester?" he asked, and I gave him a confused look.

Maester? What was he saying?

"Maester?"

"Maester. If...I...appren...tice, then...you...maester."

"Master."

"Master." He repeated my pronunciation, then murmured it several times to himself.

"I'm surprised you knew that word."

"My...owner...said."

"......"

I caught a glimpse of his life as a slave from that sentence and didn't want him to think about it anymore, so I changed the subject. I thought for a while and realized we didn't know each other's names.

"I haven't introduced myself to you yet. My name is Setsuna. I hope you can remember that. You can call me whatever you want, whether it's Setsuna or Master."

"Master." He nodded with a serious expression.

I chuckled a little.

Now...

Since I had seen his memories, I knew his parents hadn't given him a name. I was a bit frustrated that I hadn't finished looking at all of them, in case he had been given a name later. I gave an inward sigh and decided to just ask.

"What's your name?"

All expressions vanished from his face. He tore his gaze away from me and whispered, "Toalga..." He kept his eyes fixed on the ground and wouldn't look up. His tail, which had just been wagging with happiness, was now frozen.

I cursed myself for not checking his memories until the end. I couldn't take back that question now. I suppressed my sense of guilt and said, "That's not your name."

"That's...what...they...called."

"That's not your name."

I would not allow him to use a word that meant "monster" as his name. The boy's ears lay back against his head, and his shoulders shook when I firmly denied it.

Name...name... As I thought about them, I remembered something Kyoka had said.

"Did you know that the first present your parents ever give you is your name?" I remembered how happy she looked when she said that. She had a homework assignment to ask our parents what her name meant. That's how we got on that subject.

A present... I stared at the depressed little boy and thought. What would be a suitable name for him? I thought of several options, trying to settle on one that wouldn't stick out too much according to this world's languages. Then I narrowed it down to one choice.

"Hmm... Well, since you're my apprentice, I'll give you your very first present."

"Present?" He slowly looked up at me, anxiety in his eyes. I met his gaze.

"Yes. Your first present from me. Will you accept it?"

"Yes."

I could tell by the way his tail wagged that he was excited.

"Alto."

"Alto?"

"That's right. Your name is Alto. You are my first apprentice and assistant."

He stared blankly at me as if he didn't quite understand yet.

I looked down at his collar. I slowly reached out and touched the ominous-looking thing. I felt him wanting to pull away, but he suppressed the urge.

What a good boy.

An almost excessive amount of mana flowed from my finger, shattering the collar.

Now there was no longer anything holding Alto captive. His eyes widened when he saw the fragments land at his feet. He glanced up at me hesitantly.

"From now on, you and I will be together, Alto."

"Name?"

"That's right. Your name is Alto."

"Alto. My…name." He repeated it quietly, over and over again, then gave me a shy smile.

Seeing him grin for the first time filled me with the urge to see him smiling even more happily.

"My…name! First…present!" His broad, radiant smile and his perked-up ears… His tail was whipping around happily, too.

Seeing him like this and thinking how adorable he was might have been my first step to becoming a doting parent, rather than an apprentice's master.

Now I waited for Alto to calm down for another reason—he was so excited about his name and broken collar. Now that I had decided Alto would be my apprentice, it meant we would be living together from now on.

I thought about what I should do next. Honestly, there were so many things that I felt overwhelmed. I switched gears and began thinking instead about what I *needed* to do. As I stared at him, he tilted his head, looking curious. First, I should get him cleaned up and free of odors.

I'd give him a bath. I wanted one, too. There were baths in Gardir, as dipping in one was part of the lifestyle and culture here. As there were magical tools, adding hot water and draining it could be completed in an instant, which was quite the convenience.

The civilizations of this world had some aspects that were more advanced and some that were behind compared to Japan. Naturally, there were various disparities between countries in my former world as well. It might be presumptuous for someone like me, who only knew about those other countries through reading about them, to talk about such things, though.

"Alto, let's take a bath."

"Bath?"

"Yes."

Alto looked confused, wondering what that was. I picked him up, which surprised him. He glanced back and forth, at me and down at himself, then tried to jump out of my arms.

"Alto? Your feet hurt, don't they? Stay still." Even though I had healed all his wounds, there were still small scratches on his feet, since he'd been walking around barefoot.

"Master…dirty."

"Hmm?"

"Your clothes…get dirty. I…filthy."

The slave trader had said to Alto, *"You're filthy, so stay away from me."* So he was worried that he would dirty me.

"Don't worry. Even if you do, I can just change them. I'm going to take a bath anyway."

I shifted him in my arms as he struggled. I gently patted his head like you would a cat, and he simmered down. I thought it was a bit strange that he relaxed so quickly as I walked toward the lake.

I put Alto down, then used Wind magic to heal his scratches. He stared at me with interest. He really reminded me of Kyoka when she was little, and I was filled with nostalgia.

After I finished treating him, I made a bath to clean both of us. I thought I'd make it out of a barrel but had a feeling something else would be in the bag. I stuck my hand in and half-jokingly began to search for it. *Bathtub...*

" ....."

I grabbed on to the corner of something. I knew it. I pulled it out of my bag. It was a bathtub made from cypress wood, large enough to fit three grown adults inside.

I didn't even know cypress existed in this world. Huh? Did it?

" ......"

" ......"

No, wait. That wasn't the problem. This was just too ridiculous. How in the world had I picked up something so large and heavy with one hand?

And what about Kyle? He was the one who had made it out of cypress and put it in the bag to begin with.

Alto's eyes were so big that they looked like they might pop out of his head as he stared at it. No matter how you thought about it, there was just no way a bathtub of this size could fit into the bag. I certainly didn't think so, either, and was surprised. So I couldn't blame Alto for being shocked. I sighed and started transferring water from the lake to the tub with magic.

I didn't feel like using Water magic to fill the tub. After that was finished, I used Fire magic to heat it up. Steam began to steadily rise from the surface. I tested the water, and it seemed to be at a good temperature. It looked so nice...

"The bath is ready, Alto. Let's get inside." When I turned around, he looked pale and was shaking. Hmm? I wondered what he was afraid of. Me pulling the bathtub out of my bag? I didn't know what he was scared of.

"Alto?" I called his name, wanting to know the reason.

He trembled and whispered, "Pot?"

"Huh? Pot?"

I didn't see one anywhere.

"I'm...going...die?"

"What? What?!"

Pot? Why a pot?!

Alto, a bath, a pot. I tried to think of how those three things were connected. As I stared at the steam rising from the water, it finally hit me. He had never taken a bath before. In that case, this was the first time he was getting in hot water. That made sense, after all—in this world, it generally cost money to take a bath—money that wouldn't be spent on slaves.

"Alto, that's not a pot, and you're not going to die. If you get in, it will feel really good. Come on." I called out to him, but he still looked apprehensive and wouldn't budge.

I felt like he'd only get scared if I forced him. But if it didn't seem like it would work, I could always just use magic to clean him instead.

Regardless, maybe he would realize it was safe to come over if I got in first.

"Ahhh...this is the best...," I murmured. It really was the greatest feeling. This was my first outdoor bath. I was a little sad that it wasn't a natural hot spring, but since it was water from a lake, I supposed it was similar enough. Unless I put up a magical barrier, monsters would come, but I didn't mind. Right now, I was just enjoying taking a bath out in nature.

Now that Alto saw how much I was enjoying it, he hesitantly walked over. He still looked worried, though.

"Come here, Alto." He came up to me and looked back and forth between me and the water, then slowly put his hand inside. Once he realized it wasn't boiling, his nervousness subsided a little. "Can I pour some water over you?" I asked. He looked at me anxiously and nodded. I slowly splashed some onto him.

He was a little tense, but he didn't try to run away.

He reminded me of a dog taking a bath.

"Alto, I'm going to wash the mud off your head. Can you close your eyes? I want to make sure water doesn't get in your ears, either."

He seemed anxious, but he lay his ears down tightly against his head, then squeezed his eyes shut. His tail was trembling, showing me just how nervous he was.

His movements really did remind me of a dog—so pitiful that it was cute.

But I knew Alto was no animal. He was a beastfolk. However, I'd never met someone of his race before. And of course, they didn't even exist in my old world. So honestly, I wasn't sure how to best interact with him.

I decided to search Hanai and Kyle's memories. But there wasn't much information there, either. In the end, I chose to just be myself around him. He had a lot of animal characteristics, so I couldn't help but make those associations. That was how I explained it to myself. I wasn't making excuses.

I slowly poured water onto Alto's trembling head.

First, I rinsed off the mud and dirt. His injuries were healed, so he shouldn't have been in pain. After I'd rinsed off as much dirt as I could, I shampooed his head several times. I washed all the soap bubbles off and saw that Alto had tears in his eyes.

"You're all done, Alto. Great job." I petted his head and praised him. He froze like a cat that was just getting used to humans. I smiled wryly and began washing his body.

It must've tickled, because he tried to escape, but I held on to him firmly as I washed him. "Don't run away."

The first rinse didn't get rid of all the grime, so I tried again; then I told him to rinse himself. It looked like it must have tickled a lot. I turned away from Alto as he desperately tried to lather the soap and wash himself.

He had watched me very closely and tried to imitate me. He was even watching how I held the soap. I was about to tell Alto to relax and not to rush it, but I stopped myself. I didn't want to confuse him. So I thought to let him do as he pleased for now. Once he was used to living with me, I could give him more instruction.

When Alto was done washing his body, I put him inside the bathtub. He was nervous at first, but once he got inside, he surprisingly took to it. His ears perked up, and he stayed still.

The sun had completely set, so I was using Light magic to gently illuminate our surroundings. The scenery looked a little ethereal, and I gazed at it as I spoke to Alto.

"Your hair is a light sky blue. Just like your right eye."

"What?"

He stared at me.

"My...eye...white." Apparently, he didn't remember when I had told him earlier that his eye was blue. "Not...blue."

He looked confused, so I used Water magic to make a reflection in the bath. Once again, his eyes bugged out as he stared at his reflection.

"H-how?!"

His ears, his tail, his expression—his entire body seemed to scream astonishment. He was so adorable. I explained to him my theory. He didn't seem to understand it entirely, but he accepted my explanation. He did mutter that he wished his eyes were at least the same color...

Now that Alto was clean, he was even more adorable. He was definitely more cute than handsome, but at the same time, I didn't think he'd be mistaken for a girl.

His hair was a soft, clear sky blue, and his different-colored eyes had a mysterious quality. Pair that with his cute, childlike innocence and...

No wonder there were humans who would want to keep him as their pet. I realized I needed to come up with a way to protect him from slave traders. While I was busy mulling that over, I heard Alto calling me.

"Master?"

"Hmm?"

Apparently, my silence had made him feel anxious.

I looked at him and gently asked, "Alto, what do you want to do?"

"Do?"

"I want to travel around the world and see all kinds of things."

"World."

"Yes. So being with me means you'll visit all sorts of kingdoms. I'm happy that you want to be with me."

"......"

"But if you want to do something else, or if you don't like traveling, then I'll let you do what you want to do."

"I...travel with...Master," Alto declared before I could say anything else. My heart ached a little seeing him like that.

"I'm not saying you can't come with me, Alto. I'm saying that maybe there's something else you want to do, just like how I want to travel."

He thought long and hard about it. But he hung his head, perhaps because he couldn't find an answer.

I looked at him and slowly said, "It's okay if you don't know what you want to do right now."

Even though Alto hung his head, his ears were pointed forward at me the whole time.

"If you don't know, it's okay to travel around until you find what you want to do, Alto."

"I want...study?"

"......"

"You said...apprentice...study." He was beginning to form more sentences; perhaps he was gradually getting used to having conversations again. "I want...travel with Master...and study."

Study, hmm? He looked very serious about it, so I looked straight into his eyes and told him what that entailed and made sure that's what he meant, too. He nodded.

"I can teach you."

"Yes."

"But, Alto...I'm pretty strict. I might not allow you to slack on your studies in the middle of our journey."

Alto was still so young, but I asked him seriously, one last time. "Do you still want to be my apprentice?"

If he really wanted to live with me...

I didn't want him to become my apprentice just because I had been nice to him or because he wanted to stay with me. For his future, I thought it would be better if he decided on a goal and traveled with that in mind instead of following me simply because he was my apprentice. But that must be difficult for someone so young to comprehend.

Still, I wanted to tell him that. So that he could live his life the way he wanted to.

He might get hurt, being with a human like me. There might be painful times ahead, and I didn't want them to break his heart. I wanted him to be able to overcome hardships.

And to make sure he was prepared to be my apprentice.

Alto seemed a little taken aback by how serious I was, but he didn't look away from me. "I..." He seemed to be frantically thinking things through. He thought and thought, then came to an answer. I was able to see the strong resolve in his eyes at that moment. He must've balled his hands into fists, because the water around us rippled a bit.

"Master."

"Yes."

"Please make me...apprentice." He hadn't answered me right away. He'd understood the meaning of my words, considered it seriously, and arrived at his own decision.

I really respected that. And I accepted it.

"Very well. Make sure you study hard by my side."

"Yes, Master." He nodded earnestly, and just then, his stomach growled. He suddenly looked like he was about to cry as he glanced down at his stomach. He was so adorable; I couldn't help but laugh.

We were both warm enough—if we stayed in any longer, we'd probably overheat.

"Are you hungry?"

"......"

Alto didn't answer. Or maybe he couldn't answer.

"Let's eat after we get out of the tub."

He didn't respond, but he did wag his tail a little at the mention of food.

I wrapped him in a large towel and held out the new underwear, clothes, and shoes I'd bought for him, but he didn't take them. His ears folded down, and he murmured quietly, "I have...no money." He clenched his towel and stared up at me.

"You're my apprentice, so I'll provide everything you need from now on. That's a master's job."

He tilted his head.

"What do you think your job is?"

"My job...study?"

"That's right. Your job is to study."

"Yes."

"Your job is also to eat, sleep, and play a lot. And to help me with my work."

Alto nodded, accepting my answer, and he took the clothes and changed into them.

I got out of the bath and dried off, put on some fresh clothes, and made the water inside the tub disappear. I used Wind magic to dry out the tub, and I put it away in my bag.

Alto watched intently the whole time as I cleaned up, his eyes just as wide as when I had pulled it out of my bag.

He was so much cleaner; you'd hardly believe he was the same little boy I'd seen before he took a bath. Somehow, he'd gotten even cuter. I took his hand and began to walk. I held his hand because I didn't want him to fall. He looked up at me, surprised by the gesture, and gave me a shy smile.

I felt warmth spreading throughout my body when I saw how happy he was to hold hands and tag along beside me.

Back at camp, I pulled out ingredients from my bag. I lit a fire and placed a pot on top. After I sautéed the meat and vegetables, I added flour, milk, and water. Then I sprinkled in some salt and pepper for flavor, used Time magic to shorten the boiling time, and the stew was done.

I wanted it to be very tender, so I let it simmer for a bit while I prepared the bread. I cut the bread into pieces, buttered it, and put cheese on top. Alto was closely watching my every movement as I cooked the food.

"Master...what's this?"

"Hmm? What?"

He was pointing to the bread. Apparently, he didn't know what it was called. I knew from my memories that his food situation had been very cruel.

He had been given dried rations that were known as slave food. It had nutritional value, but it did not taste good. He ate that and plain salted broth. It was actually more like salted hot water. In other words, he had been given the bare minimum to keep someone alive. That was what slaves ate in this world. Everything about it made me angry...

"Master?" Alto must've noticed the glint in my eye. I felt my irritation dissipate a little.

"This is..." I explained how one could make bread from flour, but he didn't seem to understand. He had never seen wheat, and naturally he'd never seen flour before, either. I would show him my botanical guide later. I had flour because it was necessary for making stew.

I showed it to him, and he looked confused. I guess it was a bit hard to believe that this could turn into bread unless you actually saw the process yourself. His interest then shifted from the bread to the stew.

He leaned over the pot with curiosity, and I warned him to be careful to not burn himself, then told him today's menu.

"We're having bread and stew today. I hope you like it."

"Stew?"

"Yes, stew. It's a soup made from meat and vegetables, with milk to add flavor."

"M-meat! First time. Maybe first time...vegetables, too?"

I did remember seeing some leafy things in his past soups, so maybe that's why he was unsure. I'd put a lot of nutritious things in this stew. I had to check and see whether beastfolk could eat onions, but I couldn't find the answer, so I left them out, just in case. I remembered in my old world, onions were poisonous to dogs. I assumed I could kill him by accident if I wasn't careful.

I placed a plate of bread in front of an impatient Alto and set down a spoon. Then I put some stew in a bowl and put that in front of him as well. I made myself a portion, too.

"Let's eat!"

"Okay!" he replied enthusiastically.

I quietly said a prayer to give thanks for the food. In this world, apparently people prayed to the goddesses before a meal, but that had nothing to do with me.

I picked up my spoon and took a bite of the stew. Alto was staring at me. He watched how I ate and grabbed his own utensil to scoop up the stew, then took a bite just like I had.

He had watched me while we took a bath, too, and imitated my actions. I had a feeling Alto had always listened to what people said, searched for the meaning in their words, and studied on his own in that way.

That may sound simple, but it was actually quite difficult to do. But Alto had needed to do that in order to survive. That's how hungry he was to live. And I thought he was amazing for that, from the bottom of my heart.

They always say that eyes can sometimes be more expressive than mouths. In Alto's case, although his eyes were expressive, his ears and tail were even more telling than his mouth.

He didn't seem to mind that the stew was hot and chowed down.

"You should try some of the bread, too," I said, tearing off a little piece off to put in my mouth.

He watched me and set down his bowl to tear off part of the bread and eat it.

"!!!"

He wagged his tail excitedly, and his eyes sparkled. His tail was working overtime. My heart ached a little when I quietly watched how eagerly he was eating everything. I continued my meal and noticed Alto had glanced at the pot, and his ears drooped with resignation. I looked at him and said quietly, "You know that I served you first, right?"

"Yes."

"If there's food left over and you're still hungry, you can get seconds as long as you check with other people first to make sure it's all right."

"Seconds...?"

"Another serving. But does your stomach hurt?"

"No. I can...eat more?" He looked up at me with puppy dog eyes. He seemed fine.

"Ask me properly first."

"Master. May I...have...seconds?" His voice sounded a little anxious and pleading.

"Go ahead. You can serve yourself, Alto."

"What?"

He had started handing me his bowl but then stared at me with surprise. I couldn't blame him. He'd never had such a choice before and had only ever been allowed the things he was given directly. He'd never been able to say that he was still hungry.

"Hold the lid here and lift it up. You can set it down over there."

Alto nervously followed my instructions.

"Pick up your bowl. Yes, that's right. The pot is hot, so be careful."

"Okay."

"Now scoop up some stew...and put it in your bowl."

"Ohhh!" Alto laughed joyfully, his tension disappearing when he successfully did it himself.

As I watched him begin to happily eat the stew and bread, I asked him something I'd been wondering about. "How old are you, Alto?"

His mouth was full as he tried to answer, but I stopped him. "You can tell me after you swallow."

Alto nodded and hurriedly gulped down his food. "I'm twelve."

"What?"

"I'm twelve."

I was speechless. If I compared him to a human child, he looked no older than ten years old. Honestly, I thought he was seven or eight. But twelve? The years of malnutrition he'd endured must have delayed his growth. That spoke volumes about the situation he'd been living in.

After dinner, Alto said he would help clean, but I made the mistake of turning him down. That made him sad, but he perked up after I asked him to sit down and dry off the dishes after I washed them using Water magic.

Even though his body was healed, I was worried he'd start to grow fatigued.

To thank him, I handed him a cup full of warm milk with honey.

"It's a little hot, so drink it carefully."

He nodded with excitement and hesitantly brought the cup to his mouth. He licked it once to taste it, and a dreamy expression appeared on his face. He seemed to like it. There were lots of children who weren't fond of milk, so I was glad he wasn't one of them.

"Is it good?"

He nodded.

"My mouth...first time...strange."

I was wondering what he meant by "strange" but realized this must be his first time having something sweet, and he wasn't sure how to describe it.

"Strange? Oh, that's called sweet. That's from the honey."

"Honey?"

"Yes. It's made from the nectar of flowers."

"Flowers?"

"Yes, flowers." I took out my botanical encyclopedia from the bag and showed Alto the drawings while explaining it to him. He listened to me intently, showing interest in these things he was seeing for the first time.

We had a pleasant time sitting by the crackling campfire. The events from just a few hours ago seemed as though they'd never happened. I noticed Alto's head drooping a bit and thought it would be a good idea to get to sleep.

It was a little early for me, but it was probably good for a change.

"Alto, are you sleepy? Should we go to bed?"

He looked at me with eyes he could barely keep open and nodded. Even though it was early summer, it could get chilly deep in the forest. I took out some blankets from my bag. I had two, so I put the dirty one on the bottom.

I lay down on top and called Alto to come lie down next to me. "Come here, Alto."

He looked hesitant.

"I don't have any more blankets, so let's sleep together. Come on." I spoke in a gentle tone, and he timidly approached me.

He came next to me but seemed to be completely perplexed. I patted the spot beside me. He slowly lay down, keeping his eyes on me the whole time. I slipped my arm around him, lightly embracing him as I wrapped the blanket around him. I felt his body tense up for a moment, but then he seemed to be at ease.

"Are you cold?"

"Master…warm."

And he fell asleep.

"Sleep well…"

I must have been quite exhausted, too, or I felt relaxed to have a warm child beside me, because I fell right to sleep after doing a little research on beastfolk.

I woke up at the same time I always did.

The only thing different was that I had an apprentice now.

I looked at him, and my shoulders drooped. If I didn't have enough blankets, I should've just made more. I should have done that for his clothes and shoes, too. My magic and abilities were convenient, but if I didn't think to use them, I would forget about them. It would be a little longer yet before the day came when I'd take them for granted.

I quietly slipped out of bed so I wouldn't disturb Alto, who was still asleep. I walked a short distance away and began my morning training.

I had an apprentice. Someone I needed to protect. I was responsible for a child's life.

I needed to get used to combat so that I could fight even better than before.

I continued training, drawing on Hanai and Kyle's knowledge and skills.

While I was in the midst of this, Alto woke up and watched me intently. I didn't let him distract me and finished my morning routine.

* * *

"Morning, Alto. Did you sleep well?"

Alto was staring at me, seemingly deep in thought. I gave him a puzzled look. "Alto?"

He seemed to come back to his senses and raised his head. "Master. Teach. Teach…me."

"Hmm?"

"I will…fight, too. I want to…fight."

"……"

"I want…become strong." He clung onto my arm and pleaded desperately.

I gently slipped out of his grasp and knelt to be at eye level with him. "Alto, why do you want to be strong?"

"I want…fight."

"Why do you want to be able to fight? What do you want to do when you're strong?" I stared straight into his eyes, waiting for him to respond.

"I…" He trailed off, finding it difficult to put his answer into words.

I asked him more questions to figure out what he wanted. "Alto, do you want to become stronger to get revenge on humans?" I asked.

He was startled and shouted, "No!!"

"Then why do you want to be stronger?"

"I…hate humans. But…"

"Yes?"

"I like…Master."

"……"

Now it was my turn to be surprised, but I tried to not let it show so that he could finish his thought.

"So if I…travel with… Master. Then I…want be strong…too."

He was open with his fondness for me.

"Journey…dangerous. Don't want…just be…protected."

He was trying to say that since he would be with me, he wanted to help more and lighten my burden.

In a sense, Alto might know the dangers of traveling more than I did. He had been sold from place to place and had seen many dangerous things on the road.

He didn't want to become stronger to get revenge, but to be with me. That sentiment of his was so pure.

Despite his appearance, he was twelve, which meant there were only four more years until he came of age. He was still a child, but I should probably stop treating him as one.

He was clever. Although he still spoke in broken sentences, his answers were intelligent. I needed to change my perception of him.

"You're right. You should be able to protect yourself. I agree."

Alto looked at me with clear eyes and nodded.

"But first, you need to build up your stamina before I can begin training you."

"Stamina?"

"That's right. Let's start very slowly. If you push yourself, you won't grow stronger."

"Yes, Master," he replied enthusiastically with a grin, and I nodded.

"Another thing, Alto. When you wake up in the morning, say 'Good morning' and before you go to bed, say 'Good night.' I think these greetings are very important, so make sure you remember them."

Alto thought for a moment, then greeted me with a smile. "Good morning, Master!"

"Good morning."

He did a good job, so I praised him for it by petting his head. His hair felt a little stiff. Maybe because of the soap. I needed to figure out a solution to that...

I heard a low growling noise and saw Alto clutch his stomach while his ears lay against his head.

"Should we have breakfast?" I asked, wondering what we should eat.

He looked up at me hopefully.

"Hmm, why don't we use the honey from yesterday and have it on toast? Bread with butter and honey. I think that's the perfect combination."

"Honey!"

"Is that all right?" I asked, and he wagged his tail happily, as if he didn't need any other answer.

* * *

As I watched Alto merrily bite into his toast with butter and honey, I thought to ask for a favor. "Alto. I want you to listen carefully."

He suddenly sat up straight, his ears perking up when he heard how serious I sounded.

"You can listen while you eat."

"Okay."

"Do you know about abilities and magic?"

"Yes. My second owner...had abilities." He nodded as he munched on his food.

"I have them, too. I have the power to heal. I can fix anything wrong with someone's body. The bones in your arm and leg have healed, right?"

When I pointed that out, Alto nearly dropped his toast. He quickly placed it on his plate. Apparently, he hadn't noticed. A lot of things did happen the day before, but wasn't that a bit...slow?

"Healed?!"

"......"

"Master, thank you!"

"Mm, you're welcome. Thanking someone is very nice. Good job, Alto." I praised him, and he smiled shyly at me. I felt like he was grinning more and more as time went on. "Anyway, I want to keep my powers a secret between just you and me."

"Secret?"

"Yes. It means I don't want you to tell anyone else about it."

"I won't tell?"

"That's right. The reason is because if other people find out about my powers, they might arrest me."

"Wh-why?!"

"Because the ability to heal broken bones and illnesses is very rare. If it gets around that I can do those things that even magic can't fix, powerful people might come and kidnap me."

All the color drained from Alto's face when I told him that.

"Won't tell! I...won't ever tell!"

I nodded and told him not to talk about my magic, either. "I only use Wind magic in front of others. The reason is the same. Sorcerers who can use all kinds of magic are rare, and…"

Before I could finish talking, he flung his arms around my neck so violently that I thought he might take my head off. "Alto, that hurts my neck."

"I won't tell…anyone about Master's…powers or magic. I'll never tell!" He repeated that over and over again, looking quite upset.

"Alto?"

"I don't want…Master kidnapped!"

He forgot all about eating as tears welled up in his eyes, looking at me pleadingly. I realized I should've waited until after we were done with breakfast before telling him all this. I stroked his hair as he sobbed.

I could use teleportation magic, and I had the power to fight back now.

But if I got into some kind of trouble, I didn't want Alto to be targeted. That's why I had wanted to explain things to him in simple terms. Clearly, I'd done a bad job of it. I had unexpectedly made him very upset.

"Don't worry. I'll be careful. Even if someone powerful comes to take me away, I'm strong. It won't be easy for them to get me." I smiled reassuringly at him.

"Master…strong. I get strong…too," Alto said with a serious expression.

"That's right. I'll feel better if you do. So make sure you eat a lot."

A look of determination coming to his face, he picked up his toast to resume eating.

I was fond of him. Is this what it felt like to have a child? It wouldn't be unusual to have one at twenty-five, after all.

I thought about Hanai and Kyle and wondered if they'd had any children. I searched their memories, but as Kyle had told me, they were locked so that I wasn't able to see them.

He told me that keys were necessary to unlock the memories. What were the two keys he spoke of?

I'd been wondering about it, but I still had no idea what they could be. The only thing I found out from searching their memories was that neither Hanai nor Kyle had ever raised a beastfolk child.

Alto must have gotten sleepy from being full after breakfast, because he began to doze off. I put him back to bed.

There was plenty of time left before my quest deadline. If I had to hurry, I could just use Teleport. I decided to take my time going back to the castle town depending on how Alto felt.

I took a mug out of my bag and filled it with hot water using magic so that I could make some tea. I waited for it to finish brewing and took a sip. I recalled the results of my research from the night before as I watched Alto sleeping peacefully.

I'd learned that he was from a wolf clan—the Bluewolves, the rarest of all the beastfolk groups. There was no doubt in my mind that slave traders would try to kidnap him the moment they spotted him.

I had a feeling the only reason Alto had survived so long as a slave was pure coincidence.

Some beastfolk's fur or hair color changed as they got older. When Alto was younger, his had been white, and because of that disease in his eye, it had been white, too. So no one realized that he was actually a Bluewolf. He had been brought to the slave market in a filthy condition. His hair color must have only recently begun to change. If it had been common practice to bathe slaves more regularly, someone would have certainly noticed right away.

The other reason why Alto had probably managed to survive so long was that he'd fought back against his owner. The magical tool used on slaves took away their freedom, but it couldn't take away their thoughts or wills.

Regardless of whether the magical tool was made so that a slave couldn't kill their owner, Alto was beastfolk. If he attacked a human who wasn't used to fighting, his intensity alone could strike fear in their hearts. Even if his claws only inflicted scratches, that would make someone who threatened him even more scared. Especially if he never stopped fighting back no matter how much they hurt him.

Every person who had bought Alto ended up returning him to the slave trader. If he hadn't been returned that last time, he could have been bathed at some point and his identity discovered.

And after having him returned so many times, the slave trader had surely thought about getting rid of him. But his greed stopped him from doing that. If he killed him, he wouldn't get any more money out of him. So he hadn't given up on selling him, in the hopes of recouping his losses. In that sense, I thought Alto was truly lucky.

I drank my tea and shifted my thoughts to another topic. First, I ruminated over my plans for once I returned to the castle town. I had to drop by the guild to give my report. I would make Alto wear a hood so that no one would realize he was beastfolk. He was just at the age where he could sign up as an adventurer. I would consult with him and decide whether we should register him or not. Regardless of his decision, I would get armor and weapons for him.

I needed supplies for our journey, too. I didn't need to do it today, though. I could get a room at an inn somewhere after I was finished at the guild and have Alto rest there. That would be a good plan.

What else...?

I needed to leave Gardir as soon as possible. This kingdom was nothing but dangerous for Alto. It was so unsafe that I couldn't even let him walk alone outside.

But I needed to do more research about beastfolk before I left the kingdom. There were libraries here, but I didn't know whether they had the books I was seeking.

If they didn't, I would have to ask Nes for help.

I started thinking about when I should leave the kingdom and realized something. "I might not have enough money..."

I sighed. If I left the kingdom now, I might run out of money. Plus, I had another mouth to feed, so I might need to revise my travel plans.

"I need to make even more money than before..."

Alto looked so happy when he ate that I didn't want him to go without food. My gaze naturally drifted down to my hands. "That's right... I'm holding his life in my hands."

My choices could mean the difference between his life and death. For the first time, I understood the weight of the word *responsibility*.

"I have to protect him."

No matter what.

"I..." I took another sip of tea, feeling upset, and I sighed again. I placed the mug on the ground and lay down.

The sky was so blue. The only thing I could hear was the sound of the breeze passing by. My prospects were grim.

But strangely, I didn't have any regrets.

I looked at Alto, my mind busy at work. It didn't seem like he would wake anytime soon. I took a book out of my bag and read it while I lay on the ground, waiting for him to wake up.

After Alto woke up, I told him about my plan and how I was an adventurer. I told him he could register with the guild, but it was up to him. He said he wanted to, and I didn't have any reason to be against it. If we were going to travel together, it would be more convenient if he was an adventurer.

With our plans settled, we walked back to the castle town. Honestly, I wanted to use teleportation magic when I considered his condition. But we were walking instead, because Alto said he wanted to see the flowers.

Apparently, he was curious if the nectar from flowers really was sweet or not.

He found some, then widened his eyes with surprise when he discovered they *were* sweet.

His eyes sparkled as he picked fruit off trees and plopped them in his mouth, sometimes spitting them out. He frowned when he found flowers that had nectar that was not sweet.

He would be so excited when he found something delicious that he would share it with me. He asked me about things he didn't know, and once he finished memorizing my explanations, he would find something else that was new to him.

I answered his questions, slowly following behind him.

* * *

Since Alto was a wolf beastfolk, his sense of smell was very sharp, and he reacted sensitively to any little scent riding on the air. He began ambling in another direction, following the scent of something—perhaps he had found another sweet-smelling flower.

"Sweet, nice smell." He found another new flower, picked it, and licked the nectar from it. The moment he tasted it, his body trembled and froze.

"Alto, there's poison in that flower's nectar." The poison wasn't life-threatening, though. It just had a temporary paralysis effect. "That flower's nectar can paralyze people. You've been putting everything and anything into your mouth, but you should remember that there are dangerous plants out there."

Alto was still paralyzed and couldn't move, but I continued talking to him. "That flower's poison is commonly used. It won't kill you, but it's often used to paralyze others. It can be recognized by that sweet smell. So make sure you never eat any food that has that particular scent."

" . . . . . "

"There are edible grasses, flowers, and fruits. Some plants can also be used for medicine. But there are also many poisonous plants, like the one you just licked."

" . . . . . "

"Let's start learning one by one which plants are edible, which you can use for medicine, and which are poisonous, okay?" I went over to Alto and used Wind magic to cure his paralysis.

"Master, thank you!" He lay his ears down against his head and thanked me as he stared at me. He looked relieved that his paralysis was gone.

"Try to be really careful, okay? Putting everything in your mouth is dangerous."

"Okay."

As I recalled how pitiful Alto looked, I wondered if my way of teaching him that lesson had been a little tough. But I thought it was good to let children experience things for themselves, so I'd let him do as he pleased to a certain extent. Of course, I stopped him from doing anything too dangerous and warned him.

But other than that, it was good for Alto to take an interest in things, act on it, and see the result of his actions.

It was my job to take care of him and to support and protect him. I decided I wasn't going to tell him what to do, because all of his experiences would benefit him in some way.

This world placed little value on life, so I would teach him how to survive alone if he had to. That was my duty as his mentor.

I observed Alto as such things went through my mind. And I realized that I wanted to watch him do things out of curiosity. He reminded me of a puppy exploring the outside world for the first time, with sparkling eyes…

Perhaps that was one of the joys of having an apprentice, so I decided to be lenient.

Now Alto picked up a different flower. He sniffed it, thought for a bit, then slowly licked the nectar. The only difference from before was that he was more cautious about it this time. I wanted to laugh, but I managed to suppress it.

After he licked the nectar, Alto said, "Bitter. Master. My mouth, bitter."

He crouched down in discomfort, and there were tears in his eyes.

"Yes, that flower's nectar is very bitter. Their leaves are, too. But it can be used for medicine. They help settle stomachs. You should eat the leaves if you had too much food and have a stomachache."

Alto stuck out his tongue, perhaps because the inside of his mouth still felt bitter. I felt bad for him, but I suppressed those feelings and continued. "Alto."

"Yes?"

"Remember how I told you not to put everything in your mouth? So why did you still do it?"

"The flower's smell, was good."

"……"

"So I thought, it was fine."

"The flower that paralyzed you smelled sweet, too, didn't it?"

He nodded.

"So that means even if a flower smells good, it doesn't necessarily mean it's safe, right?"

Alto hung his head and drooped his ears.

"Now, how do you think you'll be able to tell apart poisonous flowers from the safe ones?"

Alto looked up at me and contemplated, then answered, "Lick it, little bit?"

"......"

Don't laugh. You can't laugh! No matter how hard it is...

I stifled my laughter and put on a serious expression. "Incorrect," I said, and Alto lowered his head again.

I didn't give him the answer, so he started thinking again. But he just couldn't figure it out. His tail started twitching.

"Hmm... I'll give you a hint. Yesterday, what did you look at with me?"

"Yesterday?"

"Yes. We looked at something while we drank milk, remember?"

"Um, book?"

"Correct!" I took out my botanical encyclopedia and handed it to Alto. He took it and glanced back and forth between me and the book.

"You can have that. So anytime you find a flower, grass, or fruit you don't recognize, you can look it up in there."

"What?"

"It has pictures of plants and their names written down. So you'll be able to tell very easily if it's edible, can be used for medicine, or if it's poisonous."

Alto hugged the book to his chest.

"And if you're in a hurry, you can remember its characteristics and look it up later."

"I can, have?"

"That's right. Don't put things in your mouth right away. Look them up first."

"Okay!" He smiled happily as he responded, and I patted his head.

"Alto," I called, and he looked up from the book.

"Say ahhh."

"Ahhh?"

"Open your mouth," I explained.

He nodded and obediently opened his mouth. I put a piece of candy inside. That flower's nectar was very bitter, so he probably still had that unpleasant aftertaste. The candy would help.

"Sweet! Yummy!"

"I'm glad you like it."

"Master, what?"

"When you want to know what something is, you ask, 'What is this?'"

He practiced my pronunciation, then asked, "Master. What, is this?"

"It's candy. It's made from melted, hardened sugar. Flavoring is added, like fruit juice. Do you like it?"

"I do!"

"Then you can have the rest. Hold out your hand."

Alto held out both his hands. I gave him a little bag of candy.

"Put them in your pocket and eat one when you feel tired. You mustn't eat them all at once, though."

"Okay."

Alto joyfully put the candy inside his pocket. "Master, thank you!" He wagged his tail, and his ears twitched, showing me how happy he was as he thanked me.

"You're welcome. Shall we keep walking?"

I urged Alto on, and we continued walking toward the castle town. He sort of rambled and wandered as he went off on his curious whims, and I rambled and wandered after him.

We had a late lunch, and then he got tired. The candy I gave Alto was the kind sold in stores, but I had infused it with magic that helped recover your stamina.

While he ate his candy, the effects slowly started to appear. I was glad the candy had been helpful, but honestly, his low stamina was a problem. The only thing I could think of was to slowly take the time to build it up.

There was still some distance until we reached the castle town. I decided he wouldn't be able to walk the rest of the way back and that we should teleport. Alto was surprised when we arrived there in an instant, but then his expression immediately tensed up.

He was wearing the hooded robe I had made for him.

I used some Light magic that would make us inconspicuous, and we entered the castle town. "Alto. I'm going to go to the guild first. Will you wait at the inn?"

"I want to come."

"Are you sure?"

"Yes."

"All right. Let me know if you're uncomfortable at all."

He nodded, and we headed for the guild. I opened the door and walked over to the reception desk. Nes greeted me like he always did. "Hey, kid. You're here awfully late today."

It was almost evening, and most of the adventurers would be returning soon. I wanted to take care of everything and get back to the inn before that happened. Since I had cast magic on us, other humans nearby didn't really notice us much. But as soon as we walked through the door, Nes and the other guild workers noticed us immediately.

"A lot happened."

"And I guess that beastfolk kid is part of it?" Nes looked at Alto, who quickly hid behind me.

Nes lowered his voice so only we could hear him. And I cast a magic spell so that only he could hear us.

"Kid...did you buy a slave?"

"Yes, I did."

"I didn't take you for that kinda person." There was an accusatory tone to his voice and the look in his eyes.

Alto jumped out from behind me and raised his voice. "No! Master, saved me!"

"Alto..."

"I'm...not slave...anymore!" he yelled desperately at Nes.

I was a little shocked that Alto had stood up for me, but at the same time, it brought me immense joy. I petted his head, praising him.

"Pfft. Ha-ha-ha-ha!" Nes had suddenly burst out laughing. "He sure is fond of you! Knowing you, I bet you showed up when he was getting beat or almost killed, and you couldn't stand for it, huh?"

Embarrassed that he'd guessed exactly what happened, I averted my gaze.

"Well, I can't say that's good, but...I understand how you feel. And it was lucky for this child." He smiled at me, his voice serious.

I looked back at him again and said, "I'm going to work very hard to make sure he's happy."

"What will you do? Take him to a shelter?"

The color drained from Alto's face when he heard the word, and he froze. I rubbed his back and told him he had nothing to worry about.

"No. He's my apprentice."

"....." I heard Nes's breath catch in his throat. He didn't say anything, though. He just nodded several times. "Your apprentice, eh? Well, that might be good. I've heard some bad things about this kingdom's shelters."

"....."

I had a feeling Nes didn't elaborate because Alto was standing here.

I thought back to when I was summoned here. When they had decided I was useless. I didn't think there was anything good about this kingdom, so I didn't need to hear the details from Nes. To be honest, I didn't want to.

"I want to register Alto with the guild. And I came to finish my quest." I changed the subject, getting back to my main goal.

"Hey, hey. You gotta be twelve to register. He's too young."

"Alto says he is twelve."

Nes was surprised to hear his age, just like I had been. He sighed and handed me the registration form. "Fill it out. You should probably write for him."

"Thanks."

I took the document and began filling it out. Alto stood next to me on his tiptoes as he looked at the sheet of paper. He probably couldn't see the whole thing.

"What should we put as your job, Alto?" I asked, remembering what I had found out about beastfolk. Beastfolk wolves had high physical and combat abilities. Under normal circumstances, they couldn't use magic, but there were exceptions. Among the wolf clans, the Bluewolves and Silverwolves were always born with magical powers, although Alto hadn't realized his yet. Since he had them, he should be able to use magic. But if people knew he could, that would just make him even more valuable, so I didn't think we should go that route in order to offer him more protection.

"Job?"

"Yes, job."

"Hmmmm."

"Hmm... What do you like more, a sword or a spear?"

"Sword! Just like Master!"

"You can fight with your fists, too."

"Wanna be just like Master!"

"Okay. We'll write down swordsman, then."

"Okay."

As for his abilities... What kind of abilities did beastfolk have? Since I didn't know, I would leave that one blank.

This should be good...

Name: Alto
Age: 12
Occupation: Swordsman
Attribute: None
Abilities: None
Skills: None
Languages: Common Language

I wasn't sure if I should put common language down for mastered languages, but I did anyway. I handed Nes the form.

"Passable." He read through it and scratched out the languages line. Then he drew a blue line on the upper right part of the form. That meant the adventurer was beastfolk. It was supposed to prevent problems that might arise when forming temporary parties or teams.

"You can explain about the guild to him later."

"Okay."

I took the booklet from him and gave it to Alto.

"Hey, kid. Put this stone on your hand."

"You're going to call him the same thing you call me?"

"Well, you're both kids, ain't ya?"

I sighed and lifted Alto up, since he couldn't reach the counter. Alto seemed a little bewildered, but he did as Nes said and put the magical tool on his hand.

"You're really fond of this kid, aren't ya?" Nes said with a smirk as he looked at Alto's hand, then at me.

I looked at the mark that appeared on Alto's hand and was speechless.

"......"

Alto's emblem was two crossed swords with camellias blooming at their hilts.

He had camellias, just like I did...even though they didn't exist in this world.

"Master?" My arms must've tensed up as I held him, because he called my name.

"I'm sorry, did I hurt you?"

"No."

"You're done registering for the guild." I put Alto down and looked at Nes, who was still grinning.

I let out another sigh and took the Cubes he handed me and gave them to Alto.

"Hey."

"What is it?"

Nes lowered his voice. His expression was very serious now. "He's a Bluewolf, ain't he?"

"I think so, yes. I don't have any solid proof, though."

"You know he'll be targeted because of how rare he is, don't you?"

"Yes."

"If he wears a slave's collar, no slave trader will be able to touch him."

"I can't do that..."

Alto was standing on his tiptoes, trying to listen in on our conversation.

Seeing this, Nes chuckled wryly. He had lowered his voice because he knew Alto's hearing was sharp, and he didn't want him to know about his suggestion regarding the slave collar.

"You should put an earring on him, then," Nes said louder. "One earring means that you're someone's apprentice. You wear one on your right ear, and your apprentice wears one on his left."

"All right."

"Plus...I'm sure he'll be targeted, but once they figure out who his guardian is, I doubt they'll try anything after that."

"Thank you." I bowed, appreciating Nes's advice.

"Good luck, Setsuna."

He called me by my name for the first time, which took me off guard. He looked at me with a sort of tenderness in his eyes. "Maybe meeting this kid will be good for you, too, Setsuna. You never seemed to have your feet planted on the ground, but maybe having someone to protect will give you a sense of purpose."

I realized Nes must have always been worried about me. Maybe he cared about me more than I knew. His feelings touched me, yet I found myself retorting, "Are you only calling me by my name so you can call him kid?"

"Why else do you think?" he said with a snort.

"I thought so." I let out a sigh, and Nes burst out laughing, then gave Alto and me a gentle look.

"You've got a long journey ahead. Just relax and take it slow. There's no rush."

"Okay. I hope I can grow along with Alto."

"I do, too. Good luck."

I nodded and picked up Alto, who was half-asleep and clinging to my clothes. I said good-bye to Nes and headed for the inn.

Alto was completely asleep, so I shifted my grip on him as I walked. He was so light, and the way he had fallen asleep with the book clutched against his chest didn't make him look like he was twelve. I thought the book would get in the way of his walking, so I'd offered to hold it, but he put his ears back and wouldn't give me the encyclopedia. That's how happy he had been to receive it.

I couldn't help but feel my heart ache when I looked at him, though. I shifted my gaze from Alto to the book and let out a sigh. I didn't mind giving it to him, but he couldn't read. I only remembered that when we were filling out the form inside the guild.

Back in Japan, a twelve-year-old would be in sixth grade. And a sixth grader could read and write well enough.

I had spoken from my experience in Japan when I told him to read the book and look up answers himself. But he had lived as a slave. He had trouble talking, so of course he had never been taught to read.

I remembered my words and behavior on the way back to the castle town, and I regretted much of it.

I thought about Alto, who was sleeping peacefully. Even though he couldn't read, he'd opened the book and looked like he was having so much fun comparing the illustrations of the flowers he found to the real thing.

His curiosity would grow even more once he learned how to read.

My new goal would be building up Alto's stamina and teaching him how to read and write. Plus showing him how to buy things.

He'd already gotten much better at conversing. If he continued at this rate, he'd have no problem speaking normally soon. He was a sore loser, a hard worker, and intensely curious.

It was exciting, thinking about all the things Alto would discover on our journey.

Various thoughts of that nature ran through my mind until we finally arrived at the inn and reserved a room. I placed Alto down on one of the beds, took off his robe, and laid him down. I didn't think he would wake up anymore tonight. I covered him with a blanket and looked at his still-boyish face as I remembered my conversation with Nes.

Once again, I thought about how dangerous Alto's hair color was.

I decided that once he woke up, I would discuss it with him and suggest changing the color.

I was consumed with the urge to research all sorts of things. But I didn't want to leave Alto alone. If I was going out, I needed to tell him first. I didn't want him to feel scared in case he woke up and saw I was gone.

At any rate, I should start on what I could do now. I decided to use my Materialize ability to create the things I would need for our journey.

First, I would make armor. I wanted something light for Alto that wouldn't inhibit his senses. I used clothes often worn by travelers as inspiration. They would be just as functional as mine. I made a hooded cloak, a shirt, pants, a belt for his sword, and shoes.

Next, I created a bag that he could carry his things in, but not like the one Kyle had made, which was like an alternate dimension inside. Since Alto was a child, I wanted to make sure he learned the importance of organization at an early age, or else he'd turn out like Kyle... The bag would be capable of holding one hundred items, regardless of size or weight.

Honestly, I didn't want it to be *that* big, but Alto was a curious child. One hundred items probably wouldn't be enough. But I thought it was important for him to figure out what to keep and what to discard after that point.

Next, I made two wallets. I decided I would give Alto one-third of all the rewards he received from guild quests as spending money. The remaining two-thirds would be saved up for his future.

Since Alto would be doing quests with me, I had a feeling he'd be making a lot of money. I wanted him to learn the value of it and how to use it at an early age. I would provide everything necessary for day-to-day living, so he would never be at a loss for spending money.

Next, I turned my thoughts to preparing weapons, so I searched inside my bag. There were many types inside, but none that I thought Alto could use right now. They all seemed much too large for a child to wield, so I decided to craft one myself. I made two shortswords. Twin blades that had camellias on their hilts, just like Alto's emblem. They were the perfect size.

Once they were finished, I took a break. I was trying to decide whether I should enchant the swords.

Fighting monsters was a matter of life and death. If you didn't want to be killed, you had to fight like your life depended on it, or they would win.

But I didn't want him to fight with weapons that were enchanted with strong magic from the very beginning. I was afraid he would get over-confident. Besides, it felt premature. If he relied on magical weapons, he wouldn't build stamina. And I had decided to make that my first priority.

After the weapons were done, I looked down at the bracelet and ear-rings in my hand. I was trying to decide whether I should enchant them with magical and physical defense properties like Kyle had done for me. Generally, you didn't want to put your apprentice in danger. But...

One day, Alto would be independent and might have an apprentice of his own. Or he might have a family and kids. If I protected him from everything, he might not be able to teach others in the future.

He wouldn't know what situations were considered dangerous or what injuries would lead to death...

If I didn't train him to learn those instincts, his ability to avoid harm wouldn't develop properly.

That was a very important skill, both for surviving and adventuring.

I had inherited my knowledge from Hanai and Kyle. I was able to respond to danger due to their cumulative experiences. They had given that to me. But Alto didn't have that. And I couldn't give it to him.

Once I thought about it that way, I realized Alto would be in trouble once he left me to raise someone else. To have your body move on instinct due to your experiences was very difficult unless you had gone through it before. The same could be said for teaching it.

I continued going back and forth over the question of enchanting the weapons. Finally, I decided to infuse them with magic under cer-tain conditions.

First, I enchanted the earring. I made it so that I'd be able to see Alto's location if something happened and he was separated from me. I also reinforced it with magical and physical defense properties that would activate if his life was at risk.

Additionally, if anyone besides me or Alto tried to remove his earring, it would break their arm.

That would render any human who was trying to do him harm powerless.

Next, I enchanted the bracelet to neutralize and detoxify deadly poisons. Neutralization would be completed in five minutes. It would also speed up wound healing. I put an anti-theft spell on that one, too, breaking anyone's arm who tried to remove it.

Just in case, I engraved Alto's name and mine on the outside of the bracelet. I put my own name on the earring because then anyone who saw it would know Alto was my apprentice.

I enchanted the two items so that the magic would only activate when he was close to death. I didn't do it to hurt him or to make him feel pain. I didn't want him to suffer from poison. But I wanted to give him the skills to live.

"......"

The armor had high defensive properties as well. Since I was with him, I doubted he would get seriously injured. Even so, I still felt conflicted as I gazed at the earring and bracelet for a while.

I settled my feelings and decided to continue preparing other necessities for him. I would have him carry medicine that I made. I also created some stationery like the ones I saw at the market and placed it on the bed. The substitute for a rubber eraser was called a letter eraser here, and they seemed to be made from monster bones.

I put it in a box with everything I'd made so far.

I opted to hold off on making bowls and silverware specifically for Alto; instead, I would have him buy some at a store so he could practice shopping.

I finished everything, made sure I wasn't missing anything, then lay down in bed. The thought of dinner crossed my mind, but I closed my eyes, thinking that eating alone would be too troublesome. I immediately felt tired and surrendered myself to sleep, drifting off.

Sometime in the middle of the night, I woke up when I felt Alto stirring. I thought he'd gotten up to go to the bathroom, but that wasn't it. He was sitting up in bed, covering his mouth like he was trying to hold something back. I wondered if he'd had a dream, and I thought about calling out to him. But it seemed as though he had covered his mouth so that he wouldn't disturb me, so I decided to watch him for a bit. I didn't want him to feel bad for waking me up.

After a while, Alto got out of his bed and quietly came over to mine and stood in front of it. I could sense him staring at me, but I didn't know why he was.

Then he must've been satisfied, because he returned to his bed. He was about to lie down when he stopped himself. He paused, then came back over to mine, looked at me, and went back to his bed again.

It seemed as though he was debating whether to wake me up, and I was just about to say something to him when he crawled into my bed. He did it very carefully and slowly, trying hard not to wake me.

After he got in bed with me, he thought about something for a while and then slowly, slowly scooted toward me.

I finally realized what he was doing, and it made my heart ache.

Alto was lonely. He was lonely but couldn't bring himself to say it. He was hesitant and stopped at the point where he was just barely touching me.

I continued pretending to be asleep and put my arms around him, just like my parents had done when I was a child when they snuggled up against me. He tensed up a bit and stared at me. But once he realized I was still sleeping, he let out a relieved sigh and dozed off.

Alto must have been craving love and affection because he had never gotten it from anyone before. He wanted someone to pat his head, hug him, and hold his hand. He wanted someone to sleep with him when he was feeling lonely. Even though he was twelve, the things he wished for were the kind a younger child would want.

Those thoughts ran through my head as I gazed at his sleeping face, and eventually, I drifted off as well.

When I woke up the next morning, I saw a shocking sight.

Alto was no longer next to me. Instead, a baby wolf lay curled up, sleeping in a ball. I stared at it in shock. It must have sensed I was looking at it, because it slowly opened its eyes. And after staring at me for a while, its eyes flew wide open, and it quickly jumped down from the bed. The moment it saw its own front legs, its entire body tensed up and began trembling.

The baby wolf put its tail between its legs and curled into a trembling ball. Almost like it wanted to disappear.

The sight of it was so sad that I could barely take it. I called out to Alto, who had turned into a baby wolf. "Alto?"

He turned his ears toward me but didn't move.

I got out of bed and walked over to him, but he just curled into an even smaller ball. "Alto? Are you okay?" I picked up the baby wolf and tried to meet his eyes, but he wouldn't look at me. His ears lay all the way down against his head, his tail still between his legs. "Alto? Can't you talk?"

I wondered if he couldn't since he was a wolf now. I cast Telepathy and asked him again. "Alto. Just think the things you want to tell me."

......

Alto remained silent, and the minutes ticked by. I just stared at him for a while... But the more time that passed by, the more I felt my mouth relax. *No, you shouldn't smile at a time like this.*

His ears were flat against his head, and his tail was between his legs. He looked just like a puppy. I felt bad for thinking it, but he was absolutely adorable.

He had a special kind of cuteness in wolf form that only animals could have. I knew he wasn't an animal, but I couldn't help but think that. Finally, I couldn't hold it in anymore and started laughing.

"Ah-ha-ha-ha!"

!!!

"Ah-ha-ha-ha!"

Alto must've been surprised by my laughter, because he finally made eye contact with me.

"Alto. I didn't know you could turn into a wolf. You're adorable," I told him earnestly. Beastfolk could turn into animals. But I had assumed Alto wouldn't be able to, since both his parents were humans.

I could tell he was flustered by my words. "I think you're cute in your normal form, but you're cute as a wolf, too," I said.

Finally, Alto began to share his thoughts. *You don't hate me, Master?*

"Hate you?"

Because I can take this form.

"I think it's adorable. I like it." Alto's tail wagged, reacting to the word *like.*

Really? You really like it?

"I do. I think both your regular and wolf forms are cute, and I adore them both."

In order to convey my true feelings to Alto, I repeated the same thing with less vocabulary. Alto seemed to hate himself, but I wanted him to grow to like himself.

You're not mad?

"Why would I be mad?"

Because I climbed into your bed last night without permission.

"You're free to sleep in bed with me whenever you want to. You don't have to ask."

Even if I look like this?

I realized that when we communicated via telepathy, our conversation was very smooth.

"As long as it's just when you're asleep, I don't mind. But during the day, I want you to be in your regular form so you can study."

Okay.

"And make sure not to turn into a wolf in front of anyone but me. I don't want anyone to kidnap you."

Yes, Master.

"Well, if you're feeling better now, I have something to give you. So you can turn back to your regular form now," I said, and Alto easily reverted back. He was wearing a happy smile.

* * *

Since I was hungry, I decided to do my daily training later and eat breakfast first.

Once we were done eating, we returned to our room. I gave Alto his weapons, armor, and bag, along with an explanation of everything. His eyes widened and sparkled when he saw the presents. He was a flurry of emotions. Finally, I put the earring on his left ear, and I did the same for my right ear.

"We match!" He beamed, apparently overjoyed that we had the same earring. I put on his bracelet and added a spell so that it would adjust sizes when he became a wolf and not fall off, and included Telepathy. I decided not to tell Alto about how his equipment was enchanted with magic. I didn't think he needed to know about it.

Finally, I told him something very important. "Alto."
"Yes?"
"Your earring and bracelet are proof that you're my apprentice."
"Proof?"
"Yes. One day, when you decide you want to leave my side, you can give me the bracelet back."
"......"
"If you want to tell me why, you can. But if you don't want to, you don't have to, either. And I won't pry. If you find something and want to go down that path, then I'll trust your judgment."

I'd asked Alto if he was prepared to be my apprentice two days ago. So I didn't think he would run away from me. He was a serious boy, and I had a feeling he would tell me why he was leaving if the time came. But if he chose not to, then it must be for a very good reason, indeed.

I was his mentor, but his life belonged to him and him alone. I wanted him to tell me without guilt when he wanted to leave, so I needed to give him the means to do that, even if that meant running away or going back down the path he'd come.

"So when you return the bracelet and decide to part ways, I'll know that you've found your own path."

Alto quietly listened to me.

"The earring is set to fall apart in three days after you remove your bracelet. Only you or I can remove your jewelry, so no one else can do it."

Alto looked down and bit his lip, balling his hands into fists.

"You don't have to think too much about it now. But just keep it in the back of your mind. You're coming on this journey to find out who you want to become."

"...Okay."

I smiled wryly at Alto, who looked a little sad. "Alto."

He didn't answer. He just looked at me with his ears laid back against his head.

"This is far into the future. You just became my apprentice. I'm going to be your master until you become an adult."

He let out a sigh of relief when he heard that. I looked at him and thought if he weren't here, I would probably be lonely, too. I was surprised when that thought crossed my mind. We'd only been together for three days, but that was how great of a presence he'd become in my life.

I opened the door to the Adventurers Guild and went up to the reception desk. Alto walked by my side, wearing his hood low over his eyes. I tried to come during a time when it would be less crowded so that fewer people would be looking at us.

Once in front of Nes, Alto took off his hood. Nes looked at him and seemed a little surprised but reverted to his usual expression. I had used magic to change Alto's hair to brown, and his eyes were now both the same shade of violet as mine.

"Hey, kid."

"Good...morning."

"Morning."

Nes returned Alto's halting greeting, then looked at me.

"Good morning."

"Morning. Pretty good, I think." He must have been talking about Alto's new hair and eye color. "I think it's a bit better. Anyway, what brings you here today?"

I'd walked right by the bulletin board, so he guessed I was here for another purpose. "Do you know a place nearby where I can rent a house for cheap?"

"I thought you were staying at the inn?" he asked, implying I should just stay there.

"I am, but I thought I should probably start saving money."

Nes stared at me for a moment and mouthed silently, "Did you get kicked out?"

He seemed so sure that I gave him a wry smile, and he stroked his chin, thinking. Alto looked puzzled, and Nes gave a faint grin. "I don't think you'll be able to rent."

At this, Alto strained his ears.

"For the same reason?"

"That's right. You shouldn't let the kid walk around town too much."

"I was thinking that, too. But I'm a little worried about how much money I have. I also need to take on more quests to earn more. Plus, it'll be too hard to leave the kingdom until Alto builds up his stamina."

"That's true."

This kingdom wasn't a friendly place for beastfolk to live. The majority of the ones I saw in the castle town were slaves. Once they noticed Alto didn't have a collar, the possibility of him getting targeted would increase. I wanted to leave the kingdom as soon as possible, but Alto didn't have the stamina for such a long journey right now.

"I suppose, worst-case scenario, I could just carry him while we travel."

Nes laughed. "Yeah... Actually, I do know one inn that would work for you two...," he said, trailing off vaguely.

"Is there some kind of problem?"

"No, there shouldn't be any issue for you guys to stay there. The person who runs it is a former adventurer who had beastfolk on their team, so I don't think you'd have anything to worry about on that front. The innkeeper is nice enough, but…" Once again, he trailed off.

"Is it expensive?"

"No, it's cheap."

"Are there too many guests there?"

"No. In fact, there probably aren't *any*."

I wondered what other problems there could be, and Nes feigned laughter, which was unusual for him. "The innkeeper's very picky…," he muttered, letting out a deep sigh.

Now I was extremely curious about what kind of inn this was.

"I see. Well, I have no other place to stay, so would you tell me where it is?"

"Ah, sure. The innkeeper's got a great personality. That much I can guarantee."

"Okay. I'll go check it out."

"I'll contact them for you."

"Thanks for going to the trouble."

"None at all. The innkeeper's real nice, so if they like you, they'll take good care of you. Although, maybe it's better if they *don't* like you…" Nes kept muttering all these cryptic things, but then he handed me a map. "You're not gonna do a quest today, are you?"

"No, I'll head to the inn." I put Alto's hood back on, bid Nes farewell, and left the guild.

Alto was interested in a vendor outside, so we took a little detour before going. The inn was about ten minutes away on foot from the guild. It was in a good location, but it felt like no one was around. It really seemed like no guests were staying there. The exterior looked a bit old-fashioned. And even though it was an inn, the interior was dim.

"Master, here?"

"Yes, this is the place he drew on the map."

Alto looked a little scared and clung to me. I rubbed his back and patted it a few times to ease his nerves. Once he calmed down, I opened the door and went inside.

"Hello?" I called. I heard a deep voice from the reception desk in the back of the room, and a woman(?) appeared.

"Yes, coming!"

"......"

"......"

The person I saw was the complete opposite of how I imagined them to be, and I was utterly shocked. Alto was looking up at the lady with eyes so wide I thought they'd pop out of his head.

"Goodness. Do I have something on my face?" she asked, smiling at Alto.

I came back to my senses and was about to apologize for being rude, but the moment I opened my mouth, Alto spoke...letting out an honest reaction.

"Beard."

I felt my back break out in a cold sweat.

"......"

"......"

An awkward mood filled the air, and I opened my mouth to apologize. "I'm so sorry. He's still just a child."

"Oh, it's fiiine! It doesn't bother me one little bit!" the lady said, but her smile looked a bit tense.

Alto tilted his head and looked back and forth between us.

"Are you the adventurers Nestor told me about, dearies?"

"Yes. The guildmaster sent us here. I'd like to rent a room. Would that be all right?"

"Of cooourse! My name is Dahlia, and I'm just the *weak little lady* who runs this inn! It's so nice to meet you!"

I wasn't really sure what to say after that introduction. Dahlia was probably over two meters tall, and since she was an ex-adventurer, her body was very muscular.

That's right... She looked like a very buff man who was wearing a dress and makeup.

She didn't seem feeble or weak to me, but I suppose everyone had their own perceptions of what that meant...

After taking things in, I decided to just introduce myself in return. "It's nice to meet you, Dahlia. My name is Setsuna. I'm a scholar, and my guild rank is blue."

After I was done, I turned to Alto. "Alto, introduce yourself."

It took a little while for him to accept reality, but he finally came back to himself and nodded. "My name...is Alto. I'm...a swordsman. My guild rank is...yellow." He had practiced that introduction very hard and was able to say it without mistakes. I patted his head to praise him.

He must've been happy about the compliment, because his tail began to wag.

"Setsu and Alty! I'll remember that! Just one room for the two of you?"

I was a bit bewildered being called by a nickname like that, but I somehow managed to respond. "Yes, we'll stay in the same room."

"You got it! I'll prepare a *wonderful* room for you!"

"Thank you."

"Alty, you're beastfolk, hmm? It's been a long time since I've seen a child. You're just adorable! Shall I teach you the basics of love?"

I quickly stepped in. "No. Alto is my apprentice, so I'll teach him everything he needs to know. He's still young, after all."

"Oh? That's a shame. What about you, Setsu? Want me to teach you?"

"No thank you. I like to study on my own." Honestly, I wasn't even sure if my answer made sense, but I couldn't think of anything else.

"Goodness! Well, whatever floats your boat, I suppose..." Dahlia nodded, accepting my answer.

I had a feeling this conversation was going completely over Alto's head. He was staring at both of us in confusion.

"Oh, I almost forgot! Nestor told me everything. You don't need to worry, Setsu. I'll protect Alty while you're gone so you can come and go as you please!"

I was surprised by Dahlia's offer.

I had a lot of preparations to make before I could leave the kingdom. And it would be a lot of trouble to take Alto with me everywhere. I had planned on leaving him in my room at the inn with some countermeasures. But...I was worried about leaving him shut up and all alone.

Yet Dahlia said she would help me. I thought I could probably trust her, since Nes was the one who introduced us. I had no reason to doubt her, after all.

But most of all, she had on a tender smile when she looked at Alto. He must've realized it, too, because although he was surprised by her appearance, he didn't seem frightened.

"I'm sorry to cause you trouble…but I'd appreciate that a lot." I bowed and made Alto do the same. "May I put up a barrier around the whole inn?"

"Why, of course."

"I'm going to make it so that no one who bears ill will against you or Alto can enter."

I imagined Dahlia must have been strong. But if a group came to attack, she and Alto might get injured. I wanted to prevent that as much as I could.

"So you're a Windmaster, then, Setsu?"

"Yes."

"In that case, can you use invisibility magic?"

"Yes, I can."

"You're a very talented sorcerer, Setsu." She complimented me with a grin. Alto looked pleased that I was being commended. "If you can use invisibility magic, could you cast it on the garden?"

"Sure."

"If no one can see the backyard, then Alty will be able to play outside with no worries."

"……"

"It'll get too stuffy if he's cooped up in here all the time."

"Are you sure?"

"Why, of course! Not a soul comes here, after all!"

"Thank you…"

I bowed deeply again, grateful for her kindness. She smiled brightly at me.

After that, I cast magic on the inn and the back garden. Dahlia gave me a key and showed us to our room.

I was grateful that Nestor had recommended such a nice and comfortable place. The room was clean, and the food was delicious. It was the most delicious food I'd tasted since coming to this world.

Alto wasn't as shy as I had expected and enjoyed chatting with Dahlia.

The night before, I thought maybe it would be okay if I left for the guild to get ready, but...

I felt a little guilty when I looked at Alto. I told him that as long as we were in this kingdom, he couldn't leave the inn. Apparently, he'd thought I was going to stay next to him the whole time. I wanted to stay close as much as I could because he was anxious without me.

But I had to get all the necessary supplies we needed to leave the kingdom. Since there'd be two of us traveling now, I had to take on more quests to make more money.

I still had the money Kyle left me, but I was the one who decided to take on Alto as my apprentice, so it was only natural that I should use the funds I had earned myself. I didn't want to touch the money Kyle had given me unless it was an absolute emergency.

Alto's ears lay back as he hung his head.

"Your job is to learn your letters today, Alto." In Japanese, it'd be called *gojūon*. In English, it would be called the alphabet. But in this world's common language, you just called it letters. I had already given him a notebook with them written inside, and his task was to practice writing them.

The night before, I had taught him their sounds for an hour before bed, plus how to write my name and his. I wrote down the letters in the notebook so that he could study on his own today. I also made an easy picture book with illustrations for him to practice reading when he had spare time.

"Master. Want to come." He looked up at me with expectation, hoping I'd say yes.

"You can't. I told you why, remember?"

"......"

"Dahlia is going to stay with you while I'm gone. And she'll make you lunch, so there's nothing for you to worry about."

"......"

"Alto, what's your answer?"

"Yes, Master," he said reluctantly.

I handed him a leatherbound notebook.

"Master?" It was a different from the one I'd given him to study with. He caressed the cover.

"This is your diary. I want you to write down what you did, what you saw, and what you felt each day. You can write about the things that made you happy or the things that made you sad, too."

"Diary?"

"That's right. You write down everything that happened to you each day in that notebook so that you can tell me about your day."

"Tell me?"

"That's right. I'll read your entry and then write back to you."

"I can't...write yet."

"That's why you're going to practice your letters, right?"

"Yes."

"At first, you'll probably only be able to write the words you learned that day, and you might not be able to read my responses. But if you practice daily, you'll be able to read and write."

It wasn't that he didn't want to write in the diary, but rather, he didn't like not being able to go out with me. I understood that, but I just couldn't take him with me.

"Alto, you became my apprentice so you could study, right?" I reminded him, and he looked up at me with wide eyes.

Then he met my gaze with a serious expression and nodded. "I'll stay home, and study."

"Good. I promise I'll come back home to you," I said. For a moment, he looked like he might cry, and he hugged me tightly. I stroked his hair and inwardly apologized to him.

I left Alto in Dahlia's care and headed to the guild. I thanked Nes, and he gave me a strange smile. To save up money for our travels, I decided to take on quests I could finish in a day and gather supplies on the way home. I was planning on making that my daily schedule for a while.

I was a little excited to see what Alto would write about while I was out doing quests every day. I hoped he would have a lot of fun experiences.

After I finished what I needed to do, I returned to the inn, and Alto happily greeted me with a smile. He hadn't spent all day in his room; he'd spent most of his time with Dahlia. We ate a meal together while he told me about his day.

He reported back excitedly about all the new things he'd learned and discovered. When I saw how his ears and tail express those feelings, too, I was relieved. I was so glad he hadn't been sad and cried while I was gone.

Alto was much more used to Dahlia than he had been the day before. But to be honest, I wasn't. The contrast was just too jarring. I didn't think I could get used to it, but I didn't hate her. I was genuinely grateful to Dahlia.

Since she looked after Alto, I tried to give her more money, but she told me she didn't need it and refused. I had a feeling she did that to help with my savings.

If it wasn't for her, I would've had to depart for my journey carrying Alto everywhere. It would've been a better choice to leave rather than stay in the kingdom with no place for Alto to sleep.

But now we had a warm place to rest, and I could go out during the day. This was all thanks to Dahlia.

I decided I wanted to do something to thank Nes and Dahlia when it was time for me to leave the kingdom.

Now that dinner was over, Alto and I helped clean up, then went back to our room. I checked his homework and read children's books with him until it was time to go to bed, then he turned into a baby wolf and curled up in my lap. I told him to sleep in bed, but he didn't leave my side.

I sat on the sofa, petting Alto and drinking alcohol by myself. Ever since I'd shared that first drink with Zigel, I had a drink nearly every day. Having some delicious alcohol while reading a book was the height of happiness for me. Right now, I was petting Alto, but that was still nice.

I sat there and thought absently to myself until I felt tired. Suddenly, the diary on the desk caught my eye. I reached out and picked it up. It was Alto's first entry. I thought it'd be probably nothing more than the vocabulary words he'd learned, but I was surprised when I opened it up.

Morning, beard gone. Night, beard there.

"......"

Beard... Beard. Were you still stuck on that, Alto?

I wondered where he'd learned to write those words, though. I hadn't taught him that. Oh no, had he asked Dahlia? Who else could it have been? Cold sweat began to run down my back.

I understood Alto's feelings. I *really* did. Dahlia had a beard like a man but wore women's clothing. I was sure that to Alto, that seemed very puzzling.

Well, to me, who was quite sheltered when it came to life experiences, I also found her quite mystifying. I wondered what had led her to live her life as a woman? On one hand, I wanted to know, but on the other hand, I thought maybe it was best if I didn't. As I went back and forth on that, I looked back down at Alto's diary.

"What should I do?"

I wasn't sure how to respond. I agonized over it as Alto slept blissfully in my lap. Agonized and agonized. Maybe I should write *Don't worry about her beard.* Or maybe I should write *She shaves her beard in the morning, so that's why she doesn't have one then.*

Or maybe I should tell him that Dahlia was really a man? But if I did that, he'd ask why she wore a dress. And how would I explain that?

Maybe I should just say even women can grow beards. It wasn't a lie...

I wanted to compliment him on his first diary entry, but I wasn't really sure what to compliment.

It was only the first day, and I was in a pickle. The night wore on. It was near dawn when I finally wrote my response.

He wouldn't be able to read my response until he got better at reading. So I decided that we would look at the diary together, and I would show him the words while I read them.

I realized just how difficult it was to teach others as I read my response.

"Dear Alto. Everyone's physical appearances are different. You can change into an adorable wolf, but I can't. Sometimes, it can be rude to comment on people's physical appearances, so you should try to keep them to yourself. You did a great job with your first diary entry."

And so I spent my time staying at Dahlia's inn battling Alto's diary entries and preparing to leave the kingdom.

Epilogue

◇Part One: Setsuna

I finished packing and cleaning our room, then headed to the front desk. Even though we'd only spent a few days here, it felt much longer than that. I was feeling sentimental about it, but if I had the choice to repeat these last few days, I didn't think I would do it.

If I didn't get caught up in Alto's and Dahlia's behavior, I'd like to stay here again. Dahlia was nice, and her cooking was delicious. She was very caring and had been wonderful with Alto.

Alto had grown fond of her as well and looked sad to leave. Dahlia was waiting for us at the desk. I returned our key and thanked her for all her help. "Thank you so much for the past few days. It's all thanks to you that I got ready so quickly."

"Of course! I had the best time with you and Alty, Setsu."

Dahlia sniffled, dabbing at her eyes with a handkerchief.

"Thank you."

"You take care, Alty. You can come back and play anytime!"

"Okay."

"We'll drop by when we visit this kingdom again."

"Yes, I'll be waiting for you!"

"All right."

Even though she knew the chances were slim that I'd return here, Dahlia gave us one last tender smile. If I ever came back, I'd like to ask her about her time as an adventurer.

"Be careful on the road. Make sure you don't get sick or injured!" She was worried about us right until the end. I said good-bye to her and put Alto's hood up.

We waved back at Dahlia and headed to the Adventurers Guild.

I opened the door, and Nes called out to me like he always did. "Hey, Setsuna. Hey, kid."

"Good morning, Nes."

"Good morning. Nes."

Nes had stopped calling me *kid* ever since I'd taken on Alto on as my apprentice. That made me happy, but when I thought about how long it took for him to stop, I felt a tad frustrated.

"You're leaving today?"

"Yes. Thanks for everything."

"Aw, I didn't do much."

"You did. You did so much for both me and Alto. If it weren't for you, it would've taken a lot longer for me to prepare for our travels." Also... "And thanks to you, I was able to meet both Agito and Dahlia." Despite what Nes wanted people to believe, he was incredibly kind, and I was grateful to him. Back when I didn't have anyone in this world to rely on or talk to and felt like I was overwhelmed with loneliness, I'd walk into the guild, and he'd look me right in the eyes and greet me with a smile.

He did the same for other novice adventurers, as well. I'm sure they knew that despite his teasing, he cared about them, too.

I started to bow to thank him, but he stopped me with his gaze. "You don't need to thank me. I just did what any guildmaster would do. If you want to thank me, do it with your actions."

"My actions?"

"Come back here as a black-rank adventurer. Then I'll work you like a horse pulling a carriage!" he said with a grin, and I laughed. We promised to see each other again.

My heart felt warm at the thought.

"I will. I'm not sure when it'll happen, but I'll work hard to become a black-rank adventurer."

"Yep. An expert one."

"Yes. Take care, Nes."

He nodded to me, then looked at Alto. "You work hard with Setsuna, kid."

Alto nodded in response.

"We'll be going now. But we'll be back someday."

Nes looked a little surprised at my good-bye, but a smile quickly spread across his face as he bid me farewell. "I'll be waiting for you."

I pulled Alto's hand as we walked. It felt like I had lived in this kingdom for a long time, but it also felt rather short. Still, I hated the place. I hated it so much that I wished I could forget about it immediately.

But this was where I had met and said good-bye to Kyle.

He had saved me from my hell.

He had given me this body and my freedom.

This was the place where he had given me everything.

This was the only place that held our memories together.

So I would never forget it, for as long as I lived.

I stood in front of the gates leading out of the castle town. Alto also paused beside me, his hood pulled low over his eyes. He glanced up at me and gave me a puzzled look.

"Alto. This is the start of our journey. I'm sure there will be lots of fun times ahead, and a lot of hard times, too. But I'm going on this journey so I can see the world."

Not as Setsuna Sugimoto. Just as plain Setsuna.

Alto nodded and spoke with resolve. "I'm going on the journey...to study. I'm traveling with Master...to find what I want to do."

*   *   *

This was the beginning of our journey.
Alto and I would live together.

After I saw him nod, the two of us slowly passed through the gate
and left Gardir.

"Let's go on our journey together now, Alto."

Another Chapter
Japanese Iris ~ Tidings ~

◇Part One: ???

As I passed through the castle gates, the sun was starting to set behind Gardir Castle. I could hear the bells tolling one o'clock.

"Hurry, the hero needs medical attention."

The hero, who was asleep in the carriage, showed no signs of waking up. He had been in a state of unconsciousness ever since using all of his mana in a fight four days ago.

The battle had happened right before we were about to rest for the night. A group of a several hundred monsters suddenly sprang up at the camp. A few mid-rank monsters were also spotted, and coupled with the sheer number of them, the soldiers lost control of the battle.

Just when we thought we would be annihilated, the hero invoked his magic.

Waves of light radiated from his body, layering on top of one another, forming a large ball of light within the darkness above his head. Then, at a diameter of five mers long, it burst without making a sound. The bursting light turned into countless arrows of light, which became meteors that cut through the dark night and expelled hundreds of monsters in an instant. Perhaps because of that, the hero had collapsed on the spot and lost consciousness.

When the hero didn't wake up the next morning, I began to fret, and we decided to temporarily withdraw from the front line.

When the allied soldiers of Ellana's camp sent an urgent messenger on horseback to inform Gardir Castle of their intention to withdraw, they carefully escorted the hero while gathering soldiers and managed to return just now.

"Anyway, be careful. Don't jostle the hero unnecessarily."

Four people moved the hero from the carriage to a stretcher.

"That's true. Who knows when the next one will awaken? We can't just let this one die so easily," Larutas, who was watching the situation with annoyance, muttered in my ear. I thought, *That's not true*, and shouted toward the stretcher. "Listen, no matter what happens, leave his clothes on and don't change them."

After confirming that the hero was brought into the castle, I ordered the entire army to line up, although at this point there were only a little over a thousand men left. There had been five thousand soldiers at the time of dispatch. There were no words for this tragic situation. However, I tried not to show it on my face and ordered the troops to disperse.

"Well, General Tylera. Guess we should go notify the king that we retreated."

My heart felt heavy that we had sent so many great soldiers to the Waterside, but it didn't seem to bother Larutas, for he had on a cold expression.

"You don't have to tell me that. Come on," I said as I headed to the throne room, where the king awaited us.

◇Part Two: Tylera

I completed my report of the war in an about an hour. My first battle was marked as a victory, based on results rather than casualties. Contrary to my somber feelings, I ordered the transfer to the second subjugation team, and the king returned to the throne room. Afterward, the prime minister ordered me to meet with the black-rank adventurer regarding the Wind ruins.

"Can't I do it tomorrow?" I couldn't help but want to quickly finish and go check on the hero's condition.

"I'm sorry for the trouble, but we have a lot of work that requires a magic monocle. I can't check the recording without you because you have the magical tool on standby. Please."

Reluctantly, I headed to the hearing room where the adventurer was waiting, as I had agreed with the prime minister beforehand. This room was enchanted with special type of magic. When a respondent told a lie, a horn went off in the questioner's head alerting him to the falsehood. For this reason, it was frequently used when dealing with merchants and reporting intelligence activities.

The hall was on the east side of the royal palace, large enough to be used for a meeting of about twenty people, but this time only one adventurer of black rank was waiting for us to come.

"Thank you for waiting." I opened the door and apologized to the adventurer who stood up to greet me.

"I've been waiting for months. A few hours is no big deal."

For a moment, I felt my face tense up when I heard the black-rank adventurer Agito's sarcastic response, but I pulled myself together and took a seat, telling him to sit down as well.

"Seems like this conquest was a tough one," he said, seeing our exhaustion. He shouldn't have been able to pick up on the mood in the castle here in this room, but somehow, he had.

"Someone as powerful as you would surely be able to get a rough idea of how many soldiers we have left and where they are, but please refrain from saying anything else," Larutas piped up before I had the chance to reply.

"No, I didn't mean to pry. I meant to thank you, but it's difficult," Agito said, then continued. "Come to think of it, after you were sent to the battle, I encountered a group of corvasals near the outskirts of Gardir. I thought maybe it was a group that the hero failed to slay..."

"Agito, please don't make unnecessary inquiries." Once again, Larutas interrupted.

"I'm not trying to overstep. I just remember that the guild wanted to know why corvasals were in that area."

"It's true that they were among the monsters we defeated. However, I don't know if the group you came across was related to the one we fought. Please tell the guild that." I didn't want to prolong this story, so I just told him the same information I was instructed to relay in advance. For a moment, Larutas looked at me disapprovingly, but I pretended not to notice.

"The princess really knows how to get to the point, huh?" Even though Agito was directing the question toward Larutas, I glared at him. Ever since I was selected as the commander of the hero's unit, I gave up my position as the fifth princess of Gardir.

"Oh, forgive me. I mean *General* Tylera." Agito deliberately corrected himself. He must have been trying to provoke me into making a mistake. However, instead of being irritated, I calmly returned to the main subject.

The information recorded by the magic monocle was reproduced on the table. The scenery of the place where Agito was when the recording began was projected there. I could feel the wind blowing as the exploration party began introducing themselves.

The monocle was a magical tool that reproduced the state of a place as if you were there in real time, and it was a treasure of the Kingdom of Gardir that had been handed down from ancient times. It was used when taking important records of archaeological sites and conducting diplomacy, but there were only three of them, and there was no end to the waiting list of people wanting to use one.

As I was looking at the recording with that thought in mind, a beautiful young man began introducing himself. He was so handsome that he could make any young woman's heart race, but it didn't matter to me right now. I was just watching the recording, hoping to end this conversation as soon as possible.

"My name is Setsuna. I am a scholar. My guild rank is green, and I can use Wind magic. I'm participating in the survey because they needed a Windmaster."

Larutas raised an eyebrow and asked to stop the playback. "This young man isn't on the Moonlight roster. Isn't that a breach of contract?"

"He's not, but because the request was so last-minute, our Wind-master wasn't available. If you didn't dispatch one for us, that's your problem. I didn't take him inside the ruins. I was planning to rely on him if something happened, and I was going to keep an eye on him if it came to that."

Perhaps convinced by that explanation, Larutas told me to continue the playback. I pressed play while thinking, *I am not your maid.* Then, after they opened the door, he made me stop it again. This time, he pointed at Setsuna as if he was looking for something, expanding and rotating and even composing it from his point of view.

"Hmm." Having finished examining whatever had bothered him, Larutas finally opened his mouth. "It looks like he was using detection magic at the same time, with a range that covered the entire ruins."

I already knew Windmasters used that kind of magic, so I thought nothing of it.

"That's right. Judging from his personality, he was probably check-ing the safety of the ruins for us. He didn't say anything at the time, but I thought he was doing something. Is there some kind of problem?"

He didn't seem to be lying. No signal went off. Larutas looked like he was pondering over something, but I wanted to get this over with, so I pressed the button again.

Agito and his son went inside, and the interior of the ruins was re-created. However, I remembered the inside without even having to watch, because I had walked that path myself just the other day when I was the hero's escort.

The Wind magical tool fitted in the center of the door absorbed the bishop's magic power and glowed white.

At the same time, a strong gust of wind blew up, left, and right from the magical tool. Pushed by the torrents, the door parted in the middle, the two halves sliding into the floor and ceiling. The magical tool stuck to the part below, and its hemispherical surface protruded from the surface of the floor.

"Let us enter, Hero." Saying this, the archbishop began to move forward with the priests carrying the ark.

"Shall we go?" I also called out to the hero.

He nodded and replied brightly, "Yes. Let's go."

I tried to follow behind him, but his movements were restricted by the green armor and helmet that covered his whole body, so his steps were stiff and awkward. As he walked in that manner, I imagined his expression beneath his helmet, and I couldn't help but laugh.

"Ah! You laughed! I'm not muscular, and you know I've said lots of times I can't wear this hero's equipment that's been passed down through the ages! Don't you think that's a bit mean?"

I imagined the delicate hero inside the armor and involuntarily burst out laughing.

"Hmph. I just told you it's mean and you're still doing it! But, well, I hope the day will come when this armor and sword won't be a burden."

The hero had faced his responsibility with seriousness, and this was his first time wearing something this heavy. I deeply bowed in embarrassment at having laughed at him.

"No, you don't have to apologize so much. If I were in the same position, I would do the same," he said with a smile. "I don't really like this armor, to be honest with you. It's rough and bumpy. I will comment on the color of it, though. I love the light green."

I knew he was trying to make me feel better, and his words made my heart feel warm.

"Yes. The goddess Endia's color is blue, so some people said that the hero's armor should also be blue. It seems it was dyed several times, but I heard that it always returned to its original color. But I think this color suits you better, Hero."

"How can you say that when you can't even see me at all?!" He wasn't joking—I really couldn't see any of the man inside the suit. I started laughing again. The hero continued to speak in a serious tone. "I never dreamed you would become a general and accompany me. Thank you. Not having anyone with you who you know is so lonely. I was so happy you came."

"Thank you for bringing me out of that stifling palace," I said quietly so that only the hero could hear.

While the hero and I were talking, the bishops and sorcerers finished investigating the interior of the ruins and found nothing remarkable other than the altar in the center.

"Just as the ancient documents say, this altar is the only one that shows the will of Goddess Endia." A temple of eight golden pillars was built on top of the seven-step stone staircase, in which a statue of a goddess made from bluesilver was enshrined. Even from a distance, I could tell it was the goddess Endia.

"An ancient document handed down to the Kingdom of Gardir states: 'Once every few hundred years, when the moon shines at its brightest blue, the Altar of Wind will appear. Offer your prayers to the enshrined goddess there, and Her will shall be revealed.' We will pray here now. Hero, if anything should happen, please lend us your assistance."

After the archbishop saw the hero nod, he went up to the altar and knelt before the statue of the goddess. The hero's band of knights stayed behind while the hero and I followed the archbishop up the steps and knelt beside him.

We stayed there by his side and prayed for a long time but sensed no change in the altar. Some began to theorize that perhaps the archbishop wasn't praying in the correct manner, or that perhaps Her will had already been shown. Then suddenly, the hero stood up and began staring intently at the statue. I rose to my feet as well and called out to him. "Is there something the matter, Hero?"

"No. I was just thinking how beautiful she is."

I nodded and looked at the statue of the goddess, which was about the same size as the hero.

"This certainly is different from my homeland. Back there, we had sacred trees..." He touched the statue's hand and continued. "And we would touch them, offering our hands in prayer."

He looked so sad that I inadvertently reached out and grabbed his hand. He looked at me with his serious eyes, and they slowly closed. "Thank you," he murmured quietly.

Suddenly, the goddess's statue began to glow, and the eight columns were illuminated. The golden light accumulated in the base of the golden pillars, as if they were storing the light.

"What's this?" The archbishop had been talking to the other priests, but he turned around and approached the hero.

"I don't know. I just touched it with my right hand and offered a prayer, and it began to glow..."

The archbishop squinted at the hero's hand, which was still on the statue. Light overflowed from it, too.

"When you offered the prayer, did you put mana into your hand, Hero?"

I couldn't use magic, so I thought the two were different things, and I figured the hero probably did, too. But apparently, the archbishop did not, and he had a mystified expression.

"Did I do something wrong?" the hero said apologetically, but the archbishop shook his head.

"No. You did precisely what I expected of the hero. We could not have found the solution without you. However..." The archbishop looked at the eight pillars. The golden light stored at the bottoms had reached the halfway points and stopped. It looked like it stopped because we were lacking something. I had a feeling the archbishop shared my sentiment. He immediately placed his right hand on the statue.

"Ooh!"

The priests exclaimed the moment the archbishop did that. It was because the light climbed the golden pillars again. But it was very slow. The archbishop must have thought so, too, as he called out to the other priests and told them to put their hands on the statue and pray while pouring magic into it.

They did as commanded, and the light regained its initial momentum, climbing the pillars and engulfing the roof of the temple. Then the light enveloped us and the temple together, and the next moment, it quietly flowed like water falling from the roof and disappeared.

When the golden light that enveloped the temple flowed, we couldn't hide our confusion at the scenery, which was illuminated by the eight pillars that held the light.

"There was no sound, no tremors, and we were..." I swallowed the words as I stood in front of a gravel road that seemed to lead somewhere, which had spread out from either side of the temple.

"......"

Unable to find words, the archbishop stepped out of the temple. There were no stairs, and the road was paved with white stones, like something out of a dream. I felt as if I was in a trance, and I neither followed nor stopped him.

"Wait a minute, Archbishop." I came to my senses when I heard the voice of the hero, who was chasing after the archbishop, and I rushed over to his side. How could I have just stood there when I was supposed to be the hero's escort? What a blunder! I felt pathetic.

"It's dangerous to walk in such darkness without a light!"

"...Right... I'm sorry I made you worry." The archbishop finally came to himself.

I looked around. It was a dark world with nothing but the light of the temple.

When I realized I couldn't even see ten steps ahead of me, I felt a chill on my back.

"Please wait, Archbishop." The priests who followed us tried to use magical tools to provide light, but the darkness snuffed them out, as if rejecting it.

"It seems there's no way to light our path forward. How troublesome." The archbishop let out a deep sigh.

"I think... Yes, this is Dark magic. It seems like this entire area is covered in it." The hero tried using Light magic, but it didn't seem to work.

"The temple's pillars were lit up, so the Dark magic must not have an effect on them, right?" I asked.

The hero tilted his head and said, "Let's try it." He stiffly walked back over to the pillars and tried using his magic again. But he shook his head and returned.

"How troublesome. I suppose we'll have to go back without being able to do anything," the archbishop muttered as he glared into the darkness.

"……" The hero crossed his arms and stared, swaying slightly. He told me when we first met that this was what he did when he was thinking about something. I hoped he would have a good idea and watched over him. The archbishop and priests were trying to create some light but glanced over at the hero.

"Maybe if we use enough mana, it will overpower the Dark magic… Hmm? It's no use. I'm using all my powers. In that case… All right, let's see if I can do it." Suddenly, he uncrossed his arms and cupped his hands together. "Come!" the moment he said that, his palms flashed with light, which then gathered like pools of water there. "Yeah, that's good. Let's go!" At that signal, the water dripped off his hands in beads of light, flowing onto the gravel path. Light kept streaming from his hands, flowing farther and farther up the road, until it shone brightly on the surface of it.

"It looks like a galaxy of stars," I murmured.

The hero smiled and nodded, then spoke to the archbishop. "I'm going to continue making the light, so you follow its path. If you see anything dangerous or you don't need the light anymore, please tell me."

The archbishop thanked the hero and led the priests down the lit path. Of course, since I was the hero's escort, I remained there. After a moment of silence, the hero murmured, "You could see a galaxy of stars in my homeland, too. That's what gave me the idea to use the magic…" He gazed at the tip of the light meandering ahead. His voice sounded depressed.

"Are you remembering your homeland?"

"…When I came here and saw the night sky for the first time, I thought about how the constellations were different and how I could see two galaxies. I wondered if the sky was connected to the one from my homeland. I remembered that just now." His voice trembled slightly. I stared at him, trying to think of what I could say, but I had been raised like a bird in a cage, so I couldn't relate to his thoughts about the world. All I could do was look at him silently.

Just then, I felt something strange. It seemed as though his entire body glowed brighter, and then a strange sensation as if it had returned to normal. Then, in the next moment, the hero's entire body—no, the hero's armor—glowed brightly.

"Hero!" It was such a bright blast of light that I shielded my eyes with my hand. I didn't know what was happening, but I felt like I had to take off his armor, so I reached out toward it.

"Aaaaah!" The hero was panicking as he reached down to his armor, too, but then pulled his hands away in order to maintain the Light magic.

"Hero, take off your helmet!" I urged him, but before I could even finish my sentence, it was over.

The change happened suddenly. He continued to change shape while tinged with light. When the glow subsided, the transformation ended. And illuminated by the light in the hero's hand was…

"A robe?" I blurted out. The helmet and armor had changed into a large hooded robe, the fabric the same light green color as before, with golden embroidery here and there. I'd never seen a robe look as divine as this one.

"Huh? Huh? Huh?!?" The hero, who didn't understand what I meant at first, let out a maddened voice as soon as he noticed the change in his equipment. He raised his hands and looked at himself to the right, then to the left, and let out several noises that sounded like *Wow* and *Hey!* And finally, he said, "My sword has turned into a staff!"

He sounded so devastated about it that I burst out laughing.

"That's terrible, Ty. Why are you laughing?!? I didn't really like the armor, but you know I liked the sword because it was cool!"

"I'm sorry, Hero." While holding back my laughter, I bowed my head to the robe-clad hero.

"……"

He didn't reply, and when I looked up at him, he turned away in a huff. His face was completely covered with a hood down to his nose.

"Also, I told you to call me by my name when we were alone, remember?"

"I—I can't do that!"

I couldn't hide my flustered reaction to the sudden change of topic and raised my voice. The hero told me that day that he wanted me to be his friend and call him by name. The offer had made me so happy.

However, for me, my feelings for the hero were more than words like *affection*, *respect*, or *friendship*, so I regrettably declined. He knew bringing it up here and now would take me by surprise, and I was blushing.

"Your guard is so tight, Ty. You're supposed to say, 'All right, I will!'" He pretended to be angry but then couldn't keep it up and started laughing. "Just now, when I remembered my homeland, I thought I wished I could go back, but strangely enough, I didn't feel lonely. I think it's because you're always here with me now, Ty." He returned his gaze to the galaxy.

I realized I had given emotional support to him, and that made me feel very proud. I also looked up at the galaxy.

After that, I don't know how long I talked with the hero. We were talking about why the hero's armor had transformed, about the hero's family, and about my family, but in the middle of our conversation a priest came back, so we had to stop talking.

Apparently, the archbishop had found a relic at the end of the gravel road, so we headed there as well.

The hero lifted both hands up toward the ceiling and then slowly lowered his arms. When he parted his hands, an arc of light spread out, following his movements, and then dispersed, disappearing. Now only the stream of light on the ground lighted the way. I wondered if that would disappear, too, and I asked him about it.

"It'll probably disappear before the day is over. It'll naturally fade away when the time comes," he said, leading the way down the path. I followed behind him. The priest looked like he wanted to say something but kept quiet.

"Don't natural rocks like these make you feel excited? I always lived in the forest, so it's unusual to me. I suppose the inside of the castle is stone, too. They're different, though." He gave a carefree smile as he lightly walked down the path. It was hard to believe he'd looked depressed a few moments ago. His robe floated elegantly behind him as he moved, almost like a gown.

We walked along the path of twinkling stars for about five minutes. We could see a set of stone stairs at the end of the gravel path. The ceiling here was about three times the height of a person, but from this area where I could see the stone steps, it suddenly became about five times taller.

There were seven stone steps, just like at the temple. At the top of the steps was a wall, so in other words, this was where the cave ended.

The archbishop had climbed to the top, but a priest called out to him as soon as he spotted us. The archbishop was staring at the wall, but he turned around and came down the stairs to greet us.

"Well, well. It looks like the hero's armor has given you its approval."

"What does that mean?"

"The hero's armor was made by the thirty-second hero and passed down to every hero since then."

I knew that already, and I had told the hero as much.

"But in reality, it did not suit the bodies of the successive heroes, and even though it was used ceremonially until the thirty-seventh hero, it was not used in actual battle. However, the thirty-eighth hero added a function that allows the armor to transform according to the strength of the hero, and since then, it seems that it has become armor that accompanies the hero both in name and reality."

The hero looked at me as if to say, *"Why didn't you tell me?"* but it was the first I'd heard of it. I shook my head, telling him I didn't know. The archbishop smiled and continued.

"We don't want the public knowing that the hero doesn't wear the hero's armor! There are other such things we don't make public, either." He took a breath. "For example, the armor you're wearing was made by the thirty-second hero's abilities, and even though the fiftieth hero was weak, he added magical recovery abilities to it."

"I see."

The hero looked down at the robe and examined it more carefully. "Then the armor I was wearing before was the hero's armor suited for the sixty-eighth hero?"

I shook my head. All I'd heard about the 68th hero was that he was isolated in a corner on the outskirts of town due to a fairly severe contagious disease. When I heard from my mother that some of the people who had taken care of him had died of the disease, I thought about how I should never go near that place.

But now that I remembered the story, a sympathy I hadn't experienced at the time bloomed inside of me. The 68th hero must have been lonely, too. Perhaps it was the effect of seeing the hero's loneliness that inspired such thoughts.

However, I told the hero only the facts, thinking I shouldn't talk about such feelings now.

"No, the sixty-eighth hero fell ill and died without ever wearing the hero's armor. The appearance of that armor must have been suited to the sixty-seventh hero."

"Oh... Poor thing. What was his name?"

"He didn't even give his name. He was in such a bad condition that he couldn't even speak."

The hero lowered his head as if thinking about something and then looked back up.

"I see. Well then, when we get back, maybe we should visit his grave."

"All right. I'll check where he was buried when we get home."

"Please."

"May we go on to the main subject?" the archbishop asked after waiting for a break in our conversation. I apologized, but he said it was fine and continued the conversation. "Looks like the goddess's will itself over there."

He pointed to a stone slab embedded in the wall of the cave. There was something carved into it, but I didn't know what it meant.

"Is that what you're looking for?" He shook his head and told me he didn't know.

"I won't know unless we take it back with us."

I immediately objected. "Archbishop, the things here are…"

"I know. That stone slab belongs to the followers of Endia and the Kingdom of Gardir. Plus, this matter is a national secret, so please don't say anything to anyone else." Before I could finish, the archbishop smiled merrily and dismissed my concerns. "Anyway, there's a problem. Even if I wanted to take it home, I couldn't remove it from the rock wall." He told us that he had tried to figure out a solution until we arrived but was at a loss for what to do.

"Archbishop. Shouldn't we put the slate in that ark?" The archbishop nodded in response to the hero's question. The hero confidently looked at me and nodded, raising his staff. In response, darkness rose like steam from between the rock wall and the stone slab and then evaporated.

"It looks like it was bound with Dark magic." The archbishop narrowed his eyes and looked for the hero to agree with him, but the hero shook his head and held his staff in front of him. At this, the stone slab separated from the wall and floated into the air. However, behind the slate, countless lights were connected to the bedrock like spider threads. When the hero swung his staff, the threads dissipated as if they were dissolved in water.

"Now we just need to put it in the arc." A band of light appeared beneath the stone slab and began flowing into it. The light even stretched down to the ark until the stone slab slowly slid down inside of it.

I was about to make a noise of surprise in response to the hero's magic, but just then there was a violent tremor, and a sound like something was crumbling came from the temple. The tremors didn't subside; in fact, they grew even more violent, and stones began to fall from the ceiling.

"It looks like this cave has served its purpose," the archbishop remarked.

I began to think of a way to escape, wondering what to do. Like Light magic, Wind magic must be canceled by this darkness. If that was the case, wasn't there no other choice but to negate this darkness so that Wind magic could be activated?

While I was thinking about it, the archbishop looked worried and pointed around. As the cave collapsed, the Dark magic that had covered the area had broken, and light began seeping from the priests' clothes.

"Since the Dark magic has cleared, the magical tools that everyone activated earlier must have started showing their effects. In this state, we can probably use teleportation magic normally."

The archbishop called over a Windmaster and ordered them to take everyone back to the ruins. The priests nodded and began using teleportation magic. Our bodies floated in the air just as another violent tremor swept over the cave.

The moment I thought the ceiling was collapsing, I suddenly saw the altar, which had lost the temple over it. I realized we had been transported to the Wind ruins, and I breathed a sigh of relief.

The magical monocle tool began to show the recording of the area around the altar. Of course, there was no temple over it. Agito stood on top of the vacant altar and wondered aloud what it could be used for. I didn't explain it to him, of course. Everything that happened at the ruins was a national secret.

We had prepared to make sure the information didn't leak. The team that had gone to the ruins was carefully chosen. The priests who came were direct apprentices of the archbishop, and the knights used to be part of the king's royal guard. In other words, everyone could be trusted.

Not only that, but only a very select number of people knew about our plans to excavate the ruins, including the king and the prime minister. Even the ministers who were at the center of national affairs believed we were jointly investigating the Wind Ruins with the Adventurers Guild.

I didn't know why they had gone to so much trouble to get that stone slab, nor did I want to know. I was in the position to find out if I wanted to. But I had no interest in slabs. My only wish was to continue being the general of the knights so that I could be by the hero's side for as long as possible.

That's why I knew what I had to do now. My mission was to complete the duties that had been assigned to me concerning these ruins. We should not arouse suspicion that we already knew about what happened in the ruins.

For the success of the mission, the prime minister devised many strategies. In order not to leak unnecessary information, he decided not to go to investigate the ruins with the adventurers. He had prepared a solid excuse for that.

Coincidentally, a large number of monsters appeared, so there was no pretext of disguise. He brought out the country's national treasure, the magical monocle, and even the hearing room, and produced a high level of interest in the investigation both inside and outside.

I couldn't afford to make a blunder in the final stages of the charade the prime minister had prepared. If there was anything in Agito's report that touched on the truth, even the slightest bit, I would quietly deny it, and after that, I would continue to prepare to answer in a safe manner.

However, acting oblivious was not so difficult. Larutas didn't know a thing, and he kept staring at the video persistently and asked Agito questions, so the adventurer didn't suspect me. He seemed to appreciate my desire to move the conversation forward.

"Setsuna's strong. He could make a living with his sword, too." Agito's voice came from the magical monocle. Once again, Larutas motioned for me to pause it. I gave an inward sigh and did so.

"Is that true? If that's true, he's an incredible talent. There is also the possibility that he is a spy from some country. He should be summoned and interrogated." He was right, but even if he was a spy, that would make things worse. I hesitated about how to respond to Larutas's remark, but Agito spoke before I could answer.

"I was just bluffing. That's what parents do with kids. I was trying to motivate him."

The room dismissed this answer as false. In other words, putting aside whether he was a spy or not, Agito seemed to be protecting Setsuna for some reason. Even though I thought it was a troublesome answer, I had already decided how to respond.

"Yes, it can happen. Parents want their children to grow up."

Agito nodded, saying that he got my point, and Larutas agreed with me and didn't pursue it any further.

Larutas didn't say anything, so I resumed playing. When Setsuna's song was faintly heard in the background, Agito made it outside of the ruins and declared the end of the recording, then it stopped.

"Well, it looks like there was nothing of interest at the Wind ruins," I commented.

"Yes, unfortunately," he agreed. With that, our meeting came to an end, and Agito left the room.

I was relieved that the job was finally finished, and I erased the recording from the magical monocle. I rang the bell inside the room and called the administrator inside. "We're done here. There weren't any problems. Record that the Adventurers Guild's messenger reported no false statements. Also, call someone else in and return the magical monocle to the prime minister."

The administrator left, and then I rose from my seat. There was only one thing left to do. My heart was racing. I hurriedly headed for the general who was waiting for me, but I was stopped by a soldier on the way.

"General Tylera. I heard that the interrogation is over. I've been looking for you."

"What is it? I'm in a hurry."

"I heard that the hero regained consciousness, and I thought I should tell you. Pardon me."

"I see. Thank you for telling me. Is he all right?"

"Yes. He's very weak, though. He's been calling your name."

Hearing that made me lose all self-control. "All right. Show me to him right away." I turned to Larutas, who was staring at me with wide eyes. "I'll leave the rest to you, Officer. Give the report on the battle accurately to the great general. Also, knowing you, I'm sure you can come up with some countermeasures against the monsters. Tell him that, too. I'm counting on you."

I rattled off the necessary things he needed to know and ignored his protests, then had the soldier take me to the hero's room.

"It's this way."

The soldier stood in front of a room in the hospital ward. I suppressed my urgency and knocked on the door, waiting for a response. The hero lay in bed, and there was a female sorcerer tending to him.

"Is he all right now?" I asked her, and she nodded.

"Yes. He lost consciousness because his mana was drained too much, but he'll be fine once it recovers and he rests."

I let out a sigh of relief, then went up to the bed to ask how he was feeling, but she stopped me and whispered, "The hero was waiting for you, but he just fell asleep. It's very important that he rest in order to recover. I'm sorry, but..."

I nodded and decided not to speak to him. Instead, I stared at him as he lay in bed, and I sat down in a nearby chair.

"I'm going to go give a report on the hero's condition. If you need anything at all, please ring that bell. A doctor and a sorcerer will come right away." She pointed to a bell by the hero's pillow and then left the room.

I didn't do anything except gaze at the hero for a few minutes. We were all alone in the room, and I listened to him breathing.

"......"

Suddenly, the hero rolled over in bed, and his blanket fell to the floor. I picked it up and quietly said his name as I put his blanket back on him.

◇Part Three: Setsuna

The morning sunlight awakened me. I absently gazed at the sunrise, the moment when the darkness of the night faded. Normally, I'd get up after I awakened, but...

The dream I had was lingering in my mind. No, what I saw wasn't a dream. I think it was a fragment of one of Kyle's memories. Although it felt like I was dreaming, in the dream I was Kyle.

The reason I knew it was Kyle's memory was because I saw the same bag he had given me. Half-asleep, I tried to calm my racing heartbeat and closed my eyes to try to chase that dream again.

Scenery I'd never seen before, towns I didn't know, ruins somewhere… There was absolutely no consistency in the passing time. Seeing things from Kyle's point of view, I could feel his strong emotions.

But even when he was talking to someone, their voices didn't reach me, and even if I squinted my eyes to read lips, I couldn't read them.

I had some thoughts about the rapidly changing scenery. However, the moment I saw something different, my thoughts disappeared like a mist. I was disappointed, but at the same time, I didn't think my incoherent thoughts seemed strange. I knew it was a contradiction, but I was convinced that's just how it was.

It was a fragment of Kyle's memory, but it was closer to a dream, I thought distantly, but then that thought faded away. Just when I thought I was on a ship, the next moment I shot down a flying monster with magic, and even though I should have been on the deck, when I closed my eyes and opened them, my feet were already on the ground.

And then, the moment I lifted my head while looking at my feet, the scenery changed again. There, under the sunlight filtering through the trees, I saw a woman who gave me a shy smile.

She had long, silvery-white hair that glistened in the soft sunlight.

Blue-gray eyes that became even bluer when light shone on them. She looked younger than me.

Rather than beautiful, I thought the word *pretty* suited her better.

She was the prettiest person I had ever seen.

Surely, when she grew up, she would become even more beautiful.

I knew she wasn't smiling at me, but at Kyle. But my heart was powerfully drawn to her. Although I knew those were my feelings and not Kyle's, they too quickly faded away.

*　*　*

I wanted to listen to the voice of the woman who spoke to me—no, to Kyle. But her voice didn't reach me. Even though Kyle was happily answering her, I couldn't understand the content of the conversation.

Even though it was frustrating, my feelings would disappear when the scene changed.

Kyle's clothes changed, and so did the woman's, when the scenery changed. Spreading a thin carpet under a big tree, Kyle, the woman, and two young men who I was seeing for the first time were chatting and drinking tea with one another.

Kyle took various items out of his bag and set them on the carpet. The other three picked up the items with smiles on their faces. I had a feeling he was giving them souvenirs.

Even though I was just watching the scene, I found myself wondering what some of the items were.

The two young men's smiles froze when Kyle began trying to give them strange items like that. But the woman looked like she enjoyed herself the whole time. She was beaming at him. I thought the feeling of being drawn to her smile was my own.

The two young men quickly chose souvenirs among the items, and it looked like they were thanking him. The woman looked like she just couldn't choose. She thought and thought and then finally chose an amber tear-shaped pendant. She pointed to it, and Kyle nodded, then gave it to her. She stared at the pendant, and then she gave Kyle a huge smile. Her smile looked like a blooming flower.

She immediately put the necklace on and asked the two young men what they thought. She pouted, so I thought they must have been teasing her. It was a gentle scene, and Kyle was happy the entire time.

However...

An intense feeling suddenly hit me, and I had to squeeze my eyes shut. The feeling was sadness, regret, and intense anger. The emotions were so strong that they were painful, and it made my head throb. I slowly opened my eyes and was speechless at what I saw next.

What in the world happened?

What happened to her? I—no, Kyle—was standing in front of the woman, whose ankles and wrists were shackled. He directed a painfully intense sadness and regret toward her. But his burning sense of anger was directed at someone else.

I saw a hand reaching out in my vision. I think Kyle was telling the woman to take his hand. She looked at his hand, and her blue-gray eyes wavered. She pressed her mouth into a line and then stared right at him, shaking her head.

"   "

Kyle said something and then gently stroked her hair.

She clutched the amber pendant that hung from her neck and gave him a faint smile as tears wet her cheeks. It almost looked like her smile said this was the last time they'd ever see each other. I...

"......!"

The moment I woke up, everything I remembered disappeared, even though I had remembered it the first time I woke up. I tried to remember my dream even though I knew that never worked out. I tried to do the same thing, even though I had forgotten the dream.

I didn't have to go back to sleep, because the memories of the dream faded the moment I woke up.

If I wanted to remember these dreams, I would just have to write them down the moment I woke up the first time. I sat up and sighed. I knew it was a futile struggle, but I tried to remember. All I could remember was that I wanted to take something away, and I couldn't remember what I saw before that. I let out another sigh of resignation and cast my gaze down on Alto, who had become a baby wolf and was sleeping curled up next to me. He was sleeping so comfortably that I couldn't help but smile.

*   *   *

I slipped out of bed, careful not to wake him, and stretched my stiff body. I woke up later than usual, but it couldn't be helped.

We should finally cross the borders of Gardir today. I made my plans in my head and let out a sigh. That intense feeling of wanting to take something away... It felt like it was burned inside of my heart and lingered for quite a while...

◆ Afterword ◆

ROKUSYOU

"Let's go on our journey together now, Alto."

That's Setsuna's last line in the main story. It's Setsuna's and Alto's first steps toward exploring a new world.

And I think it applies to me, too.

I don't think I could have stepped into the unknown world of publishing by myself. I am deeply grateful to the many people who gave me the opportunity to take the first step. I enjoy creating this world that Setsuna and Alto live in, so please join us and take a journey through this isekai.

USUASAGI

It's nice to meet you. I'm Usuasagi. Thank you so much for buying *The Ephemeral Scenes of Setsuna's Journey.* This story was originally posted on a website as a web novel, but now it has been published. It's been ten years since I first began serializing it online, so I'm incredibly touched that it's finally in print.

At the time, Rokusyou said he was bored and had nothing to do, so I suggested, "Why not write a novel?" And that was the start of this story; I'm amazed we've come so far.

By the way, regarding *The Ephemeral Scenes of Setsuna's Journey*, there was one problem in publishing it. A word of caution before we get to that, though: There will be some big spoilers from here on out, so if you started reading from the afterword and don't like spoilers, please go back to the main story.

Now on to the main topic. I decided to add to the published version so that everyone who read the web version can enjoy it, too. However, I struggled with this addition. This is because the novel is basically written in first person, from either Setsuna's perspective or by someone who knows him, which means the story is limited to the characters who appeared in the first volume. I thought that wasn't much of a surprise to the readers.

Therefore, in order to show the world inside the novel from a different point of view, we intentionally created a route that can branch off from the web version at one point and show a new kind of scenery from there. I have rewritten it to make that possible.

We are creating the published version with the intention of not changing the web one significantly, but please allow us to make that single change. On top of that, we would be happy if you could enjoy this revised world.

ROKUSYOU & USUASAGI

Finally, we'd like to thank the editors who picked *The Ephemeral Scenes of Setsuna's Journey* from all the other web novels out there, sime for drawing such lovely illustrations, everyone from the publisher, and you—our readers—for buying this book. Thank you from the bottom of our hearts.

October 5, 2020
Rokusyou & Usuasagi